The Terrible
Teague Bunch

by Gary Jennings

Gary Jennings

The Terrible Teague Bunch

W · W · NORTON & COMPANY · INC · NEW YORK

Copyright © 1975 by Gary Jennings

FIRST EDITION

Library of Congress Cataloging in Publication Data
Jennings, Gary.
  The terrible Teague bunch.
  I. Title.
PZ4.J532Te   [PS3560.E518]   813'.5'4   74–23338
ISBN 0–393–08706–9

Published simultaneously in Canada
by George J. McLeod Limited, Toronto

Drawings by the author.

This book was designed by Robert Freese.
The typefaces are Times Roman and Nubian 2.
Set by Spartan Typographers.
The book was printed and bound by the Haddon Craftsmen.
PRINTED IN THE UNITED STATES OF AMERICA

1 2 3 4 5 6 7 8 9 0

To Mary Ann and Dick Boyd
of Teague, Texas
but for whom this book would not exist

and to Glenda
but for whom *I* wouldn't

AUTHOR'S NOTE

Many of the incidents in this story actually happened, but—as old-timers will recognize—not always in exactly the way I have represented them, and not always at the places and times I have set them.

Therefore, excepting historically and geographically verifiable people, places and things—such as the still estimable town of Teague, the late Teddy Roosevelt, the now defunct Trinity & Brazos Valley Railway Co., the once-upon-a-time Seeburg Orchestrion, etc.—all the characters, appurtenances, companies and other institutions to be encountered herein are of my own invention, and any one's resemblance to any real-life entity at the turn of the century, or at any other period, is purely coincidental.

One thing more. Rather than repeatedly interrupt the story for edifying asides, let me remark here that place names in Texas and Louisiana are not always pronounced as they are spelled. Here's how the natives say them:

> Atchafalaya is *'Chaf*-falaya.
> Nacogdoches is Nacka-*do*chez.
> Brazos is *Braz*-zus.
> Bossier City is *Boze*-yer City.
> Mexia is M'*hay*-uh.
> Tehuacana is T'*wock*unny.
> Keechi rhymes with *knee*-high.
> Hell is *Hay*-ull.
> Teague, however, is just plain *Teeg*.

— G. J.

Canon for voices, banjos, concertinas and mandolins:

> 'Twas once in cold November,
> The day was very hot,
> And one could not remember
> The things he had forgot.
> The sun was shining brightly,
> While sadly fell the rain.
> Four men went out a-walking,
> *And so they took the train.*

The Terrible
Teague Bunch

1

1

THE ELDERLY, rawboned, grizzled trail boss rode a circuit around the herd, quietly cursing to himself. No words were audible; they merely came out as puffs of steam in the bitterly icy air. What with the cold freezing the skin of his face to tallow, and that frosted with the bristles of a three days' beard, the cowboy's face was just about as silvery-gray as his hair. The wide brim of his old hat was lopped down on each side to cover his ears, and held there by an extraordinarily long muffler wound over the crown of the hat, over his ears and under his chin, thence several times around his neck—still leaving a considerable length to dangle free behind him. Now he took a hitch in the muffler, to clamp his jaws tighter together and keep his teeth from chattering.

He and the crew he was ramrodding were bringing this herd down off the High Plains, through the Cap Rock escarpment, and this stretch of the drive had been a bitch. The grinding cold had slowed them—made the cattle reluctant to drift out of their bedgrounds each morning, made them lethargic on the move. So they had been four days making the haul through this blighted Cap Rock country, where no blade of grass grew, where there was no brush or even bullnettle for emergency browsing. The cattle were gaunted down, so ribby that they looked like concertinas with horns.

But the bad part was nearly over, the trail boss reminded himself. Just this one more ridge to cross and they'd be out of the Cap Rock. On the other side of the ridge, he knew, was a loamy, fertile plain full of succulent grama grass, the beginning of the Rolling Prairie country. This being winter, the grass wouldn't be grass, of course, but it would be good nutritious hay, and the critters could fill their bellies. From there on, the drive would be a snap, all the way to Wichita.

Under his horse's shoes, the rock rang as if it too was metal. The sound of the slowly shambling herd's hooves was not the customary low rumble, but a metallic clangor. The sky was a solid sheet of cloud, seeming to hang just out of arm's reach overhead, and it was the same dull, dead lead color as the solid sheet of rock underneath them.

For all the cowboys' encouraging bawling and shrill whistles, the cows moved only sullenly and grudgingly, but at least they moved. In half an hour, the leaders would breast the ridge. They would scent the good fodder below and ahead of them, and they'd take off down the other side of the ridge at the trot. In that expectation, the silver-haired cowboy uttered several further hideous words expressive of his gratitude and relief.

But then he felt a puff of wind from straight ahead, and something sudden, sharp and cold touched his cheek. With an unbelieving groan he raised his head, and another puff of wind tugged at his hat. The sky, lead-gray a moment before, had lightened to the color of dirty cotton. Even as he looked, the cotton lowered and closed around him. The air was suddenly thick with snowflakes, batting at him faster and harder as the wind ceased to puff and settled into a continuous whoosh. That first curtain of white had blotted the herd out of his sight, but he could sense the cattle slowing still more in bewilderment. He yanked at the muffler to free his jaws and uncork another spew of purple words—this time addressed to his now invisible crew.

"It's a blizzard!" he informed them, rather unnecessarily. "A real white-whiskered blizzard! Don't let 'em stop, boys! Head 'em right into it and push 'em! Hard!"

The cowboys within earshot bellowed back acknowledgment and passed the word along. In a moment every one of the crew was yawping and kiyi-ing and whistling loud enough to deafen himself, but his caterwauling could barely be heard six feet from him through the driving wind and snow.

Every one of them knew, as well as the boss did, what the hazard was. A cowboy's life is spent in intimate affinity with two creatures, the horse and the cow. He knows wherein they are similar—their intelligence, which is to say their almost vacuum lack of it—and he knows the differences between them. For example, a horse will stand bravely head on to a howling norther, or ride all day into the teeth of it. This is because the hairs of a horse's coat lie from front to back, and he is more comfortable (or less uncomfortable) when the bad weather is coming from straight ahead. But the hairs of a cow's pelt, for reasons known only to God, grow the other way, lying back to front. A cold blast coming from up ahead ruffles under his coat and chills him. So what little sense a cow has impels him to turn and stand still, butt to the blast, and wait patiently for more clement weather.

"Just to the ridge, boys!" the trail boss bawled, somehow managing to convey a prayerful pleading at the top of his lungs. "If we can just make the ridge, they'll smell the grass!"

Yelling and waving his arms, he crowded the flank of the herd, but provoked from it no promise of stampede or even a purposeful lope. The cows were barely plodding now, beginning to wall their eyes and moo in distress. With his teeth the boss yanked the heavy, fur-lined glove off his right hand, slid the instantly chilled hand beneath his sheepskin jacket and inside the bib of his overalls, and brought out his pistol. He fired several times into the air, but, even to his own ear, the pistol sounded as if he had it wrapped in a pillow, and the cattle paid no attention whatever.

Cursing more vividly by the minute, he stopped trying to push the herd and instead spurred his horse at a gallop toward the herd's leading edge. What he might have been able to do up at the point he was not to find out, for he got there too late. He arrived just in time to see the leaders stop and, there in place, do an about-face to turn their backsides to the weather. By ones and twos and bunches, all the cows following did exactly the same, with a great clashing-together of horns and bumping-together of bony hips. The animals stood there, stolid, dumb and uncomplaining, as they had stood through every lesser storm in their lifetimes, to wait for this one to blow itself out. They would stand there until they froze to death or—within an easy amble of abundant fodder—until they starved to death.

The boss turned in his saddle, from glowering at the immobile herd, to glower at the snow-shrouded ridge up yonder, maddeningly just out of reach. His point man and one of the flankers emerged from the snow curtain, stopped their horses and shrugged helplessly. He glowered at them. "No more'n a long spit further and we'd of had 'em over the hump!" One of the men mumbled, "Yes, suh," and halfheartedly gave him a sort of military salute.

The boss looked at the pistol still in his hand, as if he contemplated sticking it in his ear and pulling the trigger, then angrily jabbed it back inside the bib of his overalls. He clenched his ungloved, now blue-with-cold right hand into a fist, and shook it savagely at the heavens.

"*Goddam it to hell,* there's got to be an easier way for a man to make a living!"

That snowstorm was not otherwise very remarkable, and set no records worth enshrining in the almanacs, but it was the Texas High Plains Blizzard of 1902.

2

The summer of 1903, like most summers in far southern Louisiana, was a blisteringly hot one. It was popularly believed that only black men could work and survive in the sweltering heat of midsummertime in the Atchafalaya swamps. But the year 1903, like most years in far southern Louisiana, was "hard times," so the Evangeline Softwood Lumber Company had as many white as black men in its Atchafalaya logging camp. All the white men were

Cajuns, descendants of the Acadian French exiled from Nova Scotia
a century and a half before. All the Negroes were freejacks, descendants of the slaves freed by Andrew Jackson in reward for their
services during the Battle of New Orleans.

This was an economically enforced integration, endured by both
the white and black men with no real animosity, but with certain
reservations. The freejacks spoke "de boogalee," a yams-and-mo-
lasses dialect of English sprinkled with African and Creole words,
which was irksomely similar to the Cajuns' own peculiar brand of
English sprinkled with French and Creole. So the Cajuns haughtily
gave up English altogether, for the time, to speak only their ances-
tral French—a French, it must be said, that would have given a
native Frenchman the mullygrubs.

The whites and blacks had separate—widely separated—sleeping
tents, mess tents, even kitchen tents. And naturally they wouldn't
work together, any more than they would eat or bunk together.
They were divided into separate crews. The freejacks, with axe and
saw, did the actual cutting down of the bald cypress trees and the
cutting up of them into logs of manageable size. The Cajuns, with
axe, saw, sledgehammer and spikes, had the job of building the
portable railroad that carried the logs out of the swamp to the nearest wagon road. This job was as continuous as the actual logging
operation, because the railroad had to be dismantled and rebuilt
every time the loggers cleared all the cypress from one area and
moved to another.

The Negroes liked to say, with a chuckle, that they "couldn' tell
dem coon-ass Cajun fellas apart." Most of the Cajuns did resemble
the one who stood now waist-deep in swamp water, cursing in
French so that he fizzed like a firecracker. He had curly black hair,
black eyes, a black mustache and a skin that had once been olive
and smooth. It was now lumpy and mottled in various other colors
as a result of insect bites and stings, sunburn and several varieties
of rash and fungoid growths.

"Merde," he muttered disgustedly. "La vie doit être plus facile à
Cayenne." He paused to hawk and spit, then went on, fiercely but

disjointedly, *"Bougre boueux . . . à bas le bâtard infâme . . . sale metèque . . ."*

He was cursing the local landscape: mainly water, with here and there a relieving patch of fetid mud, or even a diminutive hummock of half-dry ground scantily haired with saw grass. For the rest, there were the double-damned bald cypress trees, trunk by trunk as far as the eye could see in every direction. The cypresses, unlovely even to a confirmed tree lover, fastidiously lifted their knobbly knees above the waterline. They were draped with vines and creepers, and shelved at intervals up their trunks with bracket fungi of every repulsive color.

The Cajun was cursing the heat and humidity that had seared his eyeballs red and raw, set his brain sizzling inside the oven of his skull, made his lungs labor for the blessing of just one clean, dry, cool breath. He was cursing the cloud of keening and ravenous mosquitoes that enveloped his head like a beekeeper's veil, and the flies and gnats that tried to get into his eyes, and the sweat-bees that bit the back of his neck.

He was cursing the swamp water he stood waist-deep in. It was evil-colored, evil-smelling, loathsomely warm and slimy, scummed with green algae and water-walking insects. Under its surface, things moved and brushed against him—nothing worse than muskrats and turtles, he hoped. But when, at day's end, he climbed out of this water and undressed, he would have to yank out of his armpits and the backs of his knees and off his belly skin the dangling black leeches that had spent the day sucking his blood.

He was cursing the numerous ever-present dangers of this repellent job. So far this season, two Cajuns and one freejack had died of snakebite. Another Cajun had died of some unidentifiable fever. One white and two black men had been crushed by falling trees. One Negro buck had simply disappeared; the consensus was that he had had an unfortunate encounter with one of the larger local alligators.

The Cajun was cursing the ten straight hours of bone-wrenching, gut-rupturing labor he had put in today, and the ten hours yesterday, and the prospect of tomorrow's ten, and the ten and the ten after that—and the six bits that was all he would be paid for each of these interminable ten-hour days.

He was cursing, in addition, the Lord God's original creation of the bald cypress tree, and His appalling ineptitude in decreeing that it should grow only in leprous and gangrenous swamps, and the lumber industry's avaricious insistence on harvesting it. He was throwing in a few side curses at the Pelican State of Louisiana, at the Atchafalaya River and its splay of swamps, at this particular swamp in Assumption Parish, and at this particular soppy spot where he stood wretchedly waiting for the little log train to come chugging along the preposterous railroad he had helped lay down for it.

And here it came: a little, antiquated, narrow-gauge, high-wheeled, wood-burning donkey engine, dragging a tender full of firewood and a string of flatcars carrying a dozen or so of the workers it was picking up at day's end to return to camp. The laboring little train came oddly—with the hesitant, humping gait of a caterpillar—because the oddest thing about this swamp railroad was its roadbed, or, rather, lack of one. The Cajun crew laid track, and kept on laying new lengths as needed, simply by chopping down thick-boled trees at convenient intervals, letting them topple into the swamp and then using them as cross-ties, spiking the rails across the recumbent trunks.

This made for unevenness, to say the least. Some of the cross-tie tree trunks would be lying across hummocks of fairly solid ground, others would lie mushily on a patch of mud, and others would simply be floating like pontoons on the water. So the railroad was a wonderfully unsteady, springy, wavy and lively thing. Riding the log train was like riding the back of a sea serpent. The Cajuns had at first found their railroad *excentrique* and *comique*. Now, after having built, dismantled and rebuilt it so many times, they found it merely *odieux*.

The black-haired, black-mustached man sloshed toward the track as the train came loping and undulating toward him. Then he stepped on something on the swamp bottom that rolled under his tread. His feet went out from under him, and, with the most extreme profanity he had uttered that day, he went full underwater with a mighty splash. The water was only waist-deep, but it was slime-bottomed, and full of snags and old vegetation, so he had to flail around considerably to get his feet planted and his head above water again.

He came up, his hair festooned with weeds and tadpoles, his mustache dripping slush, to find himself looking at another head just inches away. The other head looked back at him. It was not much bigger than a bullfrog's, but it was wedge-shaped, scaled, with slit-pupiled, lidless eyes. Abruptly it opened its mouth very wide to reveal, behind curved fangs, a palate of a corpse-white color. The Cajun was looking straight down the gullet of a cottonmouth.

The cottonmouth, or water moccasin, is one of the most venomous of all snakes, but still it is only a snake. It was facing the wettest, tiredest, maddest, don't-give-a-*merde*-est Cajun in the Atchafalaya. For a moment it seemed a toss-up: which would bite the other? Then, as if sensing that it was for the first time at a disadvantage in the matter of venom, the moccasin closed its fearsome mouth, gave a sort of shudder and swam away.

The Cajun caught the last passing flatcar of the train and heaved himself up on it. His pitch of wrath and adrenalin had not yet dwindled enough for him to feel fright at his hairbreadth escape. When he did, he would quake sleepless all night. But right now, all he did was spit weeds and mud out of his mouth, and with them the heartfelt words, *"Boudi maquarelle—quelle façon de gagner sa croûte!"* Which translates roughly as "Whore of a saint—what a way to make a living!"

3

Captain Anthony Lucas's Spindletop field in Jefferson County had been the scene of the first really big oil strike in Texas, and in 1904 was still the state's gushingest producer. In the spring of that year,

Spindletop was a forest of derricks with an undergrowth of roaring blue gas flames. Indeed, production was booming so that the carpenters were hard-pressed for lumber to build new derricks. And, as usual, that spring was a wet one. The constant drenching rains seemed to fecundate the sprouting of the derricks overhead, but underfoot they turned the whole vast area of Spindletop into one vast quagmire of thick, gummy mud—made even more unpleasant to work in by its admixture of black and stinking Texas crude.

Near one of the newer derricks, two men in work denims and hipboots stood nearly knee-deep in this mire, arguing heatedly— and as they argued they sank perceptibly into the black ooze. They were right next to the flywheel of the roaring, heaving steam engine that drove the rig, and had to shout to hear each other. They could have conversed more easily if they had moved a distance away, but to move would have required a number of separate, sucking, struggling, high-stepping steps, so they stayed where they were and bellowed above the bellow of the machinery.

One of the men standing in the rain was Captain Lucas's chief engineer, the other was one of his riggers. The chief engineer was of course superior in title, position, pay and authority, but an onlooker would have taken him to be the inferior, simply because he was so overtowered by the phenomenal height and breadth of the redheaded giant he was yelling at.

"Well, goddammit, *something's* shaking this rig apart!" the chief engineer was bawling. "That goddam derrick's gonna be falling on our heads any minute!"

"And I tell you, chief, I don't know what could be wrong!" the giant redhead roared back—though even at a roar his voice conveyed the patient tolerance of a big man toward a smaller one. "I bossed the setting-up, and I can guarantee that everything's right and tight."

"For Christ's sake, man, you can feel the whole ground shaking under us where we stand!"

"Okay, Thought damn it, something's out of kilter, but I sure as Thought can't find out what it is while the machinery's going like Mile-a-Minute Murphy." He shrugged and waved an ape-like arm.

"You'll just have to shut down and pull your string so I can take a look."

"Pull the string?!" If the chief engineer hadn't been firmly mired, he would have danced around in vexation. "Man, that string has just now got down far enough through this goddam gumbo to where the bit can get a real bite. If I pull it out for as much as ten minutes, all this jesusly muck will seep back and fill the casing and we'll have to go-devil through it all over again! We've got money down this hole! I'll be goddamned if I'll spend it tw—!"

They were spared further argument. Anyway, they were both right. As the chief engineer had said, something was definitely shaking the rig apart; as the rigger had said, it should have been shut down. Because, all in an instant, the whole thing flew apart—with the bang, clang and clatter of an explosion in a plumbing factory.

The grief stem that drove the whole drilling string of bit and pipe down through the earth was a square-sectioned metal bar nearly fifty feet long that ran the height of the derrick. Something snapped it loose from the string it was driving, and it whipped out of its seating in the rotary table at the base of the whole works. Its upper end still attached to the cable pulley at the top of the derrick, its lower end flailed out through the side of the derrick, which disintegrated immediately into kindling wood.

The swinging grief stem then whacked the governor off the top of the steam engine alongside the rig, which immediately began shrieking loud enough to be heard all across Spindletop. The end of the stem then whizzed a bare six inches over the chief engineer's head, but the other man was too big to be missed. The heavy metal bar, still moving like Honus Wagner's baseball bat, caught him full in the forehead. All of this happened practically instantaneously, but for long seconds afterward the air was still full of flying splinters of derrick, falling bits of broken machinery and an anguish of screaming steam—and every man in the vicinity was throwing himself face down in the black mud.

When things quieted at last, the men slowly, squelchingly got up again—all but the big redheaded rigger. The company sawbones was sent for, down at the headquarters buildings, and he came as fast as his horse and buggy could make it through the mire. By the time he got there, his patient was beginning to stir a bit and mumble incoherently. Several of his fellows were holding a tarpaulin over him like an umbrella, to spare him being drowned by the rain, at least. The doctor bent down, scraped some of the blood and mud off the man's face and one at a time thumbed his eyelids open.

"One pupil dilated, one contracted," he confided to the chief engineer. "Concussion at least. I'd bet on a skull fracture. If the man wasn't built like Paul Bunyan's ox, he'd be dead already. Let's get him in the buggy."

The chief engineer gave orders, and, with the combined effort of eight men, the unconscious rigger was rolled onto the tarpaulin. This improvised stretcher and its burden—really just one large coagulated lump of black mud by now—was laboriously hefted into the doctor's wagon.

Then Captain Lucas himself was on the scene. He frowned at the shambles of what was to have been his Spindletop No. 119, then leaned into the buggy to peer, half-solicitously, half-accusingly, at the shambles of what had been one of his best riggers.

"If he comes to," Captain Lucas said to the doctor, "tell him he'll go back on payroll as soon as he's fit. And he won't be docked for what happened here."

The muddy, bloody lump in the tarpaulin mumbled something; the doctor bent close to hear it.

"Sounds like he's coming around already," Captain Lucas said tartly, as if he suspected malingering. "What was that he said?"

What the big rigger actually had mumbled was for somebody please to tell Captain Lucas please to ram a drill bit up his ass, but the doctor thought it politic to translate:

"Er, he just said—and I can't say I blame him, Cap'n—that there ought to be an easier way for a man to make a living."

2

IN 1905, the best whorehouse on North Street in Nacogdoches, Texas, was Mme. Mattie Fouquet's Mahogany Parlor of Recreation, Diversion & Entertainment—as she liked to call it—mere Mother Fouquet's to its clientele. There might have been better houses elsewhere in the tonier parts of town, catering discreetly to the native nabobs and unknown to the transient element. But Mother Fouquet's was the pre-eminent establishment on North Street, and North was the "trail street," the busy, bustling honky-tonk strip, the so-called Hell's Half Acre frequented by cowboys taking a breather from a cattle drive up the Shreveport Trail, by off-duty lumberjacks from the logging camps in the pine woods roundabout, by weekending roughnecks up from the Jefferson County oil fields, by neighborhood ranchers, cotton farmers and nesters, by petty politicos in town on County Seat business, by small-bore crooks on the dodge from somewhere else, by tinhorn gamblers, medicine-show Doctors and rain-making Professors, by passing saddle tramps, by the town's own derelicts and layabouts in general.

Mme. Fouquet had been born Mattie Friggs in Louisville, Kentucky. Her current and improved surname commemorated a Cre-

26

ole gentleman with whom she had consorted—maybe even legally —during her younger days as a cabaret dancer in the Vieux Carré of New Orleans. The madam could no longer kick high enough to do a proper French cancan, but it was reliably reported that she had on several occasions kicked as high as the crotch of an obstreperous customer. Now sedately middle-aged, Mother Fouquet was a square-built woman with the hide of a Gladstone valise, tightly wound platinum curls, audibly creaking corsets, and the benevolent soul and outlook on life of a patent cash register.

But she ran a good house. The Mahogany Parlor was, as advertised, rich and warm with mahogany wainscoting, and its Recreation, Diversion & Entertainment were provided by eight pretty, convivial and accommodating young ladies with highfalutin *noms-de-chambre* like Mississippi Sal, the Carrot-top Kid, Calamity Jill and Princess Alice. (There was, of course, a Princess Alice in every brothel that had pretensions to elegance. This was a sort of left-handed salute to the President's vivacious young daughter, darling of charity balls and society photographers, the nearest thing to royalty America had, to admire and adore and to dub "Princess" Alice Roosevelt.)

It was indicative of the graded-prime quality and class of Mattie Fouquet's girls that, on their days off, wearing modestly long skirts, prim high-collared shirtwaists and their real names (Beulah Peebles, Opal Rucker, etc.), they could have strolled uptown among the fragrant gardens of Fredonia Street, and been mistaken for members of the Baptist Women's Missionary Society.

Upstairs, Mme. Fouquet's house boasted well-appointed retiring rooms (as she called them), with mahogany four-poster beds, real linen towels and mimosa-scented water in the washbasins. Downstairs were gaslight chandeliers adrip with prisms, mahogany-and-horsehair sofas and a sideboard bar well stocked with bottles of feverishly colored and poisonously sweet spirits like passion-fruit liqueur and tangerine cordial, unappealing to the male palate, and designedly so, to discourage heavy drinking on the premises. Towering and lording it over every other piece of furniture downstairs was a Seeburg KT-Special Orchestrion—the wonder of East Texas—imported at great expense all the way from Chicago.

That thing would have been a wonder anywhere. It was a head-high mahogany cabinet like an oversized upright piano, with an ivory piano keyboard across its front and, above that, a fancily etched glass window through which could be seen a complicated and compact concretion of other musical instruments. At the drop of a nickel in the slot, the Orchestrion would play any of a number of popular tunes; Mother Fouquet kept its Recordo paper rolls punctiliously up to date and à la mode.

When it played, its ivory keys would dance as if to the touch of invisible fingers, and, through the glass, you could see xylophone bars doing the same, cymbals banging each other, a mandolin and a banjo mysteriously strumming their own strings, tambourines shaking themselves, a padded mallet thumping a miniature kettledrum and sticks rattling on a snare drum.

The machinery was run by a crank-wound clockwork spring powerful enough to drive a donkey locomotive. When it was freshly cranked up, the Orchestrion played its first few selections so exuberantly—frantically, in fact—that it could make a gallows ballad sound frolicsome. As the spring gradually wound down, the music would slow to normal tempo for a while, then to solemnity, then to lugubriousness. A ragtime ditty played dolefully and funereally was something worth hearing. More than one of Mother Fouquet's clients had remarked that her house was as much fun downstairs as up.

On this Saturday night in October, the Orchestrion had been newly wound for the evening and was jangling, thumping, tinkling a frenzied quickstep rendition of the "Pomp and Circumstance March." All eight girls were unoccupied at the moment, lounging around the big front room in their colorful kimonos. A big-boned, buxom, buttocky brunette—christened Juliana Culpeper French, renamed Pepper Frenchy by Mother Fouquet, and known in every cow camp from here to the Río Grande as Scald-balls—was feeding a new nickel into the machine every time it finished a tune.

Now the girls all jumped, as a sudden and thunderous knock rattled the street door and agitated the chandeliers' prisms to chiming. The Orchestrion gave a wheezing gulp and stopped in the middle of a bar. The girls looked at each other, and long, lanky Princess Alice said, "I didn't hear any horses ride up."

The booming knock reverberated through the house once more before Mattie Fouquet, her wire hair vibrating, could stomp from her private apartment to the door. She swung it open angrily, barking, "Why act so formal and polite? Why not just kick it down and—?" She broke off as abruptly as had the Orchestrion.

The mahogany front door was uncommonly high and wide, but the man standing there was so big that his shoulders completely filled the frame from jamb to jamb, and so tall that his head was invisible somewhere above the lintel. He ducked it down and leaned it in: a hogshead of a head, hatless, with close-cropped red hair, a big, battered face, a wicked scar denting his forehead—but with surprisingly mild blue eyes and a boozily happy grin. He said in a rain-barrel bass, with a breath that had come out of no rain barrel, "Sorry, ma'am, I meant to knock as gentle as I could."

"Uh-huh," said Mother Fouquet, looking at his beerkeg fist. She dropped her gaze to his boots; they were broad as shovels, with low heels and bulbous steel-capped toes. "Well, you ain't no cowboy," she observed. "I was expecting cowboys. What do you want?"

The giant's bushy red eyebrows went up a notch. "What *would* a man want—pardon the crudity, ma'am—when he comes calling at the Mahogany Parlor after dark on a Saturday night? My pal and I crave some feminine companionship."

He moved slightly and the hall light fell on his pal. This was an ordinary-sized man, but he looked small and frail alongside the other. He was swarthy, with curly black hair, bright black eyes, a droopy black soup-strainer mustache and, under it, the twin to the big man's boozily happy grin. Each of the callers wore a plaid mackinaw, and one pocket of the smaller man's bulged with a lump the size and shape of a quart bottle.

"My name is Karnes, ma'am," said the big man. "And this is M'shoor Boudreaux. We crave some—"

"You told me. But I'm afraid you'll have to take a rain check, fellers. The gals is all reserved for tonight. There's a cattle drive due in this evening from down south. Their scout rode into town an hour ago and stopped by to book the whole house for the evening."

"We wouldn't be long," said Karnes in his most persuasive bass register. "We'll be vacated well before they get here."

"Tell it to Sweeney," said Mother Fouquet. "There's ten or a dozen waddies that'll be loping straight here to enjoy the gals. They find you here ahead of 'em, you'll be about as welcome as a turd in the punchbowl. And big as you are, you ain't bigger than ten or a dozen cowpunchers on the prod."

"*Écoutez*, I know dat bunch, me." Monsieur Boudreaux spoke up for the first time, likewise exhaling a breath that was just short of inflammable. "I pass dem when I coming into town, no more'n t'ree hour ago. Dey still five miles from here, and dem cows moving slow. We got plenty time."

Mattie Fouquet tilted her head and said contemptuously, "What the hell is a damn Cajun doing in these parts?"

"Yes'm, he's a damn Cajun, but I've never known Moon Boudreaux to lie, and I've known him real well for going on three hours now. If he says we've got time to, uh, to spend with the girls, you can bet on it we have. What in Thought's name is that thing yonder?"

Pepper Frenchy had just given the Orchestrion a kick and dropped another nickel in. It came to life and galloped madly into "Never Breathe a Word of This to Mother." Pepper Frenchy winked at the big man behind Mother Fouquet's back. The strapping and lewdly leering girl, the merry music, the warmly gaslit room—all that invitingness inspired Karnes to redoubled pleading.

"Mrs. Mattie," he boomed, "those girls are just sitting around, not earning you a picayune, and getting out of practice, like as not. Now, wouldn't it be good hospitality and good business to slip me and Moon in and out real quick before those cowpokes blow in?"

He had hit it. Good business was the one argument guaranteed to move Mother Fouquet. "We-ell . . ." she said, wavering, and looked at a gold watch on a chain around her neck. Instantly, Boudreaux dodged past her and into the front room, his arms widespread, caroling, *"Bon soir, mes mignonnes!"*

"All right," grunted Mother Fouquet. "I'll give you just exactly one hour, so don't sit around downstairs playing the music; get right on up to a retiring room." She looked in at Boudreaux and the girls. "It appears your coon-ass sidekick has already picked out Mississippi Sal. You better pick on somebody nearer your size. Take Pepper Frenchy. She's the, uh, roomiest of all the gals. If you're hung in proportion to your heft, you'll be doing her a favor."

"Yes'm," growled Karnes agreeably. He lumbered into the front room and, smiling, laid an affectionate paw on Pepper Frenchy's meaty shoulder. She staggered slightly, but smiled back up at him. The Orchestrion hiccuped and swung briskly into "When You Ain't Got No Money, Well, You Needn't Come 'Round." As if reminded, Mother Fouquet said, "Cash in advance, boys," and collected ten dollars from each of them.

The girls wagging their behinds flirtatiously, the men trudging eagerly at their heels, they started up the stairs. When Mississippi Sal was a step above him, Boudreaux took her by the waist, turned her around and plunged his mustache into the cleft between her breasts. He inhaled deeply and moaned in delight, *"Quel parfum* you wear dere, gal. It mek even my nose hard!" He exhaled and all the nearby gaslights flared momentarily. The foursome disappeared, and Mattie Fouquet sat down in the front room with the remaining girls, to wait rather nervously for the hour to be up.

Forty-five minutes passed, and then Mississippi Sal descended from Boudreaux's room. She tottered down the stairs one step at a time, clutching her lime-green kimono together with one hand and the banister with the other.

"Miz Mattie," she said weakly, "that Cajun feller's like a mink. I purely can't take no more, but he won't quit. He says send him up another gal."

"What kind of monsters have I let in my house?" snorted Mother Fouquet. She stomped to the foot of the stairs and bawled up, "You! Coon-ass! You get the hell out of that bed and get the hell down here! What do you think you bought for a measly ten dollars?"

The Cajun's voice drifted down, muffled but indignant and determined. "You say I bought me one hour, me, and I got a piece of it left. *Ma foi!* You want I tell it around that Madame Fouquet don't provide good 'nough service for one li'l hour?"

("You know what else he was doing to me?" whispered Mississippi Sal to her girl friends in the front room. "He was pulling out my —you know, them hairs—one by one, and saying, 'She loves me, she loves me not, she loves me . . .' J'ever hear the like?")

M. Boudreaux and Mme. Fouquet were still trading Gallic insults up and down the stairwell when Pepper Frenchy appeared on the landing to announce that the big man had just passed out stone cold and looked likely to sleep all night.

Mother Fouquet clutched at her metal hair and unkinked it somewhat. "Throw cold water on him! Get him dressed!"

Pepper Frenchy looked dubious, but went back into her room. A moment later there came the sound of a splash, and the house rocked, as Karnes bellowed, "Thought damn it, woman! Great Thought a'mighty!"

The madam stuck her head into the front room and barked at the other girls, "Don't just stand around gawking, you lazy hussies! Get up there and get both them drunken bums out of here!"

They all went, though joylessly. For a while the upstairs resounded to scufflings and bumpings, yells and curses. Downstairs, Mother Fouquet wrung her hands. It was bound to happen: at this juncture the cowboys arrived. Mme. Fouquet hadn't heard the shuffle of their tired horses as they came up North Street. But the riders spurred their mounts to a shambling lope for the last few yards, to draw up at the hitching rack with as much of a flourish as possible. Tired themselves, the men dismounted stiffly, but managed to raise a brave chorus of bawdy shouts addressed to the madam and the girls inside.

"Oh, Lordy!" gasped Madam Fouquet, swiveling indecisively between the street door and the staircase. But here came the two interlopers, quite sober now, descending the stairs unsteadily while buttoning up portions of their clothes. The eight girls trooped down behind them, looking as grim and man-hating as so many suffragettes. Karnes, reeking noticeably of mimosa water and carrying his tremendous boots in one hand, was confiding conversationally to Boudreaux, "Hoo*wee!* That girl Frenchy I had, she's just *got* to be the one they call Scald-balls . . ."

"Get 'em out the back way!" urged Mother Fouquet, but too late.

The front door burst open and the cowboys erupted in, shouting cheerfully, "Yee-ah-*hoooo!* . . . Howdy, Miz Mattie! . . . Bring on the gals! . . . Watch me front-foot ol' Calamity! . . ." and the like. They all stopped shouting as they saw the redheaded monster and his swarthy shadow lurching down the last few steps. There was an ominous moment; everybody in the house stood still and silent; Mattie Fouquet wrung her hands some more.

There were ten cowboys, and they formed a solid bulwark—of plaid shirts, denim dungarees or overalls, wide-brimmed hats, spurred and high-heeled boots—between Karnes and Boudreaux and the street door. They were mostly tall, rangy, broad-shouldered men, brown as cordovan leather, hard-looking cases. At any time they would have appeared quite formidable. Right now they appeared quite formidably angry.

"Miz Mattie," said one of them, very quietly, "have you been running ringers in on our game?"

"These gents was just left over from earlier," said Mother Fouquet desperately. "I'll explain it all after they—"

"Yes'm," rumbled Karnes. "If you'll explain to these boys that we're just leaving, there'll be no call for any fuss."

"You hush up!" she snarled at him. "If you've burnt your butt, you can damn well sit on the blisters!"

The cowboy at the front of the group jammed his big hat down more firmly on his head, walked over to Karnes and leaned back to look up at him. It was like David confronting Goliath.

"Howdy," said Goliath sociably. "My name's Karnes."

"Howdydo," said the cowboy, equally amiably. "I'm Cleophus Conroe." At which he swung and hit Karnes as hard as he could in the stomach just above his belt buckle.

He might as well have punched the massive mahogany front door, edge on. Karnes never so much as quivered, but Cleophus Conroe's

right arm fell to his side, paralyzed by the shock, while his eyes
widened in pain and amazement. The big man, without moving another muscle, simply opened his own hand and dropped his steel-
toed, lead-heavy boots onto his assailant's foot. Boudreaux then
calmly fetched the half-empty quart whiskey bottle out of his mackinaw pocket and belted Conroe on top of the head, squashing the
crown of his hat and dropping him like a puppet come suddenly
unstrung.

On the instant, the other cowboys made a concerted rush for
Karnes. Mother Fouquet frisked out of their path, backed into the
front room and shrieked for her girls to "Play some music! Turn it
up loud!"

The first three men to reach Karnes seemed simply to rebound,
as if they had run into a wall of stretched rubber. Another four or
five piled onto him in a seething, thrashing mound. A few headed
on past him, for Boudreaux, who was now swinging his bottle like a
maul. The girls, bleating and whinnying in terror, edged around the
battle and, skirting the walls, got into the front room with Mattie
Fouquet. A moment later, the Orchestrion began to bang out, loud
enough to drown the sounds of combat, "I've Said My Last Farewell, Toot Toot, Goodbye."

The heap of men in the hall squirmed and heaved and bucked.
One after another of its component cowboys came mysteriously un-
peeled from the mass and went careening off. Gradually the big man
again became visible—on his knees—among those who still grap-
pled with him and swung at him. But Karnes shook these off like a
horse flicking flies from its hide, and he came erect again, not even
breathing hard.

The ruckus ended with Karnes standing triumphant among a lit-
ter of bodies, some slumped around his stocking feet, others scattered up and down the hall. Boudreaux stood on the lower stairs,
now taking a long, thirsty pull at his still unbroken bottle. Most of
the cowboys just lay and groaned; a couple were painfully pulling
themselves upright, hand over hand along the wall or a chair back.

Only one of them hadn't joined in that first impetuous rush, hadn't participated in the fight at all. He remained standing now just inside the front door, uninjured and unflustered, looking without visible chagrin at the clutter of what had been his band of buddies.

He may have been wiser than the other cowboys; he looked to be old enough to have some sense. The hair that curled out from under the crumpled brim of his hat was silvery-gray. His tanned face was a craggy relief map of miles and years of experience and endurance; his pale eyes were cool and framed in skeptical-humorous crowsfeet. Of middling height, he wore faded blue Sears, Roebuck bib overalls, and under them the collarless, faded red shirt of a set of long-handled flannel underwear, his big hands and bony wrists protruding from the frayed, flared, too-short cuffs. Except for his weather-and-sweat-stained Stetson, his dusty, scuffed, high-heeled boots and his bowed legs, he might have been taken for a particularly poor-off dirt farmer.

Karnes didn't perceive all this at once. He merely saw one last antagonist still erect and waiting to be finished off. Karnes sighed and took a step toward him.

Without haste or alarm, the cowboy reached a knuckly hand inside the bib of his overalls, hauled out a pistol and pointed it at Karnes's middle, remarking mildly, "They don't call this an equalizer for nothing, big feller." The gun was not the usual cowboy's long, clean-lined Colt .45 Peacemaker single-action six-shooter. It was an elderly, medium-barreled, double-action .41 Colt Lightning with an eagle-bill butt, the wicked-looking model popularly known as a Billy-the-Kid because it had been that worthy's favorite weapon.

The giant stopped in his tracks, raised his hands above his shoulders, cleared his throat and said huskily, "My name is Karnes. Behind me, that's my pal Boudreaux."

"Howdy," said the man with the gun. "I'm L. R. Foyt. You just knocked a good pard of mine galley-west. I'd like you not to hit him ag'in. He's simple. You can put your hands down."

"Oh? Well, I'm sure sorry," rumbled Karnes. "Simple, eh?" He shrugged. "This whole bunch you brought appeared thin between the ears, if you ask me."

"They're tired," said the elderly cowboy, "or you wouldn't of mopped 'em up so quick. Had they had their strength, any six of 'em could of taken you easy."

"Oh, fewer than that," said Karnes modestly, bending down to pull on his boots. "Which one's your pard?"

"He flew into the room yonder. That's him doubled up under that pianner thing."

"Let me and Moon help you sort him out."

Foyt slid his pistol inside his bib again, and followed Karnes and Boudreaux into the front room. They brushed past the eight girls, who were now hastening out into the hall to coo and cluck over the fallen warriors. As one after another of these got up—grunting, groaning, shaking his head—Mother Fouquet made an urgent shooing motion, and the girls solicitously helped the men up the stairs.

The fracas really had been a brief one. The Orchestrion was just now racketing out its final "Toot Toot, Goodbye." It fell silent again, as Foyt and Karnes knelt beside the man lying unconscious under its keyboard. He was a very young man, with a smooth and innocent face, an Adam's apple like a crabapple, jug ears and long, lank tan hair that fell over his forehead in front and his shirt collar in back. He wore overalls like Foyt's, and was lying on his hat.

"His name is Eli Wheeler," said Foyt.

"I recollect seeing him in the crowd," said the big man. "But, for Thought's sake, all I did was bump him with my belly."

"Reckon he banged his head on the pianner," said Foyt.

"I'm mortal sorry," Karnes said gruffly. He reached up a huge hand, took the bottle from Boudreaux and began trying to pour whiskey between Wheeler's slack lips, but without much success. "This isn't working too well."

"We're all used to drinking our whiskey out of a Mason jar, not a store-bought bottle," the cowboy explained. "Anyway, I discourage Eli drinking much, him being simple and all."

"Jes' *how* simple, *hein?*" inquired Boudreaux. "Dat feller mebbe cut up wild when he wake up?"

"Oh, hell, no. He don't have fits or take spells or anything like that. Eli's just a little slow on the savvy, and he talks kinda childish sometimes. But he's a real good old boy, long as you don't expect snap. A man to ride the river with."

"He sure doesn't look very full of sand right now, does he?" growled Karnes. "Think we ought to get him out of here?"

Foyt stood up, lifted his disreputable hat and scratched in his thatch of silver hair. The deep tan of his face ended where the hat's sweatband perennially rested; above it his forehead was startlingly white; he looked removable from the eyebrows up.

The whole downstairs was empty of other people now, except for Mattie Fouquet. She had taken a stiff belt of apricot brandy from the sideboard and was at present stretched out on a sofa, her eyes closed and a vinegar rag laid across her forehead. From upstairs came indistinctly the sounds of loving foreplay. ("*Ow!* Damn it, Cleophus, the least you can do for a gal is take off the *spurs!*")

Foyt said yes, he reckoned they might as well poot along. It appeared that the other boys had got all the girls corralled, anyway. Karnes and Boudreaux hefted Wheeler's limp form, and each of them got a shoulder under one of his arms.

"There's a Chink restaurant right next door," said Foyt. He picked up Wheeler's hat and punched it back into what shape it had had. "We'll haul him over there and fill him full of black coffee. That oughta bring him around."

3

F OYT, Karnes and Boudreaux muscled Wheeler across Mother Fouquet's broad front porch and down the stairs to the plank walk. It was a crisp October night, cold for Nacogdoches at this season, and a brisk wind was whipping dust, old newspapers, stable chaff and dried horse manure down the unpaved street. The few loiterers and passersby on the street were wearing overcoats or slickers and holding on to their derbies or broad-brims. North Street had no gaslight standards, but it was adequately illuminated by the glow from various windows: on this side those of the Mahogany Parlor, on the other those of the Floradora-Six Saloon, from which spilled out, besides a lurid glare, a tumult of noises, voices and player-piano music. The four men turned right, plodding past the cowboys' ten weary, head-hanging horses distributed along three hitching racks, their manes and tails like flags in the wind.

"No other hosses here but our'n," Foyt commented. "Ain't you two fellers mounted?"

"Not me," said Karnes. "I came into town on the Beaumont stage. I don't own a horse. Do you, Moon?"

"*Non.* Me, I pass on Nacogdoches in a freight *waguine* full of yams. Damn lumpy ride."

38

"Got no hosses," muttered the lanky cowboy, shaking his head as if marveling. "Here, this is the Chink's." They stopped at a bright red door on which were painted black Chinese characters and, under them, a translation: Great Peking Water Gate Eathouse.

They eased Wheeler through the red door, propped him in a chair at the nearest table, and sat down themselves in the other three chairs. They were the only customers. The restaurant was a bleak, bare room of unpainted wooden floor, walls and ceiling. There was not a trace of decoration to be seen, nor even anything of utility, beyond the kerosene lamps bracketed on the walls, and the dozen uncovered, cheap pine tables and their rickety chairs.

"Not a very homey place," grunted Karnes, looking around.

Foyt explained that old Wu didn't invest much in fancies or pretties because the cowboys were accustomed to tear up the place every time they came to town. "As soon as they git their loads off at Mother Fouquet's, and git a load on at the Floradora, the next fun they think of is let's all go over and bust up the Chink's."

Old Wu appeared silently through a back door and shuffled up to their table, his folded arms hidden inside the voluminous sleeves of his scarlet robe, pigtail dangling behind a black silk skullcap. His face was the translucent yellow of rice paper, and just as blank, even when he glanced at the slumped and comatose Wheeler. Wu was so indescribably old that he made even Foyt look adolescent.

Boudreaux snapped his fingers. *"Café noir!"* he commanded. "Black as de devil, strong as death, sweet as love, hot as hell!" He beamed proudly at his companions, and twirled his mustache. "Dat's how we mek *Cajun* coffee down in *my* country, down on de Bayou Teche."

Wu was not impressed. He turned his impassive face to Foyt for the order. The cowboy made a pouring-and-drinking gesture and said, "Black coffee, Wu. A whole pot of it, savvy?" Wu shuffled off again, his pigtail waggling. Boudreaux looked miffed; his mustache drooped.

"Lemme see now," said Foyt. "My memory bump ain't what it used to be. You're Karnes and you're Boudreaux, right?"

"Right. Gideon Karnes."

"Euphémon Boudreaux. Dey call me Moon for short for Euphémon."

Karnes said, "And your partner there answers to Eli Wheeler when he's awake. What's *your* handle, Mister Foyt?"

"L. R."

"Nothing else?"

"Been called L. R. all my grown life."

"Oh. Were you called something else before that?"

The cowboy glared at him and said, very precisely, "Before that I was called Baby Dear."

"All right, don't get tetchy, for Thought's sake. I was just—"

"That's twice now you've blurted out 'for Thought's sake.' What is this, some new East Texas style of cussing?"

The big man fidgeted slightly. "Well, no. It's purely my own." He tried to look pious. "A matter of my religious convictions . . ."

The Cajun laughed and said to Foyt, "He explain it all to me, soon's he got drunk. Dis feller Gideon, he don't believe in a real God like we do—good, kind, old *grand'père* God wid long white beard, living up in Heaven. *Non,* he believe God no more'n a *t'ought* up in our head. Same to say we all got God inside us. *N'est-ce pas?*" he looked at Karnes for confirmation.

"Well, yes, that's close to it," the big man rumbled shyly. "Part of it, anyway. Mind you now, I'm just as Christian as anybody else, and I *cuss* just as Christian. Only I say 'Thought damn' instead of 'God damn.' Things like that."

"Not a bad idea a'tall," said Foyt. "Staves off the risk of taking the Lord's name in vain, anyhow. Here's our coffee."

Wu set on the table a battered blue enamelware coffeepot and four thick, chipped mugs. Karnes poured all around. While Foyt tilted Wheeler's head back and began dribbling coffee into his mouth, Karnes got out the whiskey bottle and spiked the other three cups. Wheeler choked and sputtered for a bit, but in a minute he was swallowing properly, his Adam's apple bouncing, and in another minute his eyes fluttered open.

He sat up and slowly, dazedly swiveled a brown-eyed, spaniel-like gaze around the table—at Karnes's big, scarred face, at Boudreaux's dark and hairy phiz. He seemed to recognize neither of them from the fight. His eyes came to Foyt's tanned and weathered countenance, and he spoke, in a washed-out, faraway voice:

"You said there'd be gals, suh. *These* ain't them?!"

"No, son, the gals are next door, but they ain't free right now, so we come over here for some coffee. You been asleep."

"Oh. Yes, suh."

"Drink that up and have some fresh."

"Yes, suh." He obediently drained his mug. Karnes poured him some more, and added a good dollop of whiskey. Wheeler said, "Thank you, suh," and sat alternately sipping and smiling.

"I never met anybody more polite," Karnes said to Foyt. "Does he say 'sir' to everybody?"

"Yep, even to ladies. Eli's an ex-sojer, you see, and he must of been a good one. He was in Cuba with the Twelfth Infantry. That's the reason Eli's simple. He took a rifle ball upside the head in the Battle of El Caney."

Karnes said to Wheeler, kindly, "I've met folks a sight more simple with a sight less excuse."

"Thankee, suh," said Wheeler, his jug ears turning pink at the praise.

"How you come to buddy-up wid dis one?" Boudreaux asked Foyt.

Foyt said well now, took a long pull at his spiked coffee, and pushed his hat back. "Well now," he said again. "After Eli got invalided out of the Army, I dunno where-all he drifted, but I come on him in a flyspeck town called Radford, up north a ways, and I could see he sure had hard-wintered some. He was doing nigger work there, cleaning out privies and suchlike. He was reckoned to be the village idjit—as if anybody else in Radford was anything but—and ev'rybody picked on him and made sport of him. Well, it was hard times, and I was riding the chuck line myself, looking for work. I got to Radford after a long ride, with my hoss crippled up so bad it looked like I'd be stuck in that piss-ant town. But I run into young Eli and he done *something* to that gelding—no more'n *talked* to him, looked to me—and old Lightning perked up like a colt. Well, I didn't have no money to pay Eli for his services, so I done him a favor instead. I pistol-whupped the town bully—big scissorbill named Bonky Bayes—that had pestered him the worst."

"I 'member that," said Wheeler, from far away. "I surely do. That was in Radford, that was."

Foyt confirmed that yes, that had happened in Radford. While bully Bayes was still stretched out in the street, and all the rest of the townspeople were gathered around to admire the improvement in him, Foyt had hoisted young Wheeler up behind his saddle. Lightning was feeling so frisky that he was even cheerful about carrying double. So Foyt and Wheeler had ridden out of town without two bits or two bites of grub between them. But then they struck it lucky. At the next spread they came to, the ramrod of the outfit hired Foyt and agreed to take on Eli, too.

"That outfit never regretted it, neither. With his touch for animals, Eli purty soon had their remuda the liveliest and handsomest string of hosses in North Texas. He's spruced up many a bunch and many a herd since then, better'n any vet-doctor. And I'm still riding that Lightning hoss—that's him I got hitched out yonder in the street—the selfsame hoss Eli doctored way back then. That was five years ago. Him and me have rode together ever since." He sighed, looking at Wheeler's sad, soft, childish smile. "The only thing Eli can't cure is his own poor addled head."

"Maybe you ought to be glad," Karnes suggested gruffly. "Suppose someday sudden-like he woke up in the morning all normal, and suppose it meant his losing that magic touch with animals. Suppose then nobody wanted to hire him."

Foyt thought about that, while he poured himself another mug of half coffee, half whiskey.

"It wouldn't matter," he decided. "We're pards. Whatever might happen, we'd look out for each other. Anyhow, neither one of us is gonna be out of work no more. We already made up our minds that this-here drive we're on right now is the last time we'll be hiring out. We won't be nobody else's hands ever ag'in. We got ambitions."

"Uh-huh," grunted the big man. "I wish I had a dollar—no, a dime—for every time *I've* said that. Here, Moon, give me another dose of that good redeye."

The Cajun shook the bottle and said, "L. R. jes' finish him."

"Oh. Sorry, fellers," said Foyt, sounding not at all sorry. "What say we decamp over to the Floradora? Their barrel whiskey ain't as good as your store-bought, but there's plenty of it. Besides, them cowboys'll be barging in here afore long."

They stood up and dropped some silver on the table for Wu, who was now silently padding about, unhooking the room's wall lamps for safekeeping. They called goodnight to the old man, wishing him an early recovery from the imminent ruination, and filed out the door.

The swinging doors of the Floradora-Six Saloon suddenly and violently flapped open as they approached, and a beefy, aproned bartender pitched an unconscious patron into the street. The man lit like a sack of meal, raising a cloud of dust, and lay peacefully still as the dust settled around and on him. The bartender disappeared back inside and Wheeler started to follow him, but Foyt raised a restraining hand. That saved Wheeler from getting banged in the nose by the swinging door, which flew open again so the bartender could scale the evictee's ten-gallon hat after him.

Now Foyt pushed through the panels, and the others followed him, into a tidal wash of noise, glare and smell. The interior of the Floradora-Six was considerably cheerier and more crowded than that of old Wu's Eathouse. It was brilliantly gaslit, even allowing for the thick miasma of tobacco smoke. There were fully four barkeeps behind the long marble-topped bar that extended the length of one side of the room, but despite their number they were kept hopping and sweating by a three- and four-deep jam of customers bellowing for service.

Behind the bartenders, and behind a protective screen of chicken wire, stretched an equally long mirror, an expensive piece of decoration, though now dismally fogged and blotched. Above it hung the obligatory life-size, full-length painting of a nude lady—this one representing some Greek-goddess-looking type, simpering, stark and supine in front of some Greek-looking truncated pillars. She appeared to be privately scratching herself, but it was impossible to judge from the expression on her face whether she was afflicted with prurience or piles. Nobody ever paid much attention to her face, anyway.

At the back of the room was the Pianola, a machine rather less elaborate and impressive than Mother Fouquet's. Three men sat abreast at the keyboard, pretending to play it, while the roll automatically hammered out "It Takes a Coon to Do the Rag Time Dance." The rest of the room was given over to small square tables —most of them occupied by men gesticulating and talking loudly over bottles and glasses—and one immense round table at which, by contrast, seven nearly motionless, tight-lipped men were playing an intense game of "Wild Annie" poker. What remained of open floor space was dotted with verdigrised brass spittoons—these, evidently, from the mess of tobacco juice all around them, not too strategically placed.

Foyt spotted a small table against the wall, occupied by only two men and they both asleep on folded arms. While Boudreaux fought his way through the teeming crowd at the bar to fetch refreshments, Foyt and Karnes tipped the chairs, gently slid the two sleepers onto the floor and nudged them up against the wall where they wouldn't be stepped on. The Cajun came back with a bottle and glasses— muttering at the outrageous price of a dollar and a half—and they all four sat down at the table.

For a few minutes they sat over their drinks, just looking around and appreciating the festive surroundings. Foyt and Wheeler nodded to a number of cowboy acquaintances in the crowd. Two men at the next table were squabbling over the comparative merits of the prize-fighters Hart and Root in their heavyweight bout at Reno this past summer. The squabble seemed to have them on the point of blows themselves, so Karnes, to quell it, leaned over and opined that

neither Hart nor Root could have licked the referee. The two quar-
relers agreed with a chuckle that that was likely so—the referee
having been the retiring champion, Jim Jeffries. They thanked
Karnes for his sage and timely adjudication, changed their subject to
the comparative merits of the Giants and Athletics, who would play
the first of their five World Series games tomorrow, and were soon
on the point of blows over that.

Foyt pulled his chair close in, so he could be heard above the
ambient uproar. He said he had been mulling over Karnes's reception of his earlier remark. "About me and Eli having ambitions not
to hire out no more. I reckon you think I was just flapping my
gums."

Karnes shrugged his massive shoulders. "I told you. I've said it
many a time myself, but I'm still a wage slave."

"But we're gonna do more'n say it," Foyt insisted. "Hell, we'll
have to. Things is closing in on the cowboy nowadays."

For example, he suggested, take a look at this drive he and
Wheeler were on right now. It hardly deserved to be called a drive.
They had hired out to one Thompson Walsh, a cow trader down
south in Giddings who didn't have a herd to start with. All the way
north up the Shreveport Trail the trader had been buying a few head
here, a few head there. Some of them from little spreads that simply
didn't have enough cows to make it worthwhile hazing them to the
nearest railhead. Some of them from big spreads—the culls and
mavericks and windies that had got left behind when the good stock
was driven to market. So the trader had collected these leftovers,
all along the way, until now they amounted to a frowsty, pick-up,
patchwork herd that was an insult to an oldtime cowboy like Foyt.

Wheeler corroborated this with a sudden laugh and the cryptic
remark, "Yea, bo! Them small-ass'ted cows!"

"That's what our cook calls 'em," Foyt explained. "You wouldn't
expect Cookie to know the diff'rence between a prize Hereford stud
and a pregnant cow buffalo, but even he refers to this bunch as 'them
small-ass'ted cows.' Christ, we got longhorns, shorthorns, old mossy-
horns, whitefaces, and some of the damndest mongrels you ever

laid eyes on. Ever see the offspring of a longhorn bull and a Jersey milk cow? We got 'em." He took a restoring drink. "Well, tomorrer we'll push on north for Shreveport, and Walsh'll pick up some more dribs and drabs betwixt here and there. We'll fetch up in the Shreveport yards with a herd we could sell to Barnum'n'Bailey sooner'n to a cattle dealer with good sense."

"Will it pay off, L. R.?" asked Karnes. "I mean, enough to make up for your lacerated sensibilities?"

Foyt said grumpily that oh, he reckoned it would. The trader had been picking up these scrubs down south for five, seven, ten dollars a head. The market was good enough right now that Walsh might get maybe an average twenty-five a head up north. He would make enough anyway to pay Foyt and Wheeler the hundred apiece they'd have coming for some six weeks' work. But, Foyt emphasized, the payoff wasn't the point.

The point he wanted to make was that, puny and pusillanimous as this little drive was, it might be *historic*—because it might be the last cattle drive there ever would be. Nobody was trail-driving overland any more. With railroads spraddling out every which way, any cattle rancher in the West could damn near carpenter himself a chute from his corrals right to the nearest railhead. Instead of the cows hiking to market half across the continent, and being all skin and skeleton when they got there, now they could trot straight into a slat-sided cattle car, and trot out of it at the market yards as fat as if they had just come off a feed lot.

"I reckon that's progress," Foyt added grudgingly. "But damn it, a cowboy don't run cows no more. He just tends meat, and a man can't take no pride in that. Moon, hand around that bottle of coyote piss ag'in."

Karnes said, "You sound bitter about progress."

"Well, I kinda hate to see the old times change, even if the new ones are an improvement. *If* they are." He sighed, pulled a cloth sack of Bull Durham out of one of his overall pockets, plucked a cigarette paper from the little folder attached, and began to roll a smoke. "In my day I've worked for ev'ry kind of outfit there is. From little boomer operators like this-here Walsh to the real big

guns like Miller & Lux that had more'n a hunderd thousand head
on spreads from Texas all the way to Montana. I've been ev'rything from reg'lar hand to rep man. I've rode the rough strings and
I've peeled broncs. On the drives, I've been ev'rything from wrangler
to trail boss. Even cooked when I had to. Any job any outfit ever
wanted to hand me, I was top ranny at it." Tapping tobacco from
the sack into the curled paper, Foyt took great care to distribute the
flakes evenly along the paper's length. "I've rode the long trails—the
Chisholm, the Sedalia, this-here Shreveport Trail—back when a drive
was something worth talking about afterwards." He had taken the
Bull Durham sack's strings in his teeth to draw its neck shut, and his
voice came indistinctly for a moment. "I've hazed cows across
hellacious alkali flats and hardpan where a man dried up like latigo
leather and the cows nearly cooked on the hoof. And I've trailed 'em
through swawmps and quicksands where I've roped out more bogged-
down cows than I've had hot meals in my life."

Foyt paused to lick one edge of the cigarette paper, roll it into a
wrinkled cylinder, twist one end of it and stick the other end in his
mouth.

"I recollect one drive in nineteen-ought-two." He recounted the
episode in the Cap Rock country when the herd was hit by the blizzard. "The cows just stood there, ass-end to the snow and the wind
and the valley, and starving where they stood. We had to rope ev'ry
blessed one of them cows and haul 'em headfirst over that ridge. It
took us a day and a night, but we done the job. We'd started that
drive with seventeen hunderd and fifty head, and I don't believe
we'd lost more'n a hunderd, time we run 'em into the Wichita
yards."

The big man and the Cajun shook their heads admiringly, and
Boudreaux murmured, *"Romantique."* Karnes said, "I'll drink to
that," and did. The bedlam of noise in the saloon died down for a
moment and they could hear the Pianola's "Would You Be True to
Eyes of Blue if You Looked into Eyes of Brown?" Foyt scraped a
kitchen match on the underside of the table and lit his cigarette. It
flared, cascaded a spew of sparks and then drew smoothly.

He squinted through the smoke, and echoed the Cajun: "Roman-

tic? I don't recall that any of us ever called our doings romantic.
Oh, there's been some good times. Poker games, some riproarious
fights, jokes we'd play on each other, a rody-o once in a while. And
we hell it up considerable in the cow towns, like here, when we can.
But them times are few and far between. The top pay I've ever
earned was sixty dollars a month and found. You don't do much
roistering on them wages. I've never owned a dress-up-to-go-to-
town suit of clo'es any better'n this Mexican serge I'm wearing right
this minute." He jabbed a thumb into the bib of his work-worn
denim overalls. "And to earn them sixty dollars I've worked ten,
twelve, fourteen hours a day, seven days a week. Never knew when
it was Sunday or Christmas or June 'Teenth, no more'n a mule would
know about Judgment Day. Why, one time we bucked through a
three-day sandstorm, had to keep them cows on the move, and I
worked sixty hours straight, pounding my tail on a saddle, not even
getting down to eat 'cept a sandwich on the grab. When that was all
over, my balls swole up like two grapefruit. For two weeks, I
couldn't sit down without leaping and screeching, and I walked like
a child bride on her honeymoon, and I thought sure I'd done gelded
myself for good. The sawbones that cured me told me I had prostrate trouble, but I've never understood that. I ain't been prostrate
enough in my whole life for it to of give me any trouble."

Karnes said, in an amused rumble, "L. R., I can't make out
whether you're bragging or complaining. They were the good old
times, and you miss them. They were the bad old times, and you
wouldn't have them back again."

The cowboy inhaled so deeply that his cigarette crinkled, and
said he reckoned he did sound contrary. But there was a difference
between then and now, and it wasn't just the obvious difference that
back then he'd been in his prime and now he wasn't. In those days,
hard as they'd been, a man could take satisfaction in a rough job
well done—because what he was bucking was nature. But now he
was bucking civilization—and even simple Eli could tell you what
civilization meant to the cowboy.

"Bob wire," Wheeler said promptly, in a melancholy voice.

"Hear that?" said Foyt. "He ain't simple beyond redemption.

Bob wire's a good enough example of civilization. It must of been the meanest man in the world, invented that stuff. You wouldn't believe how many bob wire fences we had to let down betwixt Giddings and here. And had to let 'em down gentle, and had to pick up the posts and wire ag'in after we'd crossed, and set 'em firm ag'in. It's the law."

Karnes nodded somberly. "Like you said, L. R., it's progress. We're into the twentieth century now."

Foyt's wrinkles deepened as he made a wry face. "We sure are. When the year nineteen hunderd come along, I said to myself, L. R. Foyt, I said, that's a nice round number. And that same year was when I just then turned fifty, which was another nice round number. I said to myself, L. R. Foyt, I said, this is a turning point for you, a time to make a success of yourself, settle down, quit being a mere old cow waddy on wages. But all that happened was that I met Eli about that time, and instead of one saddle stiff riding the chuck line for work or a handout, I now had two to provide for. That was five years ago. Anybody can see what a thundering success I've made of myself since then. Christ, I'm older'n the *President*." Morosely, he poured himself a brimming drink.

"Fifty-five is not exactly decrepit," said Karnes comfortingly, pouring for himself, Wheeler and Boudreaux.

"Oh, I know. I've still got my teeth and my hair and my wind. But decrepit is just what I aim *not* to be, Gideon. I've seen too many old cowboys after their useful days was over. Old and declaborated. All stove-up and wind-broke and saddle-sprung, swawmping out some bunkhouse somewhere for their bed and board. Gumming their grub like a parrot-mouth hoss that can't feed proper. Still going on working for some boss-man to the end of their days, and being grateful for it. No place to call their own, nor a woman nor a fambly nor a single dollar put away in their sock. All the happy prospects of a peckerwood in the Petrified Forest. That's not for me."

On the other hand, he admitted, cattle was all he knew. He couldn't move to some city and put on a derby hat and cloth-top shoes and go to selling insurance policies or patent medicine or whatever. But he could be his own man in his own way. If the whole West was going to be divided up and parceled out and fenced in, one of those parcels might as well be his. Ten thousand dollars would buy him five hundred head of prime stock and five thousand acres to run them on, down around Brewer's Prairie where he'd lived as a kid.

Foyt took another drag on his cigarette that brought its coal almost to his lips. He spat it on the floor and stomped on it.

"I've thought on this a long time, and me and Eli've talked many a night away. The two of us could easy rawhide a spread that size. Five thousand acres of Brewer's Prairie, a cabin, some corrals. I could draw you a pitcher right now of how the lay of our cabin and corrals will look." He broke off, shook his head with a rueful grin, and looked apologetically around the table. "Hell, I talk too much. Half the time, fellers, I'm talking to myself. A man gits in that habit when he's only had cows to converse with. Even when I talk to myself, I talk too much."

He shut up and none of the other three spoke for a while. The two cowpokes smiled dreamily into space. Karnes and the Cajun, somewhat skeptically straight-faced, avoided looking at them and instead watched two dressed-up townies Indian-arm-wrestling across a nearby table and turning purple with the effort. The noise of others' loud conversations welled about them. The Pianola tunked and tinkled in the distance, "She's Getting More like White Folks Every Day." Somewhere a bottle fell or was thrown, and broke with a brittle, liquid crash. Finally, Boudreaux asked, a little reluctantly, as if he risked pricking a pretty balloon:

"You two cowboys *got* ten t'ousand dollars?"

"No," said Foyt.

There was another silence. Karnes broke it, joshingly:

"I guess you aim to rob a bank up in Shreveport, then."

"No," said Foyt again, very quietly, as if every stranger in the room was leaning to overhear him. "We don't figger to rob no Shreveport bank." He drained his whiskey glass and said, still very quietly, "Down near a place called Teague, me and Eli, we're fixing to hold up a train."

4

1

AT ABOUT the moment that Karnes and Boudreaux were sitting thunderstruck at Foyt's ingenuous pronouncement, another man—some two hundred and fifty miles north of them—was sitting staring with distaste and dismay at a sheet of paper. He was Isaac Geller, agent for the federal Dawes Commission, at present helping administer the Kiowa Reservation in the territory which, two years from now, would become the State of Oklahoma. Geller was an efficient and dedicated civil servant, and a compassionate human being. But right now he was wishing to hell he was back in Washington, where he wouldn't have to deal personally with this piece of paper and what it represented.

He looked up at his secretary and said, "It's practically the middle of the night, Jim, and I've had a constant parade of that ragtag bunch through here all day. I'm downright bushed. Can't this one wait until tomorrow?"

The secretary shrugged his eyebrows. "This is the last of them, sir. And she's been waiting right outside all this time, chewing her fingers. Hasn't hardly budged, the livelong day."

Geller sighed. He had to admit to himself that he had deliberately —or through cowardice—put off seeing this woman to the very last, and that, if he could, he would put her off until his office expired.

51

He read again, with a grimace, the paper that sketched the history of Wilmajean Hudspeth.

"My God," he muttered. "These things used to happen in frontier days. But this is the twentieth century." Wearily he squared his shoulders. "All right, Jim, send her in."

2

As late as the 1870s, the Comanches and Kiowas were still making life generally unpleasant and often precarious for the whites in the Great Plains, and were sometimes making forays as far south as the Texas Panhandle. Their depredations in Texas usually consisted of no more than running off a few head of livestock, or desultory sniping at incautious travelers, or cutting down telegraph wires to make copper ornaments for themselves. But occasionally they committed a nuisance on a larger scale—burning out a homestead and molesting or even murdering its inhabitants.

Then they were decisively defeated in several pitched battles with the U.S. Army. The Battles of Adobe Walls, of Buffalo Wallow, of Tule and Palo Duro Canyons, all took place in the Panhandle, and all in 1874. Immediately afterward, General Ranald Mackenzie and his troops began rounding up what was left of the Comanches and Kiowas, and herding them out of Texas toward reservations in the Indian Territory to the north. "That marked the end of Indian hostilities in Texas," as one history book puts it, "except for minor incidents thereafter."

Minor incidents. One last diehard and embittered band of Kwahadi Comanche braves committed one of those minor incidents at an otherwise undistinguished spot in what is now Hemphill County, Texas, in 1877. It would not have been considered "minor" by the white family involved.

The spot was on the old Emigrant Trail that ran from Fort Smith, Arkansas, to California, the Promised Land. Wilmer Hudspeth, his wife and their daughter, in an ox-drawn Studebaker covered wagon, were members of a fifty-wagon train making that long trek when—

at this precise spot—God gave Wilmer a Sign: striking his near ox dead of old age and knocking a wheel off the wagon at the same moment. Wilmer Hudspeth had yet to see California; but he couldn't imagine that it was any more pleasant country, or offered any more opportunity for a hard-working and ambitious young farmer, than this spot right here on the Rolling Prairies of Texas. The wagon train went on without the Hudspeths, and they settled down to stake out a homestead.

By 1877, when that wrathful Kwahadi Comanche band was roaming around the vicinity on horseback, spoiling for a minor incident to commit, the Hudspeths hadn't been in residence long enough to have built up much of an estate. Their abode was only a sod house backed into a bank beside a creek. But Wilmer had built it lovingly, carefully, weathertight, and had put in an oiled-paper window, and had nicely finished the inside walls with a plaster of clay and ashes. His wife Jeannie had prettied the outside of the house by planting a profusion of wildflowers—bluebonnets, fairy thimbles, sweet William, gay-feather, widow's-tears—in the sod that roofed it.

Granted, it wasn't much. But it was even less after the Comanche band had finished galloping their ponies over it again and again, until the house was mashed flat and indistinguishable from the rest of the dirt of the creek bank. Wilmer had been right proud of that little house. He would have missed and mourned it, except that he was dead—from a bullet fired by one Kwahadi wealthy enough to possess an old Sharps carbine and intelligent enough to know how to hold it against a man's head and pull the trigger. Jeannie might have suffered a more lingering death, and endured a grueling time of it before they let her die, except that she had had the comparative good fortune to be inside the sod house when the horses rode it into the ground. There was one survivor of this minor incident: Wilmajean Hudspeth, aged ten, old enough to be of use, so when the Comanches left they took her along, and used her. Each night when they camped, the braves passed Wilmajean around at least once apiece, and there were thirteen of them.

That was the last recorded minor incident in that part of the country. By 1879, all of the Kiowas were peaceably settled on the big Kiowa Reservation that the Dawes Commission had staked out for them, and had hospitably taken in, as well, most of their former-ally Comanches. But a few bunches of Comanches—Kwahadis, Penatekas, Yamparikas—still held out, to lead a hardscrabble nomad life.

They became the gypsies of the Plains, no longer feared or hunted, merely despised and shooed from place to place. Wherever they wandered, they found more and more whites settled in, farms planted, ranches laid out, even oil derricks sprouting here and there. In this fast-civilizing and filling-up country, the Indians could no longer even contemplate going on the warpath. They could only learn to speak some English, scrounge odd jobs when they could find a white who'd trust them, commit petty thievery, knife each other once in a while, and stay as drunk as possible as often as they could get hold of some hooch or some middling-alcoholic substitute like Dr. Kilmer's Female Regulator. None of the whites in that country ever seemed to notice that one particular band of raggedy-ass Comanche tramps contained a girl child of uncommonly fair complexion. Anyway, by the time Wilmajean reached puberty, was no longer being shared around, and was "married" to just one brave, she was sufficiently filthy, smelly and verminous to be unnoticeable among the rest of the wandering bunch.

Some of the hold-out Comanches held out for years. But the Indians on the Kiowa Reservation so obviously had a good thing going, by comparison—each getting a land allotment and learning to make it prosper, each settling in to become a good and valued citizen of the imminent State of Oklahoma—that one after another of the nomad groups said the hell with the free, untrammeled and desperately impoverished life, and came asking for admission to the reservation. By the terms of the Curtis Act, they were not only admissible but welcome.

The very last hold-out group, twenty-five draggled and defeated Kwahadi Comanches who had long ago sold even their horses, and who had been subsisting for the past year mainly by eating their travois dogs, trudged surlily onto the reservation in October, 1905.

This was the bunch that agent Isaac Geller had just spent the day and much of the night "processing" through the necessary paper-work. The twenty-fourth and twenty-fifth members of the group were Wilmajean Hudspeth and her halfbreed daughter.

3

The paper before him on the desk read, in part:
HUDSPETH, Wilmajean, spinster, aged appr. 38, white Amer.
HUDSPETH, daughter, aged appr. 9, father Comanche.
Geller looked up from it, at Hudspeth, Wilmajean, nominally spinster, and was almost agreeably impressed. During her long wait to be interviewed, she had found a friendly local resident Kiowa squaw, and from her had borrowed a washtub, soap and hot water. It had required several changes of the hot water, but Wilmajean had come out of it visibly a white woman, blue-eyed, honey-blonde with just a trace of silver, and passably good-looking. She had also taken pains to put on her "best dress," a pathetic thing of once ornamen-tally beaded and quilled buckskin. Patches of the beads were missing and the buckskin was so greasy that it could have been used all by itself for waxing furniture. She sat straight and prim and proper in the chair before Geller's desk, and tried very hard to look the up-standing, chaste, deserving young matron.

Geller could have dismissed her with a few terse official phrases, but he was a compassionate man. He would try to break it to her as easily as possible. "Good evening, Miss Hudspeth," he said.

"Good evenin', sir," she replied, somewhat tremblingly, but with little trace of guttural Indian accent.

"You speak English, then." Most of the incoming Comanches did, either adequately or in pidgin fashion, but English—country English, anyway—was obviously this woman's native tongue.

"Oh, yes, sir. I wouldn't never let myself forgit my English. I learnt my li'l gal, too. O' course, I speak Injun besides."

"But we can't pretend you *are* Indian, can we?" Establish this firmly, Geller.

"Well, I bin one for nigh thirty years."

"Tell me about it, Miss Hudspeth."

She frowned uneasily. "Don't it tell it all on that-there paper yonder?"

"I'd rather hear it from you. I'm trying to find some way to help—" Geller bit his tongue; there was no way. "I'd just rather hear it from you."

"Well." She gave a shuddering sigh. "It was when I was ten years old. They kilt my pa and ma and throwed me across a pony in front of one of 'em and carried me off, me all cryin' and all. And when we'd gone a ways, they all, one after another after another, they all— well, you know." Ike Geller winced and cursed inwardly. "I was just bleedin', the whole time. We got to the tribe grounds, finally, and all the other bucks, they done it to me, too, all but the real old men. The squaws, they beat me. When I wasn't bein' beat or I wasn't bein' bedded, they worked me like a dog. Grindin' corn meal, chewin' buckskin, jerkin' buffalo meat, b'ilin' down salt, ev'rything there was *to* do. Finally I—what they call 'come of age'—and this one buck claimed me all for his own." She named him, in Comanche, a string of thorny consonants and throaty vowels. "That's John Blackwater, when he got his white name sometime later. I was —what they figger married-up to him—since I was, oh, fourteen or so."

Geller inquired tentatively, "Did you, well, love him?"

"*Love an Injun?!* No, sir, I never thunk of him as no husband. He had two other squaws, anyhow. No, I just belonged to him. I worked as hard for him as I ever worked when I belonged to the whole tribe. Harder, these last years, when times have bin so bad for us. Well, he died, five years gone. He got work as a gandy-dancer on that-there railroad they're buildin' over yonder way"— she gestured vaguely eastward—"and when he got paid off, he got drunk and come back to camp late one night after we was all asleep, and he fell down with his head in the fire, and nobody noticed him till next mornin'."

Geller swallowed. "And this, er, John Blackwater was the father of your daughter?"

"Yes, sir. Why I didn't drop twenty childer in all them years, I don't know. But I had only the one." She named the girl, too, in grunts and gutturals. "It means Feather."

Ike Geller fiddled with a pencil. "As you said, Miss Hudspeth, 'all those years.' Why in the nation didn't you ever run away?" This had nothing to do with the case; Geller was asking out of his own curiosity. "The Comanches have been degenerate for years. Weak. Played out. They couldn't have held you by force, like the old days. This is nineteen-oh-five. Why did you put up with all those years of misery? Why didn't you run away?"

With flat practicality Wilmajean asked, "Run off into the empty prairie when I was ten years old?" She looked at him; he couldn't think of anything to say. "And when I was old enough to run, by then I was an Injun. A Comanche squaw, just as Injun as Injun. Where would I of run *to?*"

"No, you were never an Indian, Miss Hudspeth." This must be kept firmly established—unless—if there might be some little loophole— "Tell me, were you ever formally adopted into the tribe?"

For the first time she shed her timidity and showed spirit. With withering scorn she asked him, "Would *you* adopt one of your *niggers?*"

Geller blinked, said no, he guessed not, he saw what she meant —and bent his head to study her sheet of paper some more. What now? He could quote to her the Curtis Act, with all its amendments and appendices and whereases, but he might as well try to tell her straight.

"Miss Hudspeth, I'm an agent of the United States government, *your* government, and as such I'm duty bound to represent your interests as an American citizen. But I am here on this reservation only in an advisory capacity. This land is ceded by treaty to the Indians. In a sense this is a foreign country and I am only an envoy."

She was staring at him with her eyes wide, as if she might comprehend through them what she couldn't through her ears.

"I know you don't understand all this fancy language. But what it amounts to is that our government specifies very strictly that this

Kiowa Reservation shall belong to the Indians and *only* to the Indians, thus you and I are merely tolerated trespassers here. In short, Miss Hudspeth, your daughter Feather is half Comanche by birth and she has a home here. As a full-blooded white American, you do not."

There was a long silence. Finally she said breathlessly, "You-all're keepin' Feather and sendin' me away?"

"Send you away, yes, I must. But no fear, we won't keep your daughter against your will." He cleared his throat. "Nevertheless, I hope you'll consider the advantages of leaving her here. Feather will certainly be adopted by some fine family; you know how the Indians cherish orphan children. And there are going to be some good schools here before long. She'll have an education, a solid life to look forward to. Someday she'll marry, and her husband will have a land allot—"

"Me go away and leave Feather?" she repeated, stunned.

"Wouldn't it be best for her? When you leave here, where will you go? What will you do? What will become of her?"

Wilmajean recovered herself and said, again with some spirit, "Mister Agent, sir, I'm close onto bein' a middle-aged woman. My whole life got throwed away. There won't never a white man have me now, nor no other white folks have anythin' to do with me. I bin an Injun squaw, and I might as well be carryin' the consumption. All I got to show for all them years is this-here old buckskin rag— and my li'l dotter. She's the one and onliest thing in this wide world that belongs to me. And you want me to give her up?"

Geller slumped in his chair. This was all damned terrible and he was a damned pencil-pushing automaton and he damned the damned laws and rules that regulated his damned machinery.

"When you leave here, Miss Hudspeth," he said miserably, "I'm not empowered—I can't offer you so much as a pony or traveling money or even traveling rations. What on earth are you and that child going to do?"

"We'll go back south, to Texas," Wilmajean said simply, as if hundreds of miles meant nothing. "I heared a while back about a

place called Brewer's Prairie where there's s'posed to be some Hudspeths livin'. I don't know 'em, but maybe they're kin. Just
maybe . . ."

There was another long silence, during which Ike Geller tussled
fiercely with his conscience.

"Go then," he said at last. "Take Feather with you. And here, my
dear, this is all I can do for you." He took out his own slender
wallet—an Indian agent of whatever government bureau was not
rich; at least no honest agent was—and handed her a ten-dollar bill.
"Maybe it will get you as far as your Brewer's Prairie."

She took it without embarrassment, but gratefully, thanked him
for it and left the room. He saw, waiting in the hallway outside, a
small and lissome girl, also clad in buckskin, also well-scrubbed,
dark-eyed as her father, honey-blonde as her mother. Wilmajean
took the child by the hand and they moved slowly off down the hall.
Isaac Geller murmured after them, in a language totally alien to any
spoken in this place or even in this century, *"Shalom aleichem . . ."*

When his secretary came in, Geller asked him, "Jim, do you
happen to know where in God's name there's a place called Brewer's Prairie?"

The secretary thought for a moment. "Yes, sir, I believe I do.
Yes, there used to be a place by that name, down in East Texas,
somewhere between the Trinity and Brazos Rivers. But they don't
call it that any more. There's a right bustling railroad town there
now, and they call it Teague."

5

IDEON KARNES goggled at L. R. Foyt. He looked all around, satisfied himself that the uproar in the Floradora-Six Saloon had not diminished, that no one was paying attention to them, and rumbled gently, "If you're truly contemplating something like a holdup, ought you to be telling us?"

Foyt raised a knuckly finger to shush him, and turned to Wheeler to say, "Did you notice, Eli, when we was coming in here, that feller the barkeep was throwing out was Dal Gaybold? The last I seen of old Dallas, he was moseying upstairs at the Mahogany Parlor. So if he's back out on the town and drunk already, some of the gals must be free by now. Why'n't you slope on over there and see can Mother Fouquet fix you up? Mind your manners, now."

"Yes, suh." The young man stood up, squared his hat, hitched up his overalls and said, "How would this do, suh? 'Mother Fouquet, I'd admire to entertain one of your young ladies . . .'"

"Do just fine, son. Tell you what—I think you'd like the one called the Carrot-top Kid. Ask if she's available."

Pouring another round of drinks, Foyt told his remaining two tablemates, "That Carrot-top's got a soft spot for crippled puppies and lost kittens and such. Eli'll appeal to her."

"That's bully," said Karnes impatiently. "Look here, are you serious, L. R.? About holding up a train? Nobody but you and that good-natured gosling?"

"I figgered you'd want to ask something like that. That's why I scooted Eli on out. But you can speak plainer'n you're doing, friend. You mean a good-natured goose like him and a spavined old poop like me, don't you? Well, you're right. We could use a couple more hands."

The Cajun grinned, his mustache bristling. "You mean you want me and Gideon in on dis, *hein?*"

Foyt sighed slightly and said no, not really. "Who I *want* is Jesse James and Sam Bass and Cole Younger. But two of them's dead and the other is retired to doing tricks in a Wild West show. Maybe there's other men as experienced as them three, but I ain't got time to look for 'em. So I've just been hoping to run onto somebody else suitable. I seen you two handle yourselves in that ruckus over at Mattie Fouquet's. And no offense, but I git the impression you ain't got no urgent engagements elsewhere right now."

Karnes and Boudreaux exchanged a look, then shook their heads.

"Okay, I can handle myself," said Karnes. "And I've got the mustard for that kind of job, I suppose. But *I've* never done anything like this. You, Moon?"

"*Non.* I been ev'ry damn t'ing, me, *but* a train robber."

"Hell, neither was the James boys afore the first time they tried it," Foyt reminded them. "They was farm boys, scissorbills, until they got tired of being it, and busted loose to turn bandit. Just like me. I aim to bust loose and better myself. That's the kind of hairpin *I* am."

"You mentioned some place called Teague," said Karnes. "That sounds like you've already fixed on some particular train."

"Yep."

"What'll it be carrying?"

"Money. Cash money. Greenbacks."

Karnes scratched meditatively with one paw in the mat of red fur on the back of the other. "How much money, L. R.? Enough to make it worthwhile for all four of us?"

"If you ain't greedy. I told you I need ten thousand spondulix to buy that spread I've been dreaming about. That's how much I expect to git, and that's how much you'd each of you and Eli git. The train'll be carrying more, but I don't aim to take it all."

"Ten. Thousand. Dollars," Karnes said slowly, his mild blue eyes fixed on some far horizon. "That would make me a grubstake and more. I could head straight out to the Superstitions." He became aware of the other two men looking mildly questioning and added, "I'm like you, L. R. I'm fed up to here with what I've been doing— mostly rigging in the oil fields. I just got laid off down at Spindletop. The field's yield has been leveling off and old Captain Lucas is running scared. So I'm on my way up to Shreveport. They've just started to prospect in the Caddo field up near there, and they'll be yelling for riggers. I get good pay, too. Fifty-five cents an hour."

"Glory!" said Foyt, looking impressed but concerned. "That's half as much as Gov'nor Lanham gits! With a good trade like yours, maybe you wouldn't want to join our little—"

Karnes waved a ham hand. "My Thought-damned 'good trade' is the hardest work there is. The insurance companies won't insure a rigger, you know that? They say the job is just too risky for them to bet we won't get killed. And I believe it." He touched the scar on his forehead. "That laid me up for three months. I still get head-aches."

He lifted the whiskey bottle to the light, eyed its content level and poured them each another drink.

"Of course, a rigger can work at just about any other kind of mining there is hereabouts. Sulphur. Gas wells. But the only way you can get at sulphur is with live steam blasted down into the ground through Frasch pipes. That's healthy work, too. I've seen men boiled like crawfish, just as pink and just as dead."

Boudreaux gagged on his drink. "Man, don't spile my taste for de good *écrevisse!*"

"Then there's natural gas. Sometime try living and working in the middle of the smell of rotten eggs. On the job you're keeling over from suffocation every five minutes, and off the job you wear a stench that would poison a polecat."

"But them good wages!" protested Foyt, still impressed. "Fifty-five cents an hour oughta buy you a good barbershop bath ev'ry payday. Hell, put in enough paydays at them wages and you can retire young."

Karnes shook his leonine head. Thought knew it was prime pay, all right, but Thought also knew there was no holding on to the money. It drizzled through a man's fingers like drill slurry. After working the field all week long, a man was inclined to blow his whole pay on the weekend, just to buy a change. In saloons like this one, to wash the taste of sulphur out of his mouth. In cathouses like Mother Fouquet's, to flush the clog of crude oil out of his ducts. Naturally, a rigger never had much chance with any kind of females except whores like Pepper Frenchy, who were paid to put up with the smell of rotten eggs.

"I'm like you, L. R.," Karnes said again. "I don't know any other trade but mining, and I'll stick with it. But I want to mine something that doesn't fart or ooze out of the ground. Something that comes out of the earth clean and hard and looking like what it's worth."

"Something like gold?" Foyt inquired shrewdly.

Karnes said Foyt had guessed it. In the middle of the Arizona desert were some mountains called the Superstitions, because they were so gloomy and mysterious and inhospitable. But somewhere in those mountains there was a lost gold mine, supposed to be the richest in the Southwest.

"It was found by an old desert rat they called the Dutchman. They say he took gold out of it right up until he died, just thirteen-fourteen years ago. He didn't leave it to anybody, or leave anybody any hint to where it is, so now they call it the Lost Dutchman Mine. But I've been studying maps and reading up on it and buttonholing every mining man that's ever heard of it. By now I've got a Thought-damned good idea where that Lost Dutchman Mine is, and I've been trying for a long time to save up a grubstake and go and look."

He took a long pull at his glass. At the back end of the barroom, the Pianola was tinkling and twanging, aptly, "Just a Bird in a Gilded Cage." Foyt turned to the Cajun.

"What about you, Moon? Ten thousand sound tempting to you?"

"*Oui, parfait.* Dat buy my way into politics."

"What?"

"I been wanting to pass on Baton Rouge"—he nodded to the southeast—"and become a politician, me."

"Politics!" said Karnes, scandalized. "Talk about farting and oozing and muck and slime . . ."

"*Comme même,*" said the Cajun calmly. "But less muck dan what dis coon-ass *been* doing. I jes' come from de hot, wet, stinking *con* of Louisiana—dem Atchafalaya swamps. Logging bald cypress I been doing, and bald cypress only grows in de hot, wet, stinking *flottants.* I feel like half-gator, me, after two years in dem damn *flottants,* working from can-see to can't-see. Now, ten t'ousand dollars ought to buy me some office like clerk of somet'ing. I mek a name for myself dere, come next election time I *run* for somet'ing —de legislature mebbe—and I win easy."

"What makes you so sure of that?"

"Hell, all de Cajuns vote for me. I mek dem proud of me. Dere ain't not one of us coon-asses ever made it higher in politics dan mebbe sheriff of some piss-pot parish. All de gover'ment is run by dem damn North Louisiana *Baptistes.* All dem perched up high, strutting de cakewalk, allatime looking down on de Cajuns, grinding down on dem. If one Cajun mek it big in de statehouse—and dat be me—all de Cajuns be proud and happy."

"I see," said Foyt. "You're out to uplift your people. I do admire a man with ideals."

The Cajun widened his black eyes and said, "Ideals? *Pas du tout!* I gonna uplift *me!* Git my own snout in dat gover'ment trough. I don't care where de boodle come from—my *people* don't care— long as I git my share."

"Well, blame it," said Karnes. "How is it going to make the Cajuns proud and happy to have you in the statehouse grinding down on them just like the Baptist politicians?"

"You don't see? One of *dere own* meks good. Dey don't notice no diff'rence in de squeeze, but now some of de squeeze lines *my* pocket. A *hometown boy* meks good. Why, sho dey be proud!"

"Well, yes, I guess . . . put it that way . . ." Karnes gave up, shook his big head and said, "I think this whiskey's getting to me again."

It was getting to all of them. Karnes's normally brick-red face was now darkened to puce, Boudreaux was slumped so low in his chair that he seemed to be hanging on the edge of the table by his mustache, and Foyt's ordinarily pale gray eyes now looked like the ends of two severed veins. None of them, probably, could have stood up and walked very gracefully, but their thinking and speaking functions seemed relatively unimpaired.

On others, the Floradora-Six's house-special brands were having other effects. From the crowd against the bar came a bellow, "Le's all go 'cross-a-street an' bust up th' Chink's!" Immediately there was a rush for the door. It emptied that side of the room of every patron wearing a wide-brimmed hat, and left the bar lined with only the derbied heads of visiting drummers, dudes and Saturday-night-slumming townies.

Foyt appeared to have satisfied himself that the motivations of his two new acquaintances—a case of gold fever in the one, political fever in the other—were sufficient to qualify them for enlistment in his project. It seemed no more than a formality to ask them, "Are you-all throwing in with me and Eli, then?"

"If you'll have us," said Karnes, slurredly but politely.

Foyt made a solemn, drunken little bow, and the other two bowed back just as owlishly.

"Tell us about this train," suggested Karnes. "Is it some kind of special run?"

"Yep."

"How did a cowboy come to know about it?"

Foyt chuckled. "If you can imagine such a thing as a black-sheep cowboy, I'm it. I come from a railroading fambly. All the rest of my kin took up iron hosses instead of four-legged ones. My cousin Norwood is a dispatcher on the Trinity & Brazos Valley line. He knows I've been waiting for an opportunity like this. And he knew I was coming north from Giddings with this drive. When we crossed the

T. & B.V. line at the Iola jerkwater, Norwood had a boy waiting for me with a copy of this-here dispatch that had come over his wire." He reached in the hip pocket of his overalls and took out a rump-curved, mashed-thin old leather wallet. "If ev'rything works out right, I've promised Norwood a thousand dollars for tipping us off. O' course, Norwood makes good wages. But his wife Blossom has social ambitions, and that keeps Norwood broke, poor cuss."

Foyt fished a frazzled yellow paper out of the wallet and handed this across the table. The paper had been so often before unfolded, read and folded again that it was now limp and fracturing along the creases. Karnes's big paws opened it with great care. He read the message silently to himself, then—after a cautious look around and behind him—began to repeat the text aloud, word by word, hiccuping occasionally:

GENERAL MANAGER, TRINITY & BRAZOS VALLEY RAIL ROAD, HOUSTON
SUPERINTENDENT, T. & B.V. R.R., TEAGUE
CHIEF DISPATCHER, T. & B.V., TEAGUE

"Them's who-all this message was telegraphed to," explained Foyt. "That last one, Chief Dispatcher at Teague, that's Cousin Norwood."

Karnes hiccuped and continued:

REA EXPRESS CAR . . .

"Not *Rea*," Foyt corrected him. "R-E-A. Stands for Railway Express Agency."

REA EXPRESS CAR NUMBER 1120 TO ARRIVE CLEBURNE ON
TRAIN NUMBER 13 AT 06:30 A.M. NOVEMBER 9 DESTINATION
HUBBARD CITY. THIS CAR CARRIES FUNDS FOR FIRST STATE
BANK HUBBARD. REA GUARDS BEING FURNISHED THROUGH
WITH CAR. PROTECT AND EXPEDITE.
V. A. ANDERSON
GENERAL MANAGER
ATCHISON, TOPEKA & SANTA FE R.R.
GALVESTON

"Well, it seems clear enough," said Karnes. " 'Funds for First State Bank Hubbard. But how do you know it's not just a sack of nickels and dimes?"

Foyt said there were three reasons. Railway Express wouldn't send a car full of armed guards with a bag of small change. And there wouldn't be a notice sent all down the line so far in advance; that car would not be arriving until November ninth, nearly a month in the future. But the best reason was to be found in the history and circumstances of Hubbard City and environs. That part of East Texas had been settled by Polacks—actually by an assortment of immigrants: Germans, Austrians, Czechs, Poles, Russians, but indiscriminately called Polacks by every Anglo Texan. These conglomerate settlers had put the prairie land in cotton, and they had prospered beyond belief. Their shipping center, Hubbard City, despite its big-sounding name, wasn't much more than a cotton compress and a loading dock alongside the railroad track. But now there was so much cash and credit slips and notes-of-hand and bills-of-lading moving in and out of little Hubbard City that the Polacks found themselves needing a bank. Hence the First State had just been chartered and was about to open its doors next month. In November.

"You mean," mused Karnes, "this special car is bringing all the money the bank will be opening with?"

"That's right. From some kind of a central bank or the mint or something in Denver. Ev'ry cent of the Hubbard City bank's working capital—the money for the vault, for the tellers' tills, for the whole operation. It can't be less'n a million dollars."

"A million dollars!" Boudreaux came quite upright in his chair and Karnes blurted, "Why, Thought damn, L. R.! That's two hundred and fifty thousand apiece for us! We'll be stinking rich. I won't have to go gold-hunting, you won't have to—"

"Whoa. Whoa." Foyt held up a big-knuckled hand. "I said at the beginning, I don't aim to cabbage ev'rything that train'll be carrying."

The other two deflated slightly. Would Foyt please elaborate on that statement?

"Reasons ag'in. For one, we ain't the James boys. That million dollars for the bank is just too big a haul for greenhorns to try for. But that same train's going to be carrying something else."

Boudreaux protested, "Man, you said we'd land cash money."

"Hush. I'm still talking cash money. But it's something y'all wouldn't know about unless you know enough about the railroad to savvy that dispatch there." He tapped the yellow paper that still lay in front of Karnes. "That car number eleven-twenty is coming east from Denver, hitched to the Santa Fe's train Number Thirteen. At the same time—and this you wouldn't know—train Number Three of the Trinity & Brazos Valley line comes south from Fort Worth bound for Houston. Them two trains make connections at Cleburne. That car eleven-twenty, full of money and full of armed guards, gits uncoupled from the Sante Fe and coupled onto the T. & B.V.'s train Number Three. It comes on south to Hubbard City. And there the car, the million dollars, the guards and their guns, all git shunted off amongst the Polacks."

"While we just stand around and pick our noses?" Karnes grumbled tipsily.

"We won't be anywhere near there. Pay attention. When it leaves Hubbard, that train keeps coming south toward Houston, but on the way it stops at a place called Teague. Now, Teague's another boom town, like Hubbard, only bigger. It grew up just because of the railroad. That piece of country used to be plain Brewer's Prairie —I told you I grew up there—and the town wasn't much more'n a wide place in the road. Few stores, a saloon, a fence-corner bank, not many houses—ev'rybody lived out on their land. But when the Trinity & Brazos Valley Rail Road was a-building, it picked that spot for a division point and gave it the new name. Now it's got a big yard, a roundhouse, back shops. There's close to a thousand men working there. What with their famblies and all the other folks that make up a town, Teague's got maybe three thousand people already, near as big as Nacogdoches, and it's not much over a year old."

Boudreaux commented languidly that all this information was interesting, but not very.

Foyt snorted. "Either one of you two smart alecks know when railroad men git paid?"

"Everybody knows that," said the big man. "Twice a month. The tenth and the twenty-fifth."

"And they git paid in cash—hard, cold cash—on account of most of 'em couldn't sign their names to a check. Now look at that dispatch ag'in."

Light began to dawn on Karnes. "To arrive . . . November nine." The light got into his eyes. "That train will be carrying the payroll for the division hands?"

"To be paid out the next day, as soon as it's counted and divvied and tucked in them little envelopes. I said there's near a thousand men working at Teague. Be modest and call it eight hunderd and fifty. Figger they make on the average a hunderd dollars a month apiece, and they'll be gitting half a month's pay. Or they would be, except that we're gonna stop that train just short of Teague and lighten it a little."

Karnes had been busily calculating with a big blunt fingertip in a puddle of spilled whiskey on the tabletop. "I make it out that that train's going to be carrying *at least* forty-two thousand five hundred dollars. A thousand for your cousin Norwood . . . leaves . . . uh, ten thousand three hundred and something for each of us. You called it, all right."

"And it oughta be easy to take," said Foyt confidently, but rapping his knuckles on the table for luck. "Say you're on the crew of that train. You're freighting a million dollars and a bunch of trigger-happy REA guards. You're *expecting* trouble. But lo and behold, you pull into Hubbard City and drop off the special car without a hitch. You're shed of the big wad of money and the gun-toting guards. So you breathe a happy sigh and go highballing on south without a worry. Sure, there's still forty-some thousand dollars on board, but *hell!* Who would pass up a million-dollar angel food cake and settle for the crumbs?"

"*We* would, *hein?*" Boudreaux barked gleefully. "Man, we got a bird nest on de ground!"

In an undertone, Foyt sketched a few more details. When that

T. & B.V. train left Cleburne after rendezvousing with the Santa Fe train, it would consist, from front to rear, of an engine—a Baldwin 4–6–0 coal-burner—a tender full of coal, the special REA million-dollar express car, then the train's regular REA express car, a U.S. mail car and finally the four passenger coaches. On arrival at Hubbard City, the train would back and fill to uncouple that special car out of its middle and shunt it onto a siding.

When the train resumed its southward journey, there would be six in the crew: the engineer and fireman, head brakeman, conductor, brakeman and one regularly assigned REA guard. That one would probably be armed, Foyt cautioned. He would have a shotgun somewhere in his express car, but he would almost certainly be either asleep or passed-out. Drunk was the usual condition of every man in a train crew on a familiar routine run, and they'd be even more likely to be relaxing after having got rid of that nervous-making money car. It would be a cinch to stop the train, throw down on the fuddled crew, persuade the REA guard to open his little tin-can safe and hand over the payroll.

"Yes, you make it sound like a cinch, L. R.," said Karnes, his forehead furrowing to his red hairline. "But a Baldwin 4–6–0 is no peewee switch engine. It'll be moving right along. And, from all I've read, stopping a highballing train is no child's play."

"Banana oil," said Foyt, with a sweeping gesture of contempt. "You been reading that *Young Wild West* or that *Police Gazette*. I know. The robbers always have to make their plans and their moves with split-second timing just to git *at* the train, and then they have to stop it or derail it by blowing up some dynamite or prizing up the tracks, and then they have to make their gitaway with some more split-second timing and skedaddling. Banana oil."

Foyt said he reckoned all that kind of rootytooting made for a good story, but it was about as necessary as the amative organ on a steer. The Baldwin 4–6–0 was a good-sized locomotive, true enough, but when it was highballing on the Trinity & Brazos Valley line, "highballing" meant maybe doing twenty miles an hour. The T. & B.V. was what railroad men scornfully called "a wooden-axle railroad," and its line wasn't to be believed, unless you'd had the mischance to ride on it. Those passengers who had were inclined to interpret the company's initials as "Travel and Be Vibrated."

The T. & B.V. roadbed was alternately sand, where the rails tended to sink, and blackland, where the rails heaved. It was something like Boudreaux's swamp-floating railroad. The line consisted of only a single track, with sidings at intervals where trains going in opposite directions could edge past each other. But there were no block signals on the line, and the telegraph equipment didn't work half the time. So every train proceeded rather cautiously, mindful of the possibility of meeting an unannounced fellow train head-on. The condition of the line was enough to make this likely, but another factor was the reasonable expectation that any and every train's crew members would be pissed to the eyeballs.

"So our train Number Three is going to be coming south at no more'n a moderate speed," said Foyt. "We make sure we're on a long straight stretch where the hoghead has got a good view ahead, even if he's fogged up as usual."

"Hoghead?"

"The engineer. So he's got a good lookout and plenty of room to make an easy stop. We don't blow up the tracks, we don't prize 'em up, we don't do nothing gaudy. All we do is run a herd of cattle onto the tracks and stall 'em there. If you was driving that train, wouldn't you stop?"

Karnes hiccuped and said he guessed he would. Sure he would. But if that was all it took, it just sounded too blamed simple.

"You mean it wouldn't make no blood-and-thunder dime novel. Well, I ain't out to be celebrated in song and story—I'm out to stop a train. What'll happen, the hoghead'll inch that engine up to where we're sitting our hosses, looking like we ain't got sense enough to move our cows. He'll cuss us out good, and let on that we've knocked the beejesus out of the whole railroad's timetable. The passengers in them coaches at the back will all just sit where they're at and grouse, figgering it's only something normal—one of the usual breakdowns or a stop to pick up some drunk that fell off. The rest of the train's crew will drift up front to help cuss us out. And when they're all up front, we unlimber our guns and tell 'em what we're there for. That's all there'll be to it, and that's all I *want* there to be to it. If you hanker to git your exploits in a book, Gideon, you can hold up another train some other time with a great big shoot-'em-up."

The big man said he guessed he wouldn't, that Foyt's plan sounded eminently practical, *hic*, even if it did lack flair. Boudreaux remarked that the Great Teague Holdup was still a month off; in the meantime, what were to be the preparations?

"We're gonna need some expense money," said Foyt, "and I got about twenty dollars. Me and Eli gotta finish this drive or we don't git paid off. It'll take us close on two weeks to git to Shreveport. Today's the eleventh of October. Can we all meet in Shreveport on the twenty-fifth?"

The big man said that was where he was headed for anyway, and the Cajun said he might as well head there as anywhere.

"Okay. Now. You boys got guns?" They said no; Foyt looked disgusted. "Not armed and not mounted. You got any money?"

Boudreaux said no again. Karnes said he had enough to get the two of them to Shreveport. He'd have two weeks before the rendezvous date to put in working at the Caddo field, and he could probably wangle a job for Boudreaux as a roughneck. He paused to do some more calculating in his puddle of whiskey. If they both worked ten hours a day, they ought to clear a hundred dollars between them by the time Foyt and Wheeler blew in.

Foyt added it up. "With our hunderd apiece, and my twenty, that'll give us three hunderd and twenty all told." He looked worried. "It's sure gonna be a shoestring operation."

The first and main thing they would need, he said, was at least a small herd of cows to drive across that railroad track. Fortunately, he had already made arrangements for that. As part of his terms of employment, he had cozened that cheeseparing trader Walsh into agreeing that Foyt could buy twenty head of his own choice at ten dollars apiece, as soon as the drive was over and before the cows were put up at market.

"So there goes my and Eli's two hunderd, but it's necessary."

Karnes objected. "Two hundred dollars shot and we have to drive twenty cows all the way back to Teague? Wouldn't it make more sense for us just to wait until we're on the scene and, uh, borrow a few of somebody else's cows for the few minutes we'll need them?"

Foyt said he had thought of that possibility but discarded it. So much of the country between Shreveport and Teague was now cotton land and farmland that there'd be no guarantee they would find any cattle anywhere near the holdup scene. To make sure of having the cows when they needed them, they would have to borrow from the first spread they came to on their way. That wouldn't cost anything, true, but they'd still have to haze the herd overland to Teague. And they wouldn't get much train-robbing done if they were being chased all across East Texas as cattle rustlers.

Karnes shrugged sleepily, said all right, Foyt was the boss, and subsided to hiccup at intervals.

"Now, I've got this old Billy-the-Kid." Foyt patted his bib front. "And a Winchester thirty-thirty back at the camp. I don't let Eli carry a gun, as a rule, him being simple and all. But I'll let him hold my carbine when the time comes. And me and Eli've got two hosses apiece. We can lend you each one. But that still leaves you-all needing saddles and guns, and all of us needing grub, and we'll only have you-all's hunderd dollars and my twenty to buy 'em all with."

Boudreaux pointed out that he and Karnes would be spending two weeks at Caddo, and that an inevitable feature of any oil camp was its running games of poker, faro and craps. They just might be able to win some money, and maybe some gear and guns, too.

"That means risking what little we've got," said Foyt. "Don't you do it. We'll just have to canvass the pawnshops at trail's end, and hope we find gear that's beat-up enough that we can afford it."

He stood up, slowly and carefully. "I got to git back to camp. I'm ramrodding this drive, and at four o'clock I got to be yelling 'Roll out!' to all them waddies snoring in their soogans." Out of one of his many overall pockets he tugged a big and dented Ingersoll watch on a braided leather fob, and closed one eye to peer at it. "Almost midnight now, and four o'clock comes almighty soon after. Damned if I ever thought I'd poot through Nacogdoches without paying my respects to one of Ma Fouquet's gals, but I'll save what cash I've got. I'll just go over and collect Eli."

The other two got up, equally carefully, and followed him weaving through the throng to the door. They had some small confusion with the swinging panels, which seemed to be more numerous and contrary than previously, but eventually they were all three outside and the racket of the Floradora-Six was fading behind them—the babble of voices, the thuds of fallings-down, the ptooies of tobacco spit, the clash of glassware, the tinny tinkle of the Pianola's "Here's Your Hat, What's Your Hurry?"

Foyt took a deep breath of the chill October night. "In case you don't know, Shreveport is a strict and straitlaced Baptist town. Don't allow no Hell's Half Acre like this-here North Street. All their high life and honkytonks is across the river from Shreveport in Bossier City. Pious and prissy damn hypocrites, all they do is sneak across a bridge."

Crash! The red door of the Great Peking Water Gate Eathouse flew outwards, off its hinges, and fell flat in the street. Across it trooped a double file of drunken, disheveled, singing cowboys, carrying at shoulder height another man with his head jammed inside a huge iron cooking pot; from under the rim of the pot dangled a pigtail. The procession went whooping and dancing off up the street.

Foyt went on as if he hadn't been interrupted. "There's a good saloon there in Bossier City called the Bad Penny—mark that name down in your hatband. That's where we'll meet. If all of us ain't there at once, don't nobody budge till we are. The night of the twenty-fifth. The Bad Penny."

ON WEDNESDAY, October 25, three things happened in and around Shreveport, Louisiana, a while before L. R. Foyt and Eli Wheeler got there.

1

Early that morning, two men rode into the stockyards on the western outskirts of Shreveport, between the fairgrounds and the Illinois Central freight depot. One of the men was medium-sized, with a medium face, medium hair, medium garb. He was nondescript and unnoticeable enough to be either a respectable range detective or the worst sort of badman. His only sartorial distinction was a gunbelt around his waist that supported a well-used-looking Colt Peacemaker sixgun in a quick-draw tiedown holster. The other man was big and fat—too fat for the spindly little mare he rode, or, rather, lopped over. He had an apoplectic-mauve face and wore the wide-brimmed hat, denim jacket and jeans of a cowboy riding trail, but his shirt was hitched at the collar with a string necktie. If he was from a trail gang, he was the boss of it. A curious companion trotted alongside his horse, a stubby-legged basset hound, panting to keep up. The fat man took off his hat to swipe out the band, revealing a sweat-shiny dome as bald and rosy as a buzzard's.

Two feedyard hands, leaning against a corral fence, watched the riders go by. One of them took his chewing straw out of his teeth to point it at the medium-looking man. "Yonder comes old Bubba."

"Uh-huh. That's Bubba, okay. Who's that fat fella with him?"

Snort. "You don't know that fat bastard? That there's Toad Walsh."

"Say which?"

Sneer. "Toad Walsh. One of them shiftless boomer cow traders. Allus talkin' some big cattle deal—*when* he ain't duckin' down alleys so as not to meet somebody he owes four bits to. Brags big, acts small. Name of Thompson Walsh, but don't nobody call him nothin' but Toad."

"How come? You git warts if you touch him?"

Spit. "Nobody knows. Don't nobody want to touch him. He's a four-flusher, a real snake in the grass, a mean old mudcat from Mississippi. See that sawed-off li'l dog he got?"

"Uh-huh."

Snicker. "Folks see Toad walkin' that dog around town on a string, they say there goes a son of a bitch on *both ends* of that string."

"Do tell. What meanness is he up to right now, you reckon?"

Shrug.

Walsh and Bubba rode without speaking, as if unaware of each other's presence. They threaded around and through corrals, chutes and pens, their horses' hooves thwocking in the churned-up mud underfoot, until they came to a plank sidewalk fronting a row of shacky little offices bearing the names of various agents, factors, packing houses and beef commission outfits. They pulled up in front of one that bore the shingle KLEINFELD & COMPANY, COMMERCIAL REPRESENTATIVES. Bubba dismounted, Walsh heaved himself down, wheezing, and they went into the office.

It consisted of little more than a tremendous rolltop desk of countless drawers and pigeonholes; a corkboard on the wall, invisible under layers and sheaves of thumbtacked notes, bills and forms; and a couple of severely upright chairs. One of these was occupied by a middle-aged woman with a face as stiff as her corseted torso, eyes like augers and a mouth like an anus. Her hair was a uniform dark brown, too uniform to be its real color, piled high over a rat into a Gibson-girl pompadour. She wore a high-collared basque with clerkish paper protectors pinned around its cuffs. She should have pinned something onto her long divided skirt, too; its hem was liberally smeared with stockyard mud and manure.

Standing atilt against the wall behind the woman were four men —each of medium size, medium features, medium attire—indistinguishable from Bubba, right down to the serviceable-looking sidearm. Bubba stepped across the little room to lean beside them, making five in a row.

Walsh stopped at the desk, smiled ingratiatingly, started to sit down in the empty chair, thought better of it, fumbled his hat off and said in a gravel voice, "Howdy, Eliza. You're lookin' just as gorgeous and charming as ever."

She gave him a wilting look and held out a peremptory hand. Walsh coughed and felt through several pockets until he found and withdrew a rumpled wad of papers. Obsequiously, with a slightly unsteady hand, he tried to smooth out the papers before giving them to her.

"Six hunderd and seventy-two head," he said. "And there's the bills for every one."

The woman took the bills but didn't immediately look at them. Instead, she raked her gimlet gaze along the row of men against the wall until it stopped at Bubba. Without appearing to move his lips, Bubba said, "I counted 'em. Six seventy-two."

Still without speaking to Walsh or even motioning for him to sit, the woman turned to the desk, went through the bills one by one, jotting down on another piece of paper the figures from each. Then she added her long column of figures. Walsh, watching over her shoulder but trying to appear not to, waited until she had the sum—672, all right—and cleared his throat to say:

"I stopped to talk to a couple of acquaintances on the way in. Bubba didn't mind, did you, Bubba? We talked market prices, and they sound right good. I estimate an average twenty-three fifty a head would be fair, Eliza."

The woman glanced again at Bubba, who said, "Ten per cent canners and cutters."

"Oh, hell, no," Walsh blustered. "Not *ten* per *cent* of 'em bad." Then his voice began to trail off. "Maybe eight per cent scrubs . . . at the most . . ."

The woman finally spoke, in a voice as kindly as a quirt. "Ten per cent, Toad. Brings your average down to twenty-one dollars and fifteen cents."

"Now that's takin' advantage, Eliza!"

"I thought I was doing you a favor. Okay, wait till your herd gets here. Put 'em up one by one, see what you average. Then pay off your cowboys, see what you got left. Bubba, show Toad out."

"Aw, hold on, Eliza." Walsh was crumpling his hat between his hands. "You're always so all-fired hasty. What would it come to at twenty-one fifteen?"

Without needing to calculate, she scribbled on the paper before her: $14,212.80.

"Well . . ." said Walsh.

"Minus five per cent for the favor I'm doing you—"

"*What?*"

"—brings it out to . . ." She scribbled again: $13,502.16.

"What's this five per cent? What's this favor?"

"Bubba counted your cowboys, too. I know what their wages would come to, if you paid 'em. When them buckaroos get here with that herd and find you've sold it and skipped, it's me they're gonna be ripping and snorting at. I figure it's worth a little cut off your price for me to put up with that."

"Hell's bells, Eliza, you're backed up by these five sons of— these five stalwart sidekicks. You ain't gonna have no trouble."

"And I ain't gonna have no Mexican haggling. I'll take your herd off your hands, sight unseen, for thirteen thousand five hundred and two dollars and sixteen cents."

"My royal ass you will! Just because I'm savin' the payroll? God-dammit, I've had other expenses! And I made the investment, took the risk. Besides, goddammit, I've worked as hard as any of them punchers. I deserve a decent return on my—"

"And I can count, Toad. Even with that five per cent off, you're ahead more'n a thousand dollars by not having to pay your gang. You'll skip out of here with close to two hundred per cent profit on that precious investment of yours."

"Jesus Christ on a crutch!"

"Okay." She turned her back on him. "Bubba—"

"No, no. Damn it all, I'll take it. But I tell the world . . ."

The woman reached into one of the rolltop's pigeonholes, plucked a check out of it and handed it to Walsh. It was already made out for exactly $13,502.16. She slid another, blank piece of paper at him.

"Give me a blanket bill of sale for the whole works. With your real name on it, Thompson. Don't sign it Toad or Benedict Arnold or something."

Muttering, Walsh scrawled it out with a trembly hand.

"Keep the pencil," said the woman. "You'll want to calculate back over the figures we've been talking. You'll find it comes out to that check price to the penny. But don't do it here. I'm busy."

"All right. But, Eliza, I just want to say—"

"You just want to go. Put some healthy distance between you and here before them cowpokes ride in this afternoon expecting payday. Bubba, show Mister Walsh out."

2

About that same time, Karnes and Boudreaux hitched a ride out of the Caddo camp on a wagon going south to Shreveport for sup-plies. They arrived in the afternoon and slid off the wagon's tailgate in midtown, on Texas Road in front of the brand-new Phoenix Ho-tel, the four-story, porticoed brick edifice that occupied a whole square block and was the pride of the city.

They looked all around, at the blocks after blocks of other buildings, plain and stodgy, but all eminently respectable-looking. All the streets seemed to be lined with big, friendly buttonwood trees, which, though the weather was still balmy, were beginning to shed their yellow leaves. The city was very quiet, except for a murmur of music coming from somewhere. Karnes stuck his big hands in his mackinaw pockets and stood leaning back to admire the Phoenix Hotel.

"Thought damn, this is a real uptown town!" he said.

Boudreaux plucked at his sleeve. "Come on, Gideon," he said, pointing east to where the Red River was visible a few squares away. "Dis street goes right over de bridge to Bossier City."

"No hurry," said the big man. "L. R. said we'd meet tonight." He started to walk the length of the hotel's long frontage, still admiring it, and the Cajun trailed along. The murmur of music got louder.

"*Dis donc,* den we got lots hours to kill," said Boudreaux. "And I bet dere ain't not one saloon on dis side de river. No room for 'em, wid a *Baptiste* church on ev'ry corner."

"Nope, no drinking, Moon. We're saving money."

"But we mek more'n we figgered, Gideon—" The Cajun broke off as they came around behind the Phoenix and the music swelled. There was a sizable crowd blocking Milam Street, over which hung a flamboyant banner stretched between two trees:

HAMLIN'S WIZARD OIL CONCERT TROUPE

Open Air Advertising Concert
Humorous and Sentimental Songs
As Sung Throughout the United States

The crowd's attention was fixed on a large, beflagged wagon with a little grandstand of benches fixed endways in the body of it. On the lowest bench sat a row of six musicians playing banjos, concertinas and mandolins. On the next higher couple of benches sat the eight male singers, all in natty suits, derbies, celluloid collars, bow ties and handlebar mustaches. On the two topmost benches sat the eight lady singers, all identical in long skirts, white shirtwaists, shawls and coiffed hair with beaucatcher side curls.

As Karnes and Boudreaux came abreast, there was a brisk rattle of banjos, exultant yowl of concertinas, and the troupe lit into a nonsense ditty. The girls sang the first line, exaggeratedly shivering and hugging tight their shawls; the men sang the second, lifting their derbies and swabbing their foreheads. And so on.

> " 'Twas once in cold November,
> The day was very hot,
> And one could not remember
> The things he had forgot.
> The sun was shining brightly,
> While sadly fell the rain.
>   [now the girls' voices, *misterioso*]
> *Four men went out a-walking* . . .
>   [girls and men together, *fortissimo furioso*]
> AND SO THEY TOOK THE TRAIN!"

"Dat damn song don't mek no sense," grumbled Boudreaux. As they moved on, he resumed wheedling. "We mek more money'n we figgered dere at Caddo. I got forty-two dollars. How much you?"

"Sixty-six." Karnes stomped his formidable boot on the bois d'arc sidewalk. "And it's tucked inside my boot and it's going to stay there until L. R. calls for it."

The Cajun counted on his fingers. "Dat's a hunner'n'eight alto-gedder. And we only told L. R. we'd kick in a hunnerd. Gideon, we got eight whole dollars we can blow."

"That eight dollars could make a big difference, Moon. No, we can find some cheaper amusement than a saloon."

He stopped in front of the Strand Opera House. A placard out-side advertised a road company presentation of *Captain Jinks of the Horse Marines*—"The Comedic Sensation of Broadway That Made Ethel Barrymore a Star!"—here offering an unknown ingénue named Laura Hope Crews in Miss Barrymore's role.

"Dat's cheaper?" Boudreaux asked sulkily.

"No, they're asking six bits a ticket. And it's not on until tonight, anyway."

They wandered on, Karnes placidly taking in the sights, such as they were, the Cajun muttering rebelliously that they had a right to wet their whistles after twelve straight days of *purgatoire* at Caddo. The big man stopped again, and Boudreaux bumped into his broad back, when they came to one of the numberless Baptist churches. This one was not, like most they had seen in Shreveport, a massive, frowning, brownstone pile, but a more inviting, white-painted frame building. The announcement board on its little patch of lawn disclosed that this very afternoon would be enlivened, after the regular Wednesday Prayer Meeting, by a Lecture on Temperance by that farfamed crusader, Sister Maybellyne Dismukes of the Order of Good Templars.

"Oh, *mon dieu,* not dat! Gideon, not dat!"

"I don't know. It sounds interesting." Karnes read off the title of the lecture: " 'If God Had Wanted Us Besotted, We'd Have Been Born Tipsy.' "

"And if de good God had wanted us to wear clo'es," said the Cajun sarcastically, "we been born wid B.V.D.s on."

"Well, it's free," Karnes pointed out. "And it'll keep us occupied. The more I think about it—what we're planning on doing—the more I think it wouldn't hurt to have a Thought-damned touch of churchgoing before we start."

He marched determinedly up to the open church door, bent his head and went in. Boudreaux did a little dance of frustration, yanked his mustache into disarray, then followed him.

There was a small and informal gathering of perhaps twoscore persons scattered among the pews toward the front of the church. Down there the Reverend Crispin Mobey was already pumping Karnes's hand, and numerous of the congregation were getting up and moving in to be presented to the newcomer. Boudreaux slid unnoticed into a pew at the very back of the building and sat watching sardonically.

". . . needs no introduction," the Reverend Mobey was now say-

ing, indicating the woman in a cane chair behind him. "Sister Maybellyne has previously spoken to this assemblage on 'There Shall Be
No More Death,' and today will be favoring us with her famous dis-
course on the curse of the demon Alcohol, which she has delivered
to great effect all over this fair nation. Sister Maybellyne Dismukes."

There was a patter of applause. The woman gave a millimetric
bow from her chair, fanning herself with a heart-shaped palm-leaf
fan imprinted "Bodine's Funeral Parlor—Behold, the Days Ap-
proach That Thou Must Die, Deut. 31:14." Sister Dismukes had
sherry-colored hair, eyes of Medford rum and a face as colorless and
astringent as gin. She wore a permanently forged little half-smile of
no discernible mirth or warmth.

"Now," the pastor went on, "I know you're all as anxious as I
am to hear Sis Maybellyne's thrilling and timely talk. But first we'll
start this afternoon's meeting with a couple of hymns and a short
prayer. So—heh heh—let's have some volunteers for a scratch
choir."

Two tremendous women and one very small man immediately
stood up and came forward. The Reverend Mobey beamed at them,
then turned to beam at Karnes, who had sat down in a front pew.
"Brother Gideon, we have here the—heh heh—hat, coat and trou-
sers of our choir. That is to say, our soprano, alto and tenor. But we
lack the boots—that is to say, our bass. Having heard you rumble
when you introduced yourself, I'd venture to guess . . ."

Karnes blushed, said aw, shucks, well, and lumbered to his feet
to tower alongside the other three. From way at the back of the
church came a small, contemptuous, Gallic snicker.

"Brother Karnes," said the preacher, "this is Sister Euri Belle
Smoot, our matchless alto. Sis Vyvyanne Phister, our superb tenor.
And Brother Rupert Barron, a deacon of our church and our in-
comparable soprano."

Karnes looked mildly surprised, and wee Brother Barron looked
daggers up at him, defying remark. The two ladies moved a little
away from the new member of the quartet and began ostentatiously
fanning themselves. Their fans were imprinted "Compliments of

Fabacher Brewery, New Orleans—Where Two or Three Are Gathered Together, JAX BEER." The Reverend Mobey handed around hymnbooks and lined out the first selection: "How firm a foundation, ye saints of the Lord . . ."

Boudreaux saw and heard everything that happened thereafter, but he never was able to give a very coherent account of it.

The foursome began to sing and, for all Deacon Barron's piglet squeal and the sheeplike bleating of Sisters Smoot and Phister, Karnes's elephantine bass was the only voice that could really be heard. Awed and overwhelmed, the congregation hesitated to join in.

> "How firm a foundation, ye saints of the Thought,
> Is laid for our faith in his excellent Word . . ."

Karnes's voice faltered a trifle here, as Brother Barron gave him an incredulous look, then stood on tiptoe and jabbed an imperious finger at the page of Karnes's hymnbook to indicate the correct wording. Karnes ignored him and thundered on:

> "Fear not, I am with thee, O be not dismayed;
> For I am thy Thought, I will still give thee aid . . ."

The hymn finally clamored to its conclusion, and the pastor stood up to say his piece.

"It's 'saints of the *Lord*'!" came Barron's resonant squeak. "To rhyme with 'his excellent *Word*'! 'Thought' don't rhyme with 'Word'!"

"Neither does 'Lord' rhyme with 'Word,' " said Karnes's rumble.

"Fight the good fight!" began the preacher, perhaps unwisely. "We believe in the work to which Jesus Christ devoted his life . . ."

Falsetto: "I'm a oldtime, Philadelphia-Confession, boiler-iron, total-immersion Babtiss, and I resent any newfangled notions!"

Profundo: "Brother Barron, I wasn't throwing off on your religion."

". . . to preach the Gospel to the poor," the Reverend Mobey went on, raising his voice. "To bind up the broken-hearted."

Falsetto, cholerically: "What are you, big feller, some kind of godless amethyst?"

Profundo, stubbornly: "I just prefer to sing 'Thought.' "

The Reverend Mobey, still louder and hurrying now: ". . . to give them beauty for ashes, the-garment-of-praise-for-the-spirit-of-heaviness . . ."

Falsetto, crackling with fury: "I'm a deacon of this-here Babtiss church, and a Babtiss church is a church of God, and by God you'll sing *'God'!*"

Profundo, sounding stirrings of anger: "Show me where it says so in the Convention articles!"

The Reverend Mobey, in a shout and at the canter: ". . . That-they-may-be-called-trees-of-righteousness, theplantingoftheLord, that-Hemaybeglorified*Amen!* We will now sing that treasured old hymn, 'He leadeth me; O blessed thought!' "

Brothers Barron and Karnes glared at each other and Sisters Smoot and Phister looked terrified, but they all obediently pitched in, and again the big man's bass overrode all:

"Thought's faithful follower, I would be,
For by Thought's hand Thought leadeth me! *Hey!*"

Barron, standing tinily tall, snatched the hymnbook out of Karnes's hand. He threw it over his shoulder; it landed in the vestal lap of Sister Maybellyne Dismukes, who almost lost her plaster smile. Veins writhing over his forehead, Barron shrilled, "God damn it to Hell, Brother, you'll sing *'God'* or you'll put up your dukes!"

Irked beyond endurance, Karnes rumbled, "Little man, if you hit me, and I ever hear about it, I'll have to mop up this church floor with you."

The little man hit him.

3

"Then what happened?" asked the bartender.

"Den all hell broke loose," said Boudreaux morosely.

He stood alone at the bar of the Bad Penny Saloon in Bossier City. At this hour, just before the evening rush, it was empty of patrons—except for a sprinkling of all-day drunks asleep at various tables—and the barkeep was bored enough to have listened patiently to this stranger's emotional and disjointed recounting of the Great Baptist Free-for-All.

"Ol' Gideon—dis big pal of mine—he never hit nobody. But he bump dat li'l feller wid his belly and dat li'l feller took off allaway across de church."

Boudreaux finished his drink, left the bar and crossed the room to the Bad Penny's princely free-lunch counter. He came back with a plate heaped high with sliced roast beef, sliced ham, sliced cheese, boiled crayfish, hard-boiled eggs, pickles, peppers and pretzels. "Dese sho good doings," he remarked parenthetically, "after dat *merde* dey fed us up at Caddo." He poured himself another drink and the bartender abstracted another dime from the little pile of change on the bar.

"So," the Cajun went on, around a mouthful of free lunch, "I never did git to hear dat Sis Maybellyne woman talk me off of booze."

The barkeep said well, that was a happy consequence, at least, and asked again what happened next.

"Well, all de women run out de church, screeching fit to bust, and all de men piled in on ol' Gideon. All but dat preacher. He jump around, yelling peace, brudders, peace. Den de whole bunch of men fighting, dey all fell over on top of dat Sis Maybellyne woman. She don't be talking nowhere for a while."

He belched, wiped pretzel crumbs and crayfish integuments out of his mustache, and polished off his drink. The bartender solicitously poured another, took another dime and said, "The police station ain't far from that church."

"You damn right. And dem church women must of run straight dere. I hear de whistles and I eench out de church and hide in de bushes. Dat big two-horse Black Maria come galloping up wid

more police dan I ever see in one bunch. Dey all go charging in de
church wid dem damn billies and come charging out dragging ol'
Gideon and batting him on de head. Hustle him in dat Black Maria
and off dey go. Dat's de last I seen of him. What you s'pose dey
do to him?"

"Jesus, I don't know," said the barkeep, scratching the perfectly
centered part in his pomaded hair. "Saloon brawls and such—nobody minds that kind of highjinks. But I never heard of anybody
that ever busted up a *church*. I reckon, if your buddy can't pay his
way out, he'll have to put in a spell on the road."

"De chain gang?!" gasped Boudreaux, horrified.

"Oh, it ain't so bad. For a white man. Grub-hoeing weeds off
the roadside and like that. It's the niggers get the hard work and the
hard time."

Boudreaux looked at the coins on the bar. Not much remained.
He sighed. "We had big plans, ol' Gideon and me."

The bartender snapped his sleeve garters and opined that rain
had a way of falling into everybody's life, one time or another; then
his attention was distracted. Two new customers came in and bel-
lied up to another part of the bar; he went to serve them; the evening
rush was starting.

Boudreaux glowered at these untroubled and carefree types. Then
he reached inside his mackinaw, inside his shirt, and unhooked the
slim wad of bills safety-pinned to his union suit. He took it out, unfolded it and counted it. Forty dollars exactly; it had not diminished; neither had it increased. He smoothed the bills on the bar
and turned to call the barkeep back with the bottle. Then he noticed
that the two newcomers had just asked for and been given a deck
of cards. He stared at the men, at the cards, at his thin sheaf of
banknotes, and a spark of new-kindled hope lit up his black eyes.

He sidled along the bar, leaning on it, to where the two men
stood. "*Excusez-moi, messieurs.*" He indicated the deck of cards.
"Do you gent'men perhaps know de game *bourrée?*"

After a moment of scrutinizing him, one of them said, "Yep."

"Ah hah." Boudreaux twirled his mustache in what he supposed was the manner of a slick professional gambler. "And do you perhaps have a quan'ity of money you would venture to risk?"

The man ptooied tobacco juice accurately into a spittoon and said, "Yep."

"*Aussi moi-même*. Den may I propose a frien'ly game?"

Another moment of scrutiny. "Yep."

Boudreaux reached across the bar, took the bottle of whiskey from the bartender's hand, beckoned enticingly to his two new acquaintances and crossed the room to an empty table, lurching considerably in progress. The two men exchanged a smile behind his back and followed him.

As they all three sat down, Boudreaux began fumblingly to shuffle the cards, and shouted to the room at large, "*Laissez le bon ton rouler!* Let de good times roll!"

7

1

I T WAS well after dark when Foyt and Wheeler got to Bossier
City, each of them riding one horse and towing another loaded with
bedroll and belongings, these hastily packed and haphazardly tied
on. They dismounted at the Bad Penny, found space for their
mounts at the crowded hitching rack and shouldered through the
saloon's swinging doors.

Foyt paused just inside, to take off his dusty old hat and swat with
it at his dusty clothing. This raised a cloud around him so that he
looked like a stage Mephistopheles making an entrance through the
floor. His red-rimmed eyes were like hot fumaroles in the dust-
caked desert of his face. His silver hair stuck out in angry spikes,
and his silver beard bristles shone like an aureole. Several customers near the door looked askance at him and moved warily away.

Foyt still wore overalls, with now a denim jacket over them. From
hat to boots, his garments were the uniform color of dust and
smelled uniformly of sweat: human, equine and bovine. Wheeler,
equally dusty and sweaty, stumped along behind him, long-faced
and vacant-eyed, looking more than ever as if he had just been hit
in the head with a maul.

Foyt craned and glared over the crowd in the room, turned to Wheeler, said in a rusty voice, "Mosey around. Find 'em," then made his own way through the crush to the bar.

"Well, if it ain't old L. R.!" the bartender with the center-parted patent leather hair hailed him. "Just get in? Heard you were bringing a drive up for old Toad Walsh."

Foyt audibly ground his teeth.

"Right, no talking till you flush out your tonsils," said the barkeep. "What's your poison?"

"Nothing," said Foyt in a dry croak. "Orville, I want to ask you—"

"Nothing?! Nothing to drink?! And you standing there looking like Lot's wife?!"

"I can't afford—oh, what the hell—gimme a shot and a schooner."

The bartender said that was more like it. While he poured, he studied Foyt's fiery eyes and thundercloud brow, and asked what had happened to put him on the prod.

Foyt drank deep and gratefully, then commenced a flavorsome commentary on Toad Walsh, Toad Walsh's mother and other antecedents, Toad Walsh's character and business ethics, Toad Walsh's prospects in the Hereafter, and how he, Foyt, personally looked forward to pissing on Toad Walsh's grave.

"You're gonna have to do some elbowing there," said the bartender. "None of this is news, L. R., to anybody that knows Thompson Walsh. What's he done now?"

Foyt growled and gnashed his teeth some more. "We bedded the herd down early last night, to rest for the last haul in to the yards. This stranger rode into camp, said he'd come out from Shreveport to meet us. Looking for Walsh, bringing word Walsh's dear old mother was sick." He paused, snarled, "Hydrophoby, I bet," knocked back the remainder of his beer and motioned for another. "So Walsh and the stranger pushed on ahead of us, early this morning, while we was still drifting the cows out. He told me where in the yards to run the herd in, who to turn it over to, and where all of us was to meet him to git paid off."

"Let me guess. The Kleinfeld office."

"Reckon I'm still not telling any news, Orville," sighed Foyt.
"Then you know the kind of reception we got. That bitch-fox
showed us her bill of sale and them five toughs of her'n showed us
their hardware. All we had to show was this." He tugged a piece of
paper out of an overall pocket and crumpled it savagely in his fist.
"The contract Walsh signed with us."

"I bet that Eliza woman got a good laugh out of that," said the
bartender. "Hereabouts, she's affectionately known as Ku Klux Kleinfeld." He moved away to draw schooners for two other customers,
but came back to Foyt. "And then I reckon you appealed to her
better nature—the rattlesnake side of her?"

"Well, yes, we did, and she did say she'd do us a favor. She
pointed and said Walsh went thataway. And them five gun waddies
made it plain that *we'd* all better go thataway, too, and fast, and
stop pestering Miss Kleinfeld."

"Missus," said the barkeep absently, snapping his sleeve garters.
"Kleinfeld was her husband's name."

"Christ. Somebody married that bitch?"

"Don't hold it against him. When he discovered his mistake, he
drank carbolic acid. Even the preacher that buried him agreed it was
preferable. Where are the rest of your boys, by the way?"

"I only got Eli with me. Last I seen of the rest of 'em they
was divvying up the remuda. Them hosses ain't worth shucks, but
them and the chuck wagon was all Walsh left us *to* divide. Me and
Eli took the four hosses that belong to us, and told the boys to share
out the rest. When they've got that settled, some of 'em may light
out after Walsh."

"They might as well," said the bartender. "There's not much
point in you-all sicking the law on him. Up here in this Ark-La-Tex
country, he can duck back and forth over the borders of all three
states and dodge whichever law is after him. He's had practice. But
you're not gonna help chase him?"

"Me and Eli got better things to do," said Foyt, adding glumly,
"If we still can. We're s'posed to meet—"

Wheeler suddenly materialized at his side, his mouth crammed with food from the free-lunch counter and his Adam's apple jigging. He handed Foyt a lopsided sandwich and said thickly, "I can't find them fellers nowhere, suh."

"That's all I needed to hear," said Foyt, sounding really worried now. He chomped moodily but voraciously at the sandwich. "Orville, draw Eli a beer, and lemme ask you something. We're s'posed to meet two fellers in here tonight. It's powerful important. If they've been in today, you couldn't miss 'em. One feller's the biggest man you ever see. Got bright red hair that would of been brushing the ceiling in here."

The bartender assumed a hard-thinking and helpful expression, but shook his head at the same time. "Would have been in today, you said? Nope, nobody like that."

Foyt looked distressed. "The other feller's about my size, only younger. A Cajun. Talks 'dese, dose, dem.' Black hair, black eyes . . ."

"Today?" the bartender said again, and frowned in deep concentration. "He got a mustache, maybe?"

"Yes," said Foyt. "Black soup-strainer."

"Real excitable type of man?" the bartender asked.

"Oh, come on, Orville! How the hell many Cajuns do you wait on in one Wednesday?"

"Well, you're right. There *was* a Cajun in today. And come to think of it, he was telling me some long rigmarole about a big man he was buddies with. He was here most all afternoon, getting well juiced up . . ."

"He oughtn't of did that," murmured Wheeler, now wearing a mustache of his own, of beer foam. "Not with the money so tight."

". . . and he's still here," the bartender added.

"Hey?" Foyt and Wheeler straightened up and began to scan the room again. Foyt said, "Talking to you, Orville, is like pulling teeth. Where's he at?"

"Relax. I've got him laid out on the boss's desk in the office out back. He won't be any use to you for a while. You couldn't prize him up with a pitchfork."

"What happened to him?"

Nothing worse than the usual, said the bartender. Boudreaux had simply passed out, somewhere around the middle of the second quart of popskull.

"Oh, hell. Then I reckon he's blown every cent he had."

"Well, yes, but it didn't all go down his gullet. He challenged a couple of the boys to a game of cards. That Cajun game, *bourrée*. He was too drunk to have took on my tads at tiddlywinks. Those two sharpers picked him clean in about forty-five minutes. Then he slid under the table. You know what they say about Cajuns—a Cajun could foul up a one-coach funeral procession."

Foyt sighed. "Well, thankee, Orville. We'll take him off your hands. But Gideon—the big feller—he never showed?"

"No," said the barkeep. "Wait a minute. He couldn't." He frowned again and scratched carefully at the precise part in his hair. "That's what the Cajun was telling me. The big guy got in trouble. He's in the calaboose."

Foyt groaned and put his head down on the bar. Wheeler asked for him, "What kind of trouble, Mistuh Orville, suh?"

The bartender recounted what he could recall of Boudreaux's story, being several times interrupted to go fill other customers' glasses. "It don't make much sense," he wound up. "Wrecking a church. But that's what the Cajun said. I'd surmise your big buddy is going to be a guest of Caddo Parish for a while. But you can find out for yourself, L. R. You'll find that police station—"

"I know where it is," Foyt said grumpily. "I've had to bail a couple of boys out in times past."

"Then you know Lootenant Huckabay is the man you see," said the barkeep. "Percy Huckabay's not a bad egg, but he's got no sense of humor. Serious as a pig pissing. And he does like to keep his Shreveport unsmirched, as he puts it. And he can be tough. Not long ago a teamster was complaining to me how Percy can add insult to injury. This feller's wagon horses had bolted and run halfway through Shreveport. It just about scared the poor bastard out of his overhalls, and like to killed him besides. But then you know what?

Percy Huckabay arrested him and fined him for 'driving at an illegal rate of speed.' You going over to see him, L. R.?"

"Yeah, I'll see him, for what good it'll do. Eli, you go out back —Orville'll show you where—and start pouring cold water on that damned Moon. Try to have him awake and up and moving by the time I git back."

"Yes, suh," said Wheeler.

"I'll take both my hosses so Gideon'll have a mount to ride, if I can pull off a miracle and spring him loose."

"Hold on," said the bartender, reaching behind him for a bottle and pouring Foyt a healthy slug. "Here's one on the house for good luck. You'll need it."

2

Foyt tied his saddle horse and pack horse to the rack outside the police station, squared his hat and his shoulders, and went in to face the Authorities. Just to enter the building was an intimidation. It was lighted by electrics that cast a hellish glare through the barred and frosted windows, and the front steps were flanked by two big lamps in green glass globes.

Coming in from the dark, Foyt had to blink for a moment at the dazzling brilliance inside. Then he picked out the uniformed man behind the high desk at the other side of the room. The policeman was hatless; his high-domed blue leather helmet stood on the desk at his elbow. He watched, expressionless, plucking at his walrus mustache, as Foyt removed his own warped old hat and meekly approached.

"Evening, Lootenant Huckabay. I've come to see about bailing somebody out."

This was business, then. Lieutenant Huckabay clapped on his helmet; it added both height and importance. He leaned over and looked more closely at the supplicant.

"I've seen you before. You're that Foyt, aren't you? We haven't picked up any of your cowboys. Not yet, anyway. What are they up to? And where?" He reached for his whistle to summon a raiding party.

"Whoa, lootenant. There ain't no cowboys in trouble. It's a friend of mine. Big feller named Gideon Karnes."

"That bull moose from up at the Caddo field?" Huckabay found Karnes's arrest sheet among those on his blotter, and glanced over it. "You have nice friends, Foyt. Can you afford this one?"

"Er, what've you got him on, lootenant?"

Huckabay cleared his throat and read with relish: "Disturbing the Peace . . . Committing a Public Nuisance . . . Malicious Mischief . . . Disturbing Religious Worship . . . Committing a Riot . . . Assault and Battery . . . Resisting Arrest." At each ellipsis, Foyt seemed to sink a little lower into his boots. Huckabay looked up and added, "Deacon Barron wanted us to book him besides for Blasphemy, Heresy and Atheism, but I told him he'd have to file suit for them. They don't come under the Civil Code."

"Well, I'm glad there's *something* he's not in for. Lootenant, what's the likely penalty for all this?"

"That depends," said Huckabay, leaning back and steepling his fingers, "on which judge he comes up in front of—Farewell Fred Baggett or Hanging Harry McSween." Foyt gulped. "Hanging Harry would probably ship him off to one of the swamp camps down on Point-au-Fer. Me, I'd sooner be hung any day." Again with seeming relish, Huckabay ticked off a catalogue: "Rain, heat, mud, slime. Damp-rot, fever, plague, dysentery. Prick your thumb on a thorn and you lose your whole arm to the gas gangrene. Mosquitoes, alligators, cottonmouths. The world's meanest gorillas for guards. Move too slow for their liking and you get the cat, and then salt rubbed into the slashes. Wrist irons, leg irons, the black hole, the hot box. Not many men ever come back from there."

Foyt wrung his hat and gulped again.

"Farewell Fred would be more lenient," Huckabay went on. "Nothing worse than the chain gang for maybe nine, maybe six months. At least your friend will come out. Maybe a little less healthy, a little less human, but you'll see him again, anyway."

"But—my God," muttered Foyt. "Gideon ain't no real criminal."

"Hell, man, we've got him down for everything except Mopery on the Public Highroad and Attempting to Sneak. Have you heard what-all he did?"

"Not exactly. I got it third-hand."

"You might as well hear it straight from the moose's mouth." Huckabay tinkled a little bell on his high desk. A uniformed constable appeared from a back room. "Emmett, take Mister Foyt to see our star boarder."

Karnes sat quietly on the bare bunk board in the barred cell, reading a book under the glare of an unshaded tantalum bulb. The constable let Foyt inside, closed the barred door after him, said to bang on the bars to be let out and went away.

"Well, L. R.!" rumbled Karnes, half-pleased, half-sheepish. "I knew you'd track me down. You met old Moon all right, then?"

"No," snarled Foyt. "It was pure luck I heard about you. Old Moon's gone raising Sam Hill. He's stiff as a plank, cuss his hide!"

"Drat," said Karnes, downcast. "I guess that's my fault, too. After I got in that fuss, he must have figured our plans were all haywire and it didn't matter what he did."

"Well, the hell with that," said Foyt. "Tell me—"

"If you've brought your wages, L. R., and if you'll bail me out, I'll make it up to you. I'm mortal sorry about this, but you can take a cut of my share of the loot when we cabbage it off that—"

"*Hush!*" hissed Foyt. "Jesus P. McChrist, shut up!" He glanced fearfully back at the corridor. "Here you sit in a jailhouse cell right under the nose of the long arm of the law and you're blatting at the top of your lungs about . . ."

"Oh, yeah. Sorry. I wasn't thinking. Well, anyhow, if you'll help put up bail . . ."

"You just don't know how things are, Gideon," Foyt said hollowly. "About the money—well, never mind that right now. The first thing is, you gotta come up before a judge."

"Oh. No bail till then, huh? Well, that'll be tomorrow, and I don't mind waiting around here that long. It's not so bad here. This is only the second or third time in my life I've been in a room lit with electrics. And I've got something to read. Back there when the ruckus started, I must've stuck this hymnbook in my pocket without noticing. So I can pass the time. And this little delay—me not getting out until tomorrow—shouldn't mess up our plans, should it?"

Foyt coughed, got out his makings, began rolling a cigarette and avoided answering that. Instead, he asked Karnes to fill in the sketchy and lunatic account he had heard of the Great Baptist Free-for-All. Karnes obliged, as well as he was able, but his tale didn't sound much less phantasmagoric than what the bartender had told. "And all because I said 'Thought,' " he concluded wistfully.

"I hope," Foyt said under his breath, "your Thought will do you some good down at Point-au-Fer."

"You hope what about what?"

"Nothing, Gideon. By the way, Orville said Moon said you got a little money of your own."

"Sixty-six dollars," said Karnes, starting to untie one of his boots. "Every penny I earned at Caddo. I thought of trying to wave it at the policemen. But then I figured I'd better wait and let you handle things. Here."

Foyt took the money somewhat gingerly, it being noticeably humid and redolent of feet, and stuck it in his jacket pocket. He said he'd see what he could do, and would be in touch. He swung one spur clanging along the bars at the bottom of the door. The constable came, let him out and led him again to the front-room desk.

Foyt came out scratching. "A clear case of self-defense," he asserted confidently. "That Barron feller swung the first punch."

"Tell it to the judge," said Percy Huckabay, smiling behind his mustache. "The judge knows Rupert Barron; evidently you don't. Hell, you could hide the little man under that hat of yours."

"Oh."

"And then you'll have to convince His Honor that Deacon Barron ran backwards—backwards, mind you—all the way across the church and bashed himself through a Beaverboard partition into the

Sunday School room and threw himself on top of all the stacked-up kiddy chairs and smashed them all to flinders and laid himself down amongst the fragments and went to sleep. Yessir, you've got a clear case, counselor. Maybe if you can get Clarence Darrow down here from Chicago to—"

"Oh, all right," said Foyt, demolished. "I don't reckon there's any way I could appeal to *you*, lootenant, to—uh—"

"Shreveport is a good Baptist town, and I'm a good Baptist. I like to keep my town unsmirched."

"Oh."

"I happen to belong to that very same Baptist church your friend tried to take to pieces."

"Oh." Foyt's defeated and dejected "oh" was sounding more and more like "ugh."

"Brother Barron and I happen to be fellow deacons of that church."

"Ugh."

"And many's the time I've wished I could stomp that sanctimonious little toadstool into the ground."

"Eh?"

"A professional Sunday Christian, smug and pious and holier-than-thou-thee-and-all-the-angels. But a puling little hypocrite the rest of the week. The tightest-fisted skinflint in Caddo Parish. And it's his wife's money. Talk about the viper that didn't have a pit to hiss in—until Brother Barron married the Widow Crabtree he couldn't afford a pew to be pious in. Now the damned little wart is holding paper on half the real estate in Shreveport. Including some of mine."

"Ah-h," said Foyt, the light dawning, and with it some hope.

"Maybe you wouldn't believe a man could strangle another man with just a piece of paper. But you haven't seen Robber Barron operate."

"Do you maybe reckon," Foyt said cautiously, cunningly, conspiratorially, "that our friend Gideon might of suspected the man's true nature? And that's why he cut loose at him?"

Huckabay again picked up Karnes's arrest record.

"All these things are misdemeanors by the book, and I can hold him on a bench warrant without anybody else's say-so. On the other hand, no aggrieved citizen has yet filed charges or sued for damages. I know damned well the deacon plans to, and I bet Maybellyne Dismukes does, too, as soon as she's up and around again. But until they do, I could legitimately spring him—if only the material breakage could be taken care of."

"How much breakage?" Foyt asked huskily.

"Well . . ." Huckabay took up a pencil and began listing: "One fractured pew, one Beaverboard partition, several palm-leaf fans, Sunday School chairs, the Reverend Mobey's spectacles . . ."

"Gideon ain't got but just sixty-six dollars to his name," said Foyt, holding up the moist and smelly little wad of bills.

"I calculate," said Percy Huckabay, scribbling busily and finishing off with a flourish, "that this breakage adds up to sixty-six dollars' worth." He reached over the desk and down, to tweak the wad out of Foyt's fingers. With the other hand, he tinkled his bell, then removed his helmet; the business had been concluded. "Emmett, go and release prisoner Karnes, G., to the custody of his eminent counsel here . . ."

3

When they left the police station, Foyt and Karnes immediately and prudently led their horses around several corners and several streets away from the risk of possible recall. As they walked, Foyt filled Karnes in on the several other depressing developments that had occurred. The big man seemed to get visibly smaller as he listened.

"It sounds like a real frost," he said, at the conclusion. "Surely we can't go ahead with our scheme now. We're as broke as the Ten Commandments."

"I'm thinking on ways and means," Foyt said grimly. "First of all, let's git our gang back together." As they passed under a gas lamp he hauled out his dented old stemwinder; it was midnight.

On a quiet, empty, white-elm-lined residential street, they

stopped to divide the pack horse's light load between both animals and to improvise a saddle for Karnes on the extra mount. The best they could manage was a folded blanket tied on with a piece of rope; for a bridle there was only the horse's halter, and for a rein its leading rope. Karnes scrambled aboard with the help of a curb-side mounting block. He sat there looking dubious, his big feet dangling, stirrupless, well below the horse's belly. The horse turned its head and looked back at him, likewise dubious.

"Don't worry," said Foyt. "It may not be comf'table, but it won't be dangerous neither. Old Lightning'll put up with it if you can."

"Ah, old Lightning," said Karnes. "I remember. This is that horse you're so fond of. The one Eli doctored, back when you two first met."

"No, that's this Lightning I'm riding," Foyt corrected him. "Your Lightning is a bit younger."

"*Both* your horses are named Lightning?"

"When I want to cuss at the hoss under me, I don't want to have to stop to recollect his name," Foyt explained. "All the hosses I've owned in forty years I've called their names Lightning."

"Well, I guess it makes sense," said Karnes. "What does Eli call his two horses?"

"Search me," said Foyt. "Something in hoss language."

He clucked his Lightning to a walk. Karnes clumped his big boot heels into his Lightning's ribs and, with a deep sigh, the horse moved after Foyt's. As they made their way down toward midtown, the streets became a little busier and livelier, with a traffic of horsemen, buggies, surreys, carriages, wagons. All of these moved with a deliberate midnight quietness, all except the horse-drawn cars—their brightly lamplit interiors mostly empty of passengers at this hour—clanging hollowly along their rails and screeching as they grated around corners.

The two men rode in silence until they were crossing the Red River bridge into Bossier City. Then Karnes spoke up:

"How far did you say we've got to ride, L. R., to meet that train?"

"It's about a hunderd and seventy-five miles from here, as the crow flies."

"Only we're not flying," said Karnes, with a groan. "Here we've come maybe just a mile and a half and already I feel split in two. I always thought I was pretty well padded in the sit-down department. But I swear I feel like I'm straddling a crosspiece on a derrick."

"Well, surely you've straddled enough of 'em."

"Derricks don't jounce up and down while you're doing it."

"Don't bitch to me, Gideon," Foyt said callously. "Look at it this way: you bought yourself Sunday School chairs instead of a saddle. At least you're mounted. It'll beat having to walk all the way to Teague."

They arrived at the Bad Penny to find that Wheeler had brought Boudreaux outside for some fresh air. The young man was standing protectively over the Cajun, who sat limp, wet and shivering on the plank walk, his back against the wall of the building. Over his bowed head were some words printed in tremendous black type, as if he himself were exclaiming:

DOOD MORNIN!

I HAPPY BABY!

Foyt and Karnes looked perplexed, looked at each other, then looked more closely at the wall. The words turned out to be printed on a gigantic and garish poster, bearing the picture of a fat, pink baby, grinning and purportedly saying:

DOOD MORNIN!

I HAPPY BABY!

Tause My Mamma Always Uses

TARRANT'S SELTZER APERIENT

Foyt and Karnes got down from their horses and came to stand with Wheeler, gazing down at Boudreaux in a silence that was loud with exasperation. The Cajun raised his head—he looked about as ghastly as the baby on the poster—and began making broken apologies and excuses.

"*Je suis honteux,* fellers, honest to God I am . . . I t'ought ev'ryt'ing go bust unless I did somet'ing, me . . . so I tried win some money . . ." He took out a large and dirty red bandanna and loudly blew his nose, dampening his mustache. "So what I do? I lose ev'ry damn t'ing . . . *Je suis honteux . . . stupide . . . bête . . .*"

"Oh, pipe down," said Foyt irritably. "Can't-help-it don't mend it. But what's done is done. We ain't gonna shoot you for it."

"Shoot . . . aha!" said the Cajun, reminded of something. He looked up at them appealingly. "I *ain't* lost ev'ryt'ing, me. I do got a gun, L. R. I have it some time now." He began going through his pockets. "I didn't say so before, because I li'l bit 'shamed about it."

"What? Why? Where'd you git it?"

"Well, dat's how-come I was *embarrassé*. I stole it."

"Here? At the Bad Penny?"

"*Non, non.* Back in Nacogdoches, at Madame Fouquet's. Before I even knew I'd need one. I lift it from de *chiffonier* when dat Mississippi Sal was out de room."

Wheeler chided him mildly, "That wasn't no nice thing to do, Mistuh Moon, suh."

"No," said Karnes, though smiling. "I didn't think we'd start our blackhearted career of crime by pilfering from a little girl in a cathouse."

Foyt said the hell with that; it was worth a good deal to them to have one more gun. "Where is it, Moon?"

"Right here in my hand."

"Huh?" Foyt bent down to peer, then stood up again and said with feeling, "Oh, my aching crotch!" If he hadn't been so depressed by everything that had happened that day, he'd have burst out laughing. The stolen gun was small enough for Boudreaux to hide in his palm simply by closing his fingers. It was a lady's muff pistol, a tiny, two-barreled, two-shot .22 derringer with a mother-of-pearl butt and arty engraving all over it.

"You crazy coon-ass! If you got up real close to a man and stuck that little hooter right up his nostril and fired it off, you might give him a nosebleed."

"It ain't no good?" said Boudreaux, dashed. "I figgered a gun's a gun, and I helped myself to it. Hell, L. R., I don't know not'ing about guns, me."

"Let's hope that train crew don't neither," said Foyt. "They might die laughing and we'll be on the dodge for murder instead of robbery. Okay, Moon, you've done your best. Now git up from there and see can you set a hoss. Eli, here's a dollar. Go back in yonder and ask Orville for a bottle of his cheapest sheep-dip whiskey."

"Where are we going, L. R.?" asked Karnes. "What are we going to do? What the hell is there to do?"

Foyt was already busy, tying a blanket on Wheeler's extra horse to improvise for Boudreaux a saddle—or pad—like the one Karnes was riding. Without turning his head, he said with heavy irony, "We're gonna continue that blackhearted career of crime we started with stealing a toy popgun from a whore's dresser drawer. Only now we're moving on to the big time. Yessir, afore you know it, we'll be making the Jameses and the Youngers look like a needlework society."

"What in Thought's name are you talking about?"

"I ain't talking about pushing a pygmy deacon around, Gideon, so start flexing your muscles and bracing your nerve. We're gonna go rustle ourselves a herd of cattle. This is something I ain't never done, even in the hardest of my hard times, and I never thought I'd turn long-rope artist at my age. But I got a heavy stake in that-there herd, and I find it hard to convince my conscience that this'll really be stealing. Here comes Eli with the bottle. Mount up, you-all. From here on, it's root-hog-or-die."

8

OR THE last time, they crossed the Red River bridge from Bossier City to Shreveport, by which time Boudreaux was already complaining even more piteously than Karnes about the miseries of riding an ambulatory ridgepole with nothing but a blanket between him and it. He got no sympathy from Foyt, who told him he'd just better get used to it.

"Now let's all keep our traps shut," Foyt added, "and mosey through this damn town as quiet as we can. I don't want none of Lootenant Huckabay's bluecoats to spot us and start wondering if we're out to beat up a bishop this time around. We're already too blamed notorious in these parts to suit me."

They had to cross the whole east-west width of the city to get to the stockyards on the far side. The streets were entirely empty by now, the horsecars had stopped running, and practically every building was dark. The only sound was the muffled clop and rustle of their horses' hooves in the drifts of fallen leaves. They made it to the yards without encountering a single other night rider or stroller, much less a policeman. They stopped at a fence on the perimeter of the yards, where, a little way inside, there was a shack showing a feeble glow of lamplight from its one window. They dismounted, tied their horses to the fence, and Foyt motioned them all into a huddle.

"This ought not to be too risky," he said in a low voice. "Prob'ly nobody's ever heard of cows being rustled out of a stockyard before, or even thought of such a crackbrained thing. There's only the one watchman, old Orlando Benbow. That's his shack yonder. We can handle him. But that Kleinfeld female is bound to have a night guard standing watch over that herd we brought in."

"Handling *him* may be something else again," said Karnes. "From what you told me about the kind of toughs in her employ."

"We'll see," said Foyt. "But first things first. If old Benbow ain't drunk already, I want him that way. Eli, you take that bottle of whiskey and go over and knock on his door."

"Yes, suh."

"Orlando knows you and me; he won't suspicion nothing. Tell him you're s'posed to meet me here and you've just dropped in on him to kill the time. Git him started drinking—*but don't you*—and keep pouring till he's plumb ossified. We gotta drive a sizable herd of cattle past that shack in just a little while, without him knowing about it."

"Yes, suh."

"It's important now, Eli. We're depending on you."

"Important, suh." He assumed an expression of grave responsibility. "I'll do it, all right."

"Stay there with him till you hear us coming back with the cows. Then slip out and come along with us."

"Yes, suh." He gave Foyt a snappy military salute, bent and slithered through the rails of the fence, and tromped off toward the watchman's shack, rehearsing in an undertone, "It's me, Mistuh Orlando, suh. Thought you might like a nice drink."

They waited until Wheeler had knocked and was admitted. Then Foyt reached up to his saddle and slid his Winchester out of its boot. "You two come with me." Karnes and Boudreaux followed him through the fence, big Karnes with some difficulty, and all three of them tiptoed—which was hardly necessary in this mucky terrain of mixed mud, cowpats and horseapples—past the watchman's shack, around and through pens, corrals, chutes and squeezers. There was a quarter moon, giving just enough light for them to see their way. Only an occasional corral contained cows, and those were mostly lying down asleep or sleepily chewing their cuds. Some raised their heads as the three men tiptoed past, and two or three lowed gently.

"Wait for me here," whispered Foyt, when they came to a slaughter pen well within the yards. "Stay outa sight and don't make a sound." Karnes and Boudreaux obediently shrank into the shadow of the pen's hoisting wheel. Foyt moved off into the pale blue moonlight, knees bent to lower his profile, carrying his .30–30 at port arms.

He was gone about ten minutes. He came back as noiselessly as he had left, hunkered down beside the hoisting wheel and said, barely audibly:

"I was right, she's set a night guard. But only one. A feller I've seen twice before and I heard 'em call Bubba. He's setting on the fence, rolling hisself a smoke, so he's wide awake—and he's wearing a sixgun like he knows how to use it. Damn him. Now here's what we're gonna do. We're only gonna take the canners and cutters."

"I t'ought we come for cows," breathed Boudreaux.

Foyt gave him a look that went unnoticed in the darkness. "I told y'all this was a sorry herd to begin with. Well, the canners and cutters are the *real* sorry ones—sick, scrawny, wormy—the ones that would make a butcher gag. They're not fit to be whacked up into steaks and roasts and chops and put in a meat market showcase. So they're sold dirt-cheap to the processors that make 'em into wienies and canned beef stew and stuff like that. Things that people don't know what goes into 'em."

"Ugh!" grunted Karnes. "I used to like wienies."

"*Ssh.* Keep your damn voice down. All right, now. Kleinfeld's boys have already cut 'em out and they're in a side corral, fifty or more of 'em. Plenty for our purposes. And if we absquatulate with just them worthless canners and cutters, there ain't nobody going to go to *too* much trouble to chase after us and fetch 'em back."

"Worthless they may be," muttered Karnes. "But your Bubba boy won't just hand them over to us. How do we go about this?"

Foyt hunkered around to face Boudreaux. "Moon, I want you to sidle over to the far fence of the corral from where Bubba's setting. Me and Gideon will be inching up behind him. When you git over there, count to one hunderd. You *can* count?"

Boudreaux looked insulted. "*Un, deux, trois, quatre—*"

"Okay, okay. Count to a hunderd and then make some kind of a noise to catch his attention."

"What kind noise, L. R.?"

"Christ, I don't care. Yodel like a coyote, chirp like a butterfly, cuss in Cajun. Do any damn thing, as long as it turns his head your way so we can git the bulge on him."

"Butterflies don't chirp, L. R.," Boudreaux informed him in all solemnity, but he followed along as Foyt and Karnes tiptoed toward the Kleinfeld & Company corral. When they came near it, Foyt motioned the way for Boudreaux to go; the Cajun went left around the fence, the other two right.

Foyt and Karnes could see Bubba silhouetted against the moonlit sky, perched on the top rail of the corral fence. The cattle inside were even more phlegmatic than those they had passed on their way in through the yards. These, besides being generally punier than any other cows in Shreveport right now, were resting from their long hike, all lying still and quiet, not even ruminating. Some time passed, during which Foyt and Karnes crept, step by slow step, as close to Bubba as they dared to get.

Then the night suddenly resounded to a surprisingly good tenor voice, singing from the far side of the corral an old Cajun folk song, "*Dansez, mes enfants, tandis que vous êtes jeune!* . . ."

Bubba's head jerked up. For a moment he sat stiff with astonishment at the apparent miracle of one of his cows having been this moment endowed with a voice, with which it was melodiously exhorting its fellow cows to get up and dance while they were young. Indeed, a dozen or so of the animals, as startled as he, did unfold to their feet. Then Bubba threw away his cigarette, slowly got down from the fence and, peering across the dark humps of his herd, slowly withdrew his long Peacemaker from its tiedown holster. It was the last thing Bubba did for a very long time.

Foyt swung his carbine by the barrel, and he didn't swing it just to annoy or even to stun temporarily. He put into the blow all his pent-up feelings for Thompson Walsh, Eliza Kleinfeld and Bubba as well. The stock caught the man at the base of his skull, lifted him right off his feet and pitched him fully three yards through the air before he fell on his face in the mud.

"Great Thought a'mighty, L. R.," Karnes said in horror. "You may have killed him."

"Hell won't thank me for it, if I did," Foyt said, no longer bothering to lower his voice. "That thug would make trouble even for Old Scratch." He yelled across the corral to where Boudreaux was still warbling. "Moon, you can stop them operatics now!"

Foyt scrambled through the fence and bent over Bubba. "Don't fret, he's still breathing," he assured Karnes, as the latter came wedging his big body between the rails. "Take an Act of God to kill that breed of bastard." He took the Colt revolver out of Bubba's limp hand and gave it to Karnes. "Here's a bonus. Shuck off his gunbelt, too, and put it on." Karnes did as he was told, at the same time thoughtfully turning Bubba's head so his nose wasn't buried in the mud.

Moon joined them, looked down at the unconscious man without comment, looked back over the herd and asked, "Which cows you want, L. R.? And how we get 'em out of here?"

"Not these," said Foyt. "Believe it or not, these are the choice specimens. Ours are over yonder." He led them through another fence, into an adjoining corral that was only sparsely populated with sleeping cows. He opened the gate and propped it open with a rock. "Start kicking 'em up on their feet. Yell. Whistle. Git 'em moving out that gate and back the way we come in here."

Boudreaux began doing just that, bawling his "Dance, my children!" song and kicking right and left. One after another, the cows arose, humping their rear ends first, then standing on all fours—

though many of them tottered from weakness and weariness. Once erect, they began blatting anxiously.

"Does it occur to you, L. R.," Karnes asked above the noise, "that we're committing this little crime with all the secrecy of a wooden-legged burglar having a fit on a tin roof?"

"Don't matter," said Foyt, also beginning to boot at sleeping cows. "Bubba was all we had to worry about. If there's other night guards around these yards, they'll only be concerned with their own herds. They'll just figger we're making some kind of a hurry-up delivery someplace."

Karnes, kicking cows awake, could tell even in the dim moonlight that what was now "their" herd was not much to be proud of. Some of the animals had a horn knocked off, others a knocked-down hip. Some had eyes running with pus, others running sores on their flanks.

"You said nobody'd be too eager to chase after this bunch," he remarked to Foyt, panting from exertion. "Thought damn it, man, we ought to get a gold medal and a big cash prize just for running them out of here."

"I can't gainsay you, Gideon," admitted Foyt, also panting. "They got pinkeye, screwworms, blackleg, rednose, Texas tick fever—you name it. But I expect they'll serve to stop that train, don't you expect?"

"Hell, yes, it'll stop. It'll probably back up."

"Well, that's all I want. Then the poor damned critters can go on to their destiny, for all I care. A string of P. D. Armour's wienies."

If these cattle had been halfway healthy, they'd have refused to be prodded awake and pushed around in the middle of the night. As it was, about a score of them were flatly too sick and too feeble to have been roused with railroad torpedoes. The rest—thirty-seven head in all—while in condition to move, were in no condition to protest. With Karnes whooping at them, Boudreaux chunking rocks, Foyt belting their backsides with his Winchester, the afflicted animals moved insensibly, unhappily to the corral gate and through it, and stumbled off through the runways of the yards.

The men and their herd made slow progress and a deal of noise, but no one showed up to challenge them. As the herd shuffled and shambled past old Benbow's shack, Wheeler came out of it to report that Orlando was past caring even if they kidnaped him along with the cows. "And look, suh," he said proudly, holding up the bottle he had carried in. "I done it on just half a quart."

"Good going, son," said Foyt. "Them leftovers will come in useful on the way." To prove it, he tilted the bottle and took a drink. Then he choked, sputtered, turned colors and said, "Hoo*wee,* what rotgut! If old Orlando had good sense, he'd of just hit hisself over the head with the bottle." He handed it to Karnes and Boudreaux, saying, "Take a drink, but take it walking. Don't let them cows stop or they may fall down dead."

Wheeler slipped through the fence again to collect their horses, while the other three hazed the herd along the inside of the same fence until they came to the main gate to the road. Wheeler met them, leading the horses. Before they mounted, as he rammed his .30–30 back in the saddle scabbard, Foyt made a little speech:

"I don't want you-all to even start calculating when you're going to git to go to sleep next, and I don't want to hear no bitching about it neither. Moon, you had a nice drunk snooze, and Gideon, you had at least a laydown in that calaboose. Me and Eli've been on the go ever since last four A.M. Now we're all gonna be on the go for maybe another whole round of the clock. We're heading first for Bethany, just the other side of the border, and that's twenty-three miles. Once we make that, we're in Texas, and we don't have to worry about no Louisiana law chasing after us. About the Kleinfeld woman and her pistoleros, I can't say. I do believe they'll write off these pissy few scrubs, sooner'n waste time looking for 'em. Bubba may feel diff'rent, when he wakes up with iron in his head and none on his hip. But he never got a look at us, and nobody's got no reason to think we'd be chousing these cows right back where we brought 'em from. Hell, any of the other cowboys we come up with could of done the stealing, and them fellers have prob'ly scattered all over the compass by now. Not even Bubba can track down ev'rybody what had a grudge ag'inst him. So add it all up and I'm figgering we ain't gonna have to fight no rear-guard action. But that still don't mean we're gonna have a picnic of it. A decent herd can do twenty miles easy between dawn and dark. With this stumble-bum bunch we got, we'll be lucky if we make Bethany by this time tomorrer. That works our top speed out to maybe ten miles a day. And after Bethany we got another hunderd and fifty miles to go to git to that railroad—at the very least, not counting detours we maybe'll have to make, and two big rivers we got to cross. And we only got fifteen days to do all this in. So we're gonna be pushing just as goddam hard as we can the whole goddam way. That's all I got to say, pards. Now let's mount up."

When they were all aboard, Foyt made a cavalry troop leader's slicing motion with his arm, toward the west, and barked, "Move 'em out!" Wheeler led at the point, Boudreaux and Karnes rode left and right flank, Foyt brought up the rear. Immediately and unconsciously, he began the tuneless whistling that every cowboy does incessantly, to assure the cows that they're being accompanied and looked after.

Consciously, he was thinking, "Wellsir, if this ain't one fine band of bandits going out to rob a train. One grayheaded old fart that oughta be stashed in a chimbley-corner, cackling over his corncob. One softhearted giant that wouldn't step on an ant, but that seems to of been born to trouble. One crazy Cajun with a little whistle-pecker pocketbook pistol, and about as dependable as a dust devil. One young twitterwit with only forty-six cards in his deck, so simple he couldn't tie his shoestrings, if he wore any. And all of 'em driving the goddamndest miserable-est bunch of wore-out cows ever seen this side of Mexico. Now if we could only recruit, say, a sideshow midget and one of Converse & Petrie's Ethiopian Minstrels . . ."

But then he thought back on the place they were leaving, and what its esteemed and upstanding citizens called each other—Toad Walsh, Robber Barron, Ku Klux Kleinfeld. He raised his head and looked out at Wheeler, up at the point, also whistling tunelessly, at Karnes and Boudreaux, valiantly jiggling and jostling on their pitiful jury-rigs—and decided what the hell, he could be in worse company.

9

ALKING was no novelty or hardship to either Wilmajean or Feather Hudspeth. Even back when their Comanche group had had horses, only the braves, the old men and the boys rode. The girls and squaws, even the most aged and crippled crones, walked in file behind, uncomplaining, squelching stoically through the horses' droppings.

No doubt Wilmajean and Feather could have trudged the whole way from the Kiowa Reservation to the middle of Texas, and could have done it on no more nutriment than the few strings of jerky they carried to chew on. Indeed, they had done just that, for good stretches of the way, but they had also enjoyed a stroke of luck now and then. The kindly brakeman of a southbound Gulf, Colorado & Santa Fe freight train had let them ride in the caboose, as far as he was going, and had even fed them a welcome meal of bacon, beans, fried johnnycake and coffee, cooked up on the caboose's little potbellied stove. A traveling anvil salesman had given them another lift, in the massive header barge in which he carried his wares—though riding on top of a wagonload of anvils was not much of an improvement on walking. They had hitched rides on occasional other wagons, once on the baggage rack of a Butterfield Overland

stagecoach; they had hiked; they had sloshed across streams; they
had stopped to rest from time to time.

At the infrequent farmhouse or ranchhouse they passed, Wilmajean would brave the dogs that raged at her and inquire at the
kitchen door, with eyes downcast but without cringing, "Could you
spare me and my li'l gal a bite to eat, missus?" At maybe two out
of three places they would be given, usually grudgingly, a meager
handout—it seldom consisted of more than gluey cold grits, a bis-
cuit and a dipperful of water. They slept most nights on the hard
prairie ground, under the open sky, rolled in the two threadbare old
trade blankets they carried.

And finally, weary, dusty, travel-worn and hungry, they arrived
at the town that was no longer called Brewer's Prairie—except by a
few unregenerate old cusses who had lived thereabouts all their lives
and would be damned if they'd drop the noble and resounding old
name for the tacked-on and mimsey-sounding new one of Teague.
The land which, like the town, had once been Brewer's Prairie had
long since become Freestone County. It was still mostly "country,"
given over to corn fields, pea farms, cotton fields, peach orchards—
and not much else of note, except its raw and jerry-built but booming railroad town.

This was the biggest, most populous and prosperous, most metro-
politan and sophisticated community the two ex-Comanche Hudspeth women had ever been in; they were overwhelmed. The town's
dusty, seven-block-long Main Street had such a flurry of traffic—
horses, wagons, buggies, buckboards, going past at the rate of at
least one a minute—that Wilmajean dragged Feather across it in a
breathless dash, lest they be run over. A solid new plank sidewalk
ran the whole length of each side of Main Street, and each walk was
an arcade, roofed over with the wooden or corrugated-iron awnings
of shops and offices and stores and a bank and a funeral parlor and
saloons and restaurants. The sidewalks absolutely swarmed with
people, dozens of them, mostly men. The side streets off Main were
spiky with newly set out buttonwood saplings that would one day be
shade trees.

To the wide-eyed Hudspeth women, the bilious yellow brick Yoakum Hotel, on Third Avenue across from the T. & B.V. depot, looked manorially majestic. So did the Hubbard House, on another side street called Cedar, which had yet to know a cedar. Both the Yoakum Hotel and the Hubbard boardinghouse were obviously fully booked and thriving. Their verandas were crowded with local railroad biggies and visiting drummers, lounging against the porch pillars, impressive as fashion plates in curly-brimmed derbies, narrow-lapeled suits and cloth-top shoes, smoking big cigars and swapping shoptalk, farmer's-daughter jokes and braggedy lies about their big deals. The Acropolis Restaurant on Main Street, Alexandros Apostolides, prop., was brightly lighted—even in daytime, to show off—by real electric bulbs. The Main Street ginmills were all jammed to the doors; Wilmajean wrinkled her nose and hurried Feather past them.

Tired though they were, the two of them wandered Teague's busy streets for more than an hour—merely marveling at the glamour and magnificence of the town, gawking in the shopwindows that flaunted unbelievable goodies and luxuries—before they began stopping passersby to ask where they might find the resident Hudspeths they had once heard about. Practically every passerby was passing by at a brisk trot; evidently on important business; late for a crucial appointment; on his way to sign some epochal contract. Each time Wilmajean managed to address one, or touch a timid hand to his sleeve, he stopped impatiently and replied brusquely.

It was always no. No, sorry, ma'am, I'm a stranger here myself. Or no, sorry, ma'am, I never knowed of any Hudspeths in these parts. The "ma'am" was always added rather derisively, after the speaker had taken a look at Wilmajean's grubby get-up and the ratty bedroll that was all her baggage. To the impatient eye, the handsome woman and the pretty little girl were not discernible under those Injun buckskins, that hobo trail dust and sweat and weariness. One or two men suggested, after sizing them up, that if they were searching for kinfolk, they'd likely find them out in the countryside someplace—implying that any relatives of these two were bound to be nesters or squatters or sheepherders or some similar no-good rabble.

So Wilmajean and Feather spent a week roaming all over Freestone County, stopping at every habitation they encountered, from imposing farmhouses set among rich orchards to fishing shanties on the banks of the creeks, everywhere asking the same question, meanwhile living marginally on what handouts they could beg, and getting more downcast and more desperate each time the name Hudspeth elicited only a shrug and a shake of the head.

Then, at one puny pea patch of a farm, the accordion-necked old farmer said yes, by God, he did remember some Hudspeths. They used to have a place over yonder way—which way he didn't specify—but it was such a pisspoor piece of ground that it wouldn't grow anything more than rocks, and the Hudspeths were such pisspoorly shiftless farmers that they hadn't the gumption even to grow good-sized rocks. So they had pulled up stakes a few years back and headed off toward the Río Grande Valley with the announced intention of planting orange groves and getting filthy rich, after which they were going to return to Freestone and lord it over all their former neighbors who had called them pisspoorly and shiftless. Maybe, said the old man, they *had* grown the oranges and had grown rich doing it, as far as he knew, but to date they had not come back to Freestone County, in splendor or otherwise.

Wilmajean tried not to let Feather see how discouraged and disheartened she was. But finding the elusive Hudspeths was still the only hope, the only goal she had. Foolish and fruitless though it must be, this endless search for them—until Doomsday if necessary —was the one and only thing she could think to do.

The very next day, near sundown, Wilmajean and Feather climbed a rise of ground. It was only a gentle rise, but they were so fatigued and weak from undernourishment that they could barely make the top of it. When they did, they looked down upon the handsomest and neatest farmyard and buildings they had seen in all of Texas.

Even the most imposing farmhouses they had stopped at had seldom boasted a coat of anything more decorative than whitewash slapped on with a broom. As any Anglo Texan would point out, paint was expensive, painting was laborious and time-consuming, and decoration for the sake of decoration never put a penny in any man's pocket. But the house below—set about with half a dozen towering pecan trees and one windmill derrick—was a gleaming white with a blue roof, trim, shutters and porches. Still more amazing, even the barn behind was similarly painted white with a blue hipped roof. The water in the vast stock tank beyond the yard shone bright orange in the low sunlight. Blue smoke wafted lazily from the house's two chimneys. The sight as a whole was attractive and refreshing enough to make both Wilmajean and Feather momentarily forget their tiredness and aches and dejectedness. They didn't pause to rest atop the rise, but kept on down the far side toward the blue-and-white house.

As usual, they went around back, to the screened kitchen door. As she knocked gently on it, Wilmajean debated with herself whether to ask first for a dab of grits or for news of the Hudspeths. When the door was opened by a big, motherly-looking, chocolate-brown Negro woman in turban and apron, Wilmajean was so taken aback that she could only stutter, "Missus . . . uh, missus, we . . ."

"Lawd bless you, chile, I ain't de missus heah. I'm Willie Pearl. Dey used to be a missus, but she passed, rest her soul, long yeahs ago. I keep house heah for de mistuh."

"Oh." There didn't seem much point in asking about Hudspeths, so Wilmajean asked instead, "Do you reckon me and my li'l gal could have just a bite to eat? Anythin'? You could hand it out-chere on the porch. We bin walkin' a long way and—"

" 'Pears to me you young ladies needs more'n a bite," said Willie Pearl, looking at them almost severely. She swung the screen door wide.

Wonderingly, almost fearfully, Wilmajean and Feather followed Willie Pearl into a kitchen that fairly glittered. There were windows all around the room, and blue-and-white curtains at every one of them. The big cast-iron range was so meticulously black-polished that it looked brand-new. The walls were hung with copper pots, pans and utensils, burnished with sand, vinegar and soda until they glowed like red gold. Wilmajean suddenly felt how very dirty and ugly she and Feather were; how out of place in these, to her, palatial surroundings.

"Dere's de sink and dere's de pump," said Willie Pearl in a voice of command. "And heah's a pan and a warshrag and a towel and some soap." She went to the range and used the socket end of the stovelid-lifter to give the grate a good shaking down. "Y'all kin warsh off dat top layer of Texas, anyways, whilst I git somep'n cooking heah. You wants to eat right quick, I 'spect." She poured coal from a scuttle into the stove's firebox. "Whilst you're eatin', I'll heat up some good hot water, and after you've et you kin git out of dem clo'es and have a sponge bath at least."

Dazedly, Wilmajean said, "We—we didn't mean to be no trouble . . ." She began scrubbing the more visible areas of Feather with the rough washcloth and cold water.

"No trouble, chile. I'se jes' startin' to fix de mistuh's supper, anyhow. He be's in fum de field pooty soon now."

"Oh," said Wilmajean, with a pang of anxiety. "Well, we better git gone afore he gits here. He might not like you fixin' for us." She began scrubbing her own face, fast and vigorously.

"Mistuh Fritz, he lift my scalp if'n I let two young ladies go out of heah skin-and-bones like you-all is." Willie Pearl slapped a skillet and saucepans onto the stove. "Ain't nothin' he like better'n to see somebody set down and eat for de hunger to come." She began carving and chopping and peeling things. "You heahs allatime 'bout south'n horspitality—*huh!* De mistuh ain't no South'nah, but he know a sight mo' 'bout horspitality dan any o' dese Texas scissor-bills 'round heah."

"If he ain't a Texan," said Wilmajean, her voice muffled by the thick towel, "what is he?"

"He a Polack."

"What's a Polack?"

"Dat's a German. His name Fritz Altdorfer. He come fum Germany, place dere called Bavaria. Dat's how-come ev'rythin' 'round dis place is blue and white. He say dem de state colors of Bavaria. You know, like Texas's colors is red, white and blue."

"It sho is purty." Feather spoke for the first time, shyly, wistfully. "All the blue and white. This is the purtiest place I ever seen."

"Well, I *wondered* could you talk, li'l lady. Now I wonder kin you tell me yo' name."

"My name's called Feather Hudspeth."

" 'Magine dat! Pleased to make yo' 'quaintance, Miss Feather."

"She's Feather and I'm Wilmajean Hudspeth. And we're both mighty proud to know *you*, Aunt Willie Pearl. You sho are bein' good to us."

Willie Pearl gravely bowed her head, then went back to her cooking. Mouth-watering aromas began to fill the kitchen.

"Dis place used to be pootier even dan now," she said conversationally. "Back when Miz Hannylory was alive, rest her soul. Flowers all ev'ywhere. She jes' couldn't *have* enough flowers 'round de house. But de mistuh, he can't keep up de yard and de farm both, po' man. He gittin' on, and he pooty crippled up. Dey's near fo' hunderd acres heah, and best he kin do is work maybe forty of 'em all by hisself. I sorry to say, things bin goin' downhill heah for quite a spell now. Dey ain't no he'p to be hired; ev'y workin' man in Freestone County is a-workin' on dat railroad nowadays. And po' Mistuh Fritz, it's 'bout all he kin do to drag hisself around. Wouldn't hurt none to have a good woman's touch 'round heah ag'in. Y'all set down to de table."

They did, and almost fainted when Willie Pearl laid the meal before them. After the starvation rations they had been living on for as long as they could remember, just the greens and the beans and the succotash and the potatoes and the corn bread and the coffee would have sustained them for a month. But then Willie Pearl slid onto each of their plates a golden-brown "chicken-fried" beefsteak. It was the first meat they had had since the bit of bacon in the

freight-train caboose, nearly two weeks ago. This steak was the biggest piece of meat Wilmajean had ever eaten; really the biggest piece
she had ever even *seen,* since the long-ago days of her childhood
among the Comanches, when there were still buffalo to hunt.

Willie Pearl, who had never before seen an Indian eat, looked
shocked, but said nothing, when both the woman and girl picked
up their steaks in their hands and began tearing at them like
panthers.

She shook her head disapprovingly, and went to tidy the sink
where they had washed. She poured out the pan water, reflecting
that it could have passed for stove polish, wrung out the washcloth,
then picked up the towel. It might have just wiped down a T. & B.V.
locomotive. Holding it between finger and thumb, she took it out to
the back porch and discarded it in a carton of old rags and cotton
waste saved for use on the farm machinery. By the time she finished
cleaning the pots and pans she had cooked in, Wilmajean and
Feather had eaten pretty nearly everything on the table but the ta-
blecloth. They were looking, in fact, rather glassy-eyed. But they
also looked contented and measurably healthier; it did Willie Pearl's
heart good.

"Now, Miz Wilmajean, Miss Feather, dat kettle on de stove is
steamin' good. Y'all two skin out of dem clo'es and I fetch a tub and
y'all git in it." She added sternly, "If'n you don't come out clean as
clean, I go' fetch a wire brush, you heah me tell you?"

Wilmajean glanced apprehensively at a window. "But you said
the mister'd be comin' in . . ."

"I keep an eye out. If he come, I send him 'round de front way
so he don't see you till you look human ag'in. 'Sides, he gittin' later
ev'y night now gittin' home, it seem. I told you he's poorly nowadays, and he walk slower'n slower. He all crippled up with authoritis. His right arm and leg, dey completely authorized. Now, I ain't
go' tell you twice: *peel!*"

Bashfully, Wilmajean and Feather shucked off their moccasins
and slipped their buckskin dresses over their heads. Willie Pearl
could not repress an appalled gasp when she saw that neither of

them wore a stitch under the dresses. The slim and unformed nine-year-old merely looked nude. But the grown woman, fully and admirably shaped, looked stark naked. While they busied themselves filling the tub and whipping up suds in the hot water, Willie Pearl bustled off—clucking, muttering and shaking her head—out of the kitchen, through the front hall and up the stairs.

It took her quite a while of rummaging in a long shut-up closet to find what she sought. By the time she returned to the kitchen, her two guests had finished their baths and were happily toweling their now shining blonde hair. They were both still as naked as *September Morn.*

Willie Pearl had already noticed that, despite their identically golden hair, Wilmajean's eyes were blue and Feather's brown. But now that the two were clean, she noticed for the first time that mother and daughter were of otherwise subtly different coloring. Wilmajean's skin was creamy-white, her nipples pink. Feather's skin was creamy-fawn, her diminutive nipples brown. It occurred to Willie Pearl that the difference might be something interesting to speculate about, when she had time. Right now, she simply held out the armload of clothing she carried.

"Miz Wilmajean, I 'spect you tired of wearin' dat mangy old buckskin thing. It look like *it* tired. Now, Miz Hannylory, she was a Polack like Mistuh Fritz, and Polack ladies is built consid'able more plump dan what you is. But I found dis gingham what was de smallest she owned. How 'bout you try it on?"

The sun had gone down some time ago and the kitchen was in deep dusk, but the brightening of Wilmajean's face almost lighted the whole room up again. She took the green gingham dress from Willie Pearl with something between disbelief and reverence.

"Jes' hold on one minute," Willie Pearl said severely. She shook out the other garments she held. "In case you don't know, chile, dese li'l pieces goes on first. Underneath."

While Wilmajean struggled into the unfamiliar clothing, and the still nude Feather regarded the process with interest and envy, Willie

Pearl said, "I go direckly and see kin I find you some decent shoes. But dere ain't nothin' hereabouts to fit de li'l gal. Maybe we kin cut down somep'n else of Miz Hannylory's. My ol' eyes ain't much good for sewin' no more, but I reckon I kin whomp somep'n togedder. Meantime, you Feather, don't stand around and git chilled. Put back on dat buckskin o' yours, for now."

It was nearly full dark when Fritz Altdorfer opened the back-yard gate, using his good left hand, limped across the yard to the back porch and carefully cleaned his boots on the piece of old saw blade affixed to the bottom step for a bootscraper. Slowly, favoring his stiff right leg, he climbed the steps, limped across the porch, opened the door and entered the kitchen. Willie Pearl had lighted the lamps by now, and in the golden lamplight stood a golden vision. She stood tall and slender and shyly proud, in a floor-length green gingham dress that Fritz Altdorfer dimly recognized. She had eyes as blue as Hannelore's had been, and hair as golden, with a strand or two turning silver, just as he remembered Hannelore's.

"Mistuh Fritz, we got comp'ny," said Willie Pearl, with the ges-ture of a conjurer. "Dis here's Miz Wilmajean Hudspeth and her li'l gal Feather."

Wilmajean swallowed nervously as she looked back at him. Fritz Altdorfer was near the age her father Wilmer would have been if he had lived, and he was as big a man as she remembered her father to have been. Or he should have been big; his arthritis had crum-pled him some. His shoulders were bowed, his right leg was almost rigid, his right arm was permanently bent at the elbow, and both hands were gnarled like tree roots. His hair was iron gray. His face was furrowed and held expressionless as if he was determined not to reveal the grinding pain that he bore always with him. But Wil-majean could see the pain and, behind it, behind the mask he af-fected, she could see more: kindliness and honesty and good nature. Maybe he had kept those qualities shuttered up for a long time, but they shone out all of a sudden—even Willie Pearl was startled and delighted—when he smiled, spontaneously, warmly, and said:

"*Guten Abend*, Frau Hudspeth. And welcome." His smile broadened still farther. "You are a surprise. A most pleasant surprise. I never thought this old house would see such beauty ever again."

It is hardly to be believed—she could hardly believe it herself—but this was the very first time in all her life that she could recollect, the very first time that any human being, redskin, black or white, had ever smiled at Wilmajean Hudspeth.

10

1

FOYT called to Karnes and instructed him to peel out of the formation. It was midafternoon, and they were skirting at a cautious distance around the little crossroads hamlet of Greenwood. They had not paused since they left Shreveport, now fifteen miles behind them, and there was still no sign of pursuit.

"Gideon, right at the crossing yonder you'll find Slagle's Store." Foyt handed Karnes his entire stock of money, some eleven dollars. "I'd go myself, but old Slagle knows me and I don't want him asking questions. Here's a list of groceries I made up. Git what you can of 'em. We'll keep pushing on." He gestured at their herd, which was leaving a most distinctive trail because the cows were dragging their feet so, and said drily, "You won't have no trouble tracking us and catching up."

When Karnes did rejoin them, a mile or so farther on, he was leading his Lightning. And it appeared, from the two bulging croker sacks, one humped on each side of the horse, that he had coped pretty well with their slim funds and Slagle's slim inventory. He was also wearing a broad-brim, blocked-crown, ten-cent straw hat, and had brought one for Boudreaux. They both now felt they looked more like cowboys, not knowing that a cowboy seldom wore anything but a John B. Stetson.

"You were right about the questioning," said Karnes. "I never met such a picky old peckerwood. I had to invent all kinds of twaddle about who I am and where I came from and what I'm doing up in this Ark-La-Tex country and how do I like it and what my mother's maiden name was and what she died of and was there a good attendance at the funeral and I don't know what-all. Then I had to tell him the reason I was riding Injun fashion was because my saddle had been stolen and I was on the track of the thief and it might be a long chase and that was why I was buying so much grub. Anyhow, he was sympathetic. He even threw in a paper sack of raisins and dried apples, free of charge, as his contribution to righteous revenge, and said he hoped I'd catch up to the lowdown son of a bitch this side of the prairie, so there'd be a tree to hang him on."

"You done the old feller a kindness," said Foyt. "Nothing much interesting ever happens out here, you bet. Now he's got conversational fodder for a month." He lifted his own John B. and squinted up at the sky. "I do hate to stop, but it's long past time for noon bait, not to mention breakfast, and I'm about to swoon from hunger." The other three said by damn so were they. "Okay. In that beech grove over to the right."

When the herd was allowed to halt, the cows all lay down—or fell down—simultaneously and thankfully, as if they had come to some legendary dying ground like that of the elephants in Africa.

Since Foyt had once said that he had had occasion to play cook on other drives, he was unanimously accorded the job now. While Boudreaux and Wheeler watched with keen interest, he began taking the supplies out of the croker sacks, fairly licking his chops at each item: a good-sized flitch of bacon, a fragrant five-pound bag of Arbuckle's ready-ground coffee, numerous cans of Campbell's pork-and-beans, more cans of Del Monte stewed tomatoes, a ten-pound bag of Queen of the Pantry white flour, a pound of brown rice, three cans of Borden's condensed milk, a box of Imperial sugar and another of Morton's salt, a paper twist of pepper, a can of K.C. baking powder and a box of Arm & Hammer baking soda, a bottle of Heinz's ketchup, plus the little gift bag of raisins and dried apples.

"From Slagle's prices," grumbled Karnes, "you'd think his is the only general store between here and Forth Worth. Maybe it is. Anyway, I've got not quite five dollars left."

"You done good," said Foyt.

"But no peaches," Wheeler murmured sadly, looking over the assortment. "I do love canned peaches."

"So does every other cowboy, apparently," said Karnes. "Old Slagle told me he just can't keep peaches on his shelves. Seems every cowboy that comes through buys him out of them—and eats every one of them out of the cans right there on his porch. Sorry, Eli. But I did bring these." He took from a pocket and handed to Foyt two sacks of Bull Durham.

"Why, that *was* thoughty of you, Gideon!" exclaimed Foyt with pleasure. "I didn't put tobacco on the list. Say, don't you smoke a'tall?"

"No, I chew now and then." To demonstrate, he took out a plug of Red Apple and bit off a hearty hunk. "You get out of the habit of smoking, when you're half the time on top of a derrick in the wind, where you can't roll a cigarette. And I'd have to fight half the roughnecks and roustabouts on the field if I was to turn sissy and start smoking tailor-mades."

Wheeler and Boudreaux collected fallen branches for firewood, and Foyt got his cooking utensils—an extremely rudimentary kit—out of his horse's pack. He went to work with an expert-seeming bustle and hum, while Wheeler divided his and Foyt's mess gear with Karnes and the Cajun. But it turned out that, as a cook, L. R. Foyt was a good cowpuncher. When he distributed his refection among their tin dishes, only Wheeler fell to without hesitation; the other two stared at it for a while before they tasted it. Foyt had somehow combined the store-bought provisions into an unrecognizable hodgepodge and spooned this swill on top of a fibrous fried hoecake; all put together, the dish looked like a cowflop.

"Horreur," said Boudreaux at first mouthful. He was hungry, God knows, and he had been hungry before in his time, and God knows he'd been poor enough often enough to eat whatever was set before him, but still he was of French descent, inbred with the Frenchman's respect for cuisine. He remarked that this mess was sure to give him a *crise de foie,* and then sat muttering *horreur* at intervals throughout the meal. Even the normally imperturbable Karnes remarked mildly, "L. R., you'd have to fix this up some to throw it away. I might just swallow my quid instead of eating. And could I have a couple fingers of that creosote whiskey to gentle this coffee down a trifle?"

Foyt simply said humph, they ought to be glad they weren't in *West* Texas, where there was nary a stick to burn and they'd have to bolt their fixings cold. Then he himself ate gluttonously and smacked his lips over the coffee, which he dosed liberally with condensed milk and about eight spoons of sugar. Ordinarily, he and Wheeler would not have spoken a word while they ate. Out of some long-standing tradition or some peculiar courtesy or just plain concentration on eating, cowboys never did talk at the table. But Karnes and Boudreaux had inquiries they wanted to make.

The Cajun asked, "What's it like, dis town we're passing on?"

"Teague?" said Foyt, swallowing. "Well, I wouldn't call it the armpit of the United States. Radford's that, I reckon. But it ain't no big, grand Shreveport nor Fort Worth neither." He described the town's physical aspects, not very glowingly. Then he ate a bit before resuming. "And it ain't no prodigious center of culture, like New Or-*leens,* say. I remember, there was a young feller—Buford Noseworthy—went off and joined the Navy and was gone four-five years. He come back tattooed all over with little red and blue boats and eagles and anchors, and carrying a big sea turtle with a painted-up shell under his arm. Ever since, Buford has been pointed out to visitors as Teague's leading patron of the arts."

Wheeler nodded in verification, as solemn as Sunday. Foyt chewed for a minute.

"Then there was the Pike brothers. Jasper M. Pike and T. Eustace Pike. They owned the Brewer's Prairie Bank & Trust. That was in the days when Teague was still Brewer's Prairie, and no bigger'n that runty little Greenwood back yonder. But then the T. & B.V. picked it to be their division point. It was plain that the town was set to boom, and natur'ly the bank would have to git bigger and more responsible and all. So the Texas state board of whatever-it-is sent an examiner up from Austin to audit the bank's books. Pure routine, it was. But when that bookkeeper walked into the Pikes' bank, wearing spectacles and carrying a satchel, and said what he was there for, that Eustace was so all-fired outraged that he took out the pistol he kept in his desk drawer and shot the man dead where he stood. I'll bet that's the first and only time such a thing ever happened in Texas. Usually, it's the *banker* what gits shot by somebody."

"I'll be Thought damned," said Karnes. "Did he swing for it?"

"That T. Eustace Pike? No, sir. They say never trust a man that parts his hair in the middle or his name on the side, and T. Eustace fitted the saying both ways. It was a matter of debate around Teague—which was the fuller of meanness, him or his brother Jasper. They was both cordially hated. Partly because they was the richest men in town—in them days that wasn't something hard to be—but mostly because they was the most rancorous and ill-tempered curmudgeons Teague has hatched to this day. I been knowing 'em since we was all three just pimply little whelps. They'd pull the wings off butterflies, turpentine dogs' balls, set fire to cats. Ev'rybody predicted they'd both be hung, as soon as their lower extremities got heavy enough that their necks would break."

"Well, come on, L. R.! What happened to them?"

"Nothing. Besides being as bloodthirsty as weasels, they was just as sneaky. The only other employee in that bank was their old teller, Ambrose Weems. The Pike boys bribed him to confess that *he* shot the examiner—in a fit of passion. With that plea, he wouldn't hang, just go to prison, and they arranged to pay him a thousand dollars for ev'ry year he'd be in there, which was twice what his wages had been at the bank. Well, talk about a farce! Ambrose was about seventy years old, and so mole-blind he couldn't of hit the bank floor with his ledger, and so trembly he had to set down to pee, and about as liable to a fit of passion as one of them sick cows yonder. Ev'rybody in town knew he'd been bought and framed by the brothers Pike. At the trial, Judge Muckleroy ranted a lot about miscabbage of justice and such, but old Ambrose stuck to his confession. So, just out of spite, Judge Muckleroy sentenced him to a measly six months in Huntsville Penitentiary. That graveled old Ambrose Weems, lemme tell you. He'd figgered on five years at least, at a thousand dollars a year, and to come out a rich man."

"But what happened to the Pikes?"

"I told you: nothing. O' course they lost the bank. That state board wouldn't let 'em run no bank no more, not after such shenanigans. So Eustace and Jasper picked up and left town together. The story has it that they went out West and turned desperadoes— seeing as how you might say they'd had some experience at gunslinging now. But I don't know why I'm telling all this gossip about my old hometown. We ain't really going to Teague, not if we can help it. I don't aim to hold up Number Three in the middle of town. We're gonna hit for the railroad about seven miles west of there, at a nice, straight, empty, lonesome stretch of track purty near midway between Teague and Mexia. Mexia's the next stop up the line and the train'll be coming towards us from there."

They had all finished eating by now, and Boudreaux had finished retching, so Wheeler began picking up the mess gear and cookery ware and scouring them with sand. The cows had recuperated to some degree, and had got up and started grazing the grass under the trees. All except those too short-toothed—or absolutely toothless— to be able to crop at the grass. These mooned unhappily among the undergrowth, browsing leaves, twigs and tendrils off the bushes, and lipping up fallen beechnuts from the ground. Karnes watched them for a minute and then said:

"L. R., I don't know any more about rustling than I do about robbing trains or knitting bootees. But haven't I read that rustlers doctor the brands on the cows they steal? Change them somehow, so they won't be a giveaway?"

Foyt laughed. "Go take a closer look at that bunch, Gideon. Them cows haye been around some. They already got so many brands and road brands and vent brands that they're burnt till ev'ry one of 'em looks like a walking brand book. And they've been punched with a diff'rent earmark by ev'ry owner they've had—swallerforks, overslopes, steepleforks—till their ears are in tatters. They won't give us away to nobody short of a fortuneteller. Now let's git 'em moving ag'in. They got to learn to graze and browse while they're trailing."

2

Late that night, the four rustlers and their stolen herd crossed the border. Foyt, Karnes, Wheeler and Boudreaux all exhaled a sigh of relief that even the cows seemed to share in. They were clear at least of Louisiana lawmen. The little border town of Bethany—one of the oldest towns in Texas, Foyt informed them—was dark and quiet and empty at that hour, so they didn't skirt around it but pushed the herd straight on through and a mile beyond, before camping for the night. Again, as soon as they were let stop, the cows collapsed as if each had been that instant dismantled.

Here in East Texas, even on the brink of November, the days were still mild and pleasant, even warm, but the nights were getting snappy. Foyt and Wheeler shared out their soogans—each had a rubberized canvas tarpaulin and two frowsty blankets (these the big man and the Cajun had been riding on). They raked together a bed of dried fallen leaves, laid the tarpaulins side by side on that and spread two blankets over each. Then two men crawled into each layout, fully clothed but for their footwear. Like the cows, they all fell asleep as if they'd been pole-axed. Though they never consciously felt the cold as it clamped down, and never came even glim-

meringly awake, they spent the night squirming and scrunching the
dead leaves under them and wrestling for a better share of the blankets—Karnes, being the biggest, came off best in the struggle—and
by morning were all intertwined with the blankets, tarps and each
other, like a nest of snakes.

At the first graying of dawn, Foyt was trumpeting, "Roll out, you
waddies!" Wheeler got right up; the other two had to be shaken and
cussed at and finally kicked awake. When they were erect, grum-
bling, shivering, rubbing their eyes and scratching their stubble,
Foyt said in a voice as cold as the daybreak's dew, "Four o'clock
is really roll-out time, and from now on it's gonna be. I let y'all sleep
late this morning because—"

"Late?!" rasped Karnes and the Cajun together.

"—because yesterday was such a long and hard one. Now look.
I been plugging harder'n longer'n you two put together, don't you
dare deny it. But here I been up already and got coffee made, good
and hot. Hunker down and warm your bellies with it, while I git
some bacon frying."

"My Thought, L. R.," Karnes said creakily. "We're in Texas
now. We don't have to scamper any longer. Or get up before the
Thought-damned birds do."

"I said warm your belly, not to start bellyaching. We still got a
hunderd and fifty miles or more to go, and if we miss that train by
one minute we might as well not of started this rootytoot a'tall.
Drink some coffee, dammit, and then saddle up the hosses whilst I
git the rest of breakfast fixed."

That morning, and every morning to come, the cows humped to
their feet without seeming even to wake up, and continued their
dreary march, pitching into rabbit holes, stumbling over roots and
stumps and their own feet, limping even on clear and level ground.
Now and then, one would utter a mournful, despairing moo, or be
racked by a ropy cough, but otherwise they made no complaint and
gave no trouble. They were far too sapless, spunkless and sorefooted
to stampede. Stolidly, numbly, forlornly, they went where they were
driven. But the driving had to be ceaseless, just to keep them mov-

ing forward at a walk; a trot was beyond hoping for. The driving consisted of constant whistling, hooting, kiyi-ing and yelling of encouragement from all four men, until they were as hoarse as so many frogs.

The first animal to fall out was a brindle steer of ambiguous breed that died between one step and the next. Foyt got down from his saddle to examine it and decide if it was fit to eat.

"We eat off him, mebbe we die, too," warned Boudreaux.

"What killed him," Foyt diagnosed, "is killing us, anyway."

"*Hein?*" gasped Boudreaux, alarmed.

"Time. That poor critter must of been damn near half as old as I am."

He cut four large hunks out of its flank for their supper that night. They moved on and left the carcass to the timber wolves, coyotes and buzzards, who probably enjoyed their portion more than the men did theirs.

"Why didn't you just saw off one of his horns, L. R.?" asked Karnes over the campfire. "It would have been tenderer."

As the drive progressed, the big man and the Cajun privately came to the conclusion that cowboying was not at all a skilled profession; it was 50 per cent boredom and monotony. They'd have made that a round 100 per cent, but, ill-mounted as they were, they allowed the other 50 per cent for blistered behinds and skinned-raw thighs. Then one day they came to the Sabine River, and changed their minds. The boredom, monotony and nagging pain might add up to as much as 90 per cent—but the other 10 per cent was hectic and harrowing hard work.

They got to the river just at sundown; Foyt said they'd camp here on the eastern bank and cross in the morning; Karnes asked why.

"There's plenty of light left to make it across," he said, "and still make a couple more miles west on the other side before dark. As long as the cows are moving, let's push them right on into it."

Foyt shook his head. "If we was going the other direction, I'd say sure, push on. But that sun's setting right smack in front of us. It glints red off the water and them cows get spooked. They always do; I never have known why; I reckon they think it's fire. Anyhow, they'd scatter ev'ry whichaway, upstream and down. We'd be here till Christmas, rounding 'em up ag'in. No, we'll camp. Git a long night's sleep for a change."

It was just as well that they were fresh next morning—or as fresh as they could be after a "long night's sleep" that ended at four A.M., and after a Foyt-cooked breakfast of bacon fried brittle and coffee that filed down the teeth. Before they mounted up, Foyt brought out the remains of their bottle of whiskey and said they might as well polish off what was left; they could use the extra energy. It went the rounds, Foyt gulped the last couple of ounces and then grinned at the bottle.

"I never can take a drink nowadays," he said, "without remembering last year's elections." He threw the bottle into the water.

"In Thought's name, why?" asked Karnes. "What's the connection?"

"Don't you recall who run for President on the Prohibition ticket? I thought his name was just so blamed perfect for a puckered-up Prohibitionist that I'd of *voted* for him, if I'd ever lived anywhere long enough to have the privilege. Silas C. Swallow for President!"

Karnes laughed a laugh that put ripples on the river. "No, I didn't remember his name. But you're right, L. R., that's one for the books." He was still laughing as he hauled himself aboard his blanket-padded Lightning, but he soon sobered and had no further occasion to laugh that day.

The cows knew the river was there; they had drunk from it the night before. And in their longer-than-cow-average lifetimes of frequent travelings, they had crossed plenty of other rivers. But a cow is deficient in the memory department, as well as in intellect and courage. These let themselves be driven into the water, but, as soon as it was up to their bellies and threatened to lift them off their feet, they balked and began bawling as if they'd never encountered a river before.

Boudreaux stood on the bank and threw into the water behind them the biggest rocks he could lift and heave, so the surge of waves at their back might frighten them into the calmer water ahead. Meanwhile, Wheeler, Foyt and Karnes rode in among the leaders, Karnes firing off a good deal of Bubba's ammunition, Foyt batting at the cows with his carbine butt, Wheeler whacking at them with his rolled-up tarpaulin.

The combined commotion goaded the leaders on again, and the rest of the herd followed, though walling their eyes in terror and complaining loudly. The water lifted their hooves off the bottom, they floated, they began swimming. Boudreaux leaped onto his horse and rode after the others. The four men were soon up to their thighs in water, their horses swimming staunchly under them. Foyt led them along the downriver side of the slowly paddling little herd.

"Keep them leaders moving!" shouted Foyt. "Don't let none of 'em turn and look back or they'll just swim for the nearer shore. Keep pushing 'em till they forget this side and they'll figger the west bank's the nearer one."

Now the current began to take both the cows and the horses. Though swimming straight ahead, they were slipping sideways— southward—at the same time, crossing the river on a long downstream diagonal.

Foyt shouted again, "Stay downriver of 'em, boys! One of us behind another, like a fence. Rein your hosses ag'inst the current so you're crowding the cows. That way we'll keep 'em bunched and none won't drift apart."

It should have been a cinch, and would have been, if all four of the men had been experienced riders. At this particular reach, the Sabine was not very broad, and its deepest part, where the animals had to swim, was no more than a fifty-yard-wide channel down the very middle. The cows and horses would have had footing again in a few minutes. But then both Karnes and Boudreaux fell off their mounts. They managed to grab the ropes that secured their blanket pads, but from then on it was all they could do to hold tight and be towed by the vigorously kicking and plunging horses. They had no way to steer their animals, and their weight was a drag besides, so they went off on an even longer diagonal than the rest of the flotilla.

Foyt looked back from the leading edge of the herd, to see half his human "fence" gone wallowing downstream, and their trailing half of the herd beginning to disintegrate. For a while there, all four men were shouting (or spluttering) enough Old Testament words that the Sabine should have parted for them like the Red Sea. Foyt's own horse would have been walking on the bottom of the western shallows any minute, but he yanked the reins and Lightning obediently turned back into the deep water. Foyt yelled to Wheeler to keep the lead cows moving, and aimed Lightning to swim with the current in a long curve and get beyond the several cows that were, now, not just drifting apart from the bunch but apparently had decided to say the hell with it and float all the way to the Gulf of Mexico.

Hurriedly, Foyt untied the latigo thong that held his coiled rope to the saddle skirt, and went for the shorthorn that had sailed farthest downstream. The rope was soaked, limp and heavy; it took several throws, but he finally managed to get a loop over the cow's horns, and Lightning towed the thrashing beast into the far shallows, a good way south of where they had originally started across. The cow found its footing and began to splash toward the bank. As he retrieved and coiled his rope, Foyt threw a glance back up the river. Wheeler also had the leaders lurching through the shallows now, and what was left of the bunched herd was following. Closer to Foyt, the horses of Karnes and Boudreaux had likewise found river bottom under their hooves, had stopped swimming, and their riders were trying to heave themselves back aboard. Foyt turned Lightning and went after the remaining cows—there were five—that were still drifting south.

After a deal of cursing and splashing around and slinging loops that missed their mark, he finally roped and hauled ashore two of the cows, each of them farther downstream. The last seen of the other three, they were still floating Gulfward, but by then they had drowned and turned turtle; all that could be glimpsed were their stiff hocks and hooves sticking up above the water. They rounded a bend in the river and disappeared.

Foyt found a place on the western bank that Lightning could climb, and rode north up the river—he was nearly a mile from where they had started to cross—collecting along the way the three cows he had rescued. Each of them stood in the shallows, dejected, shivering and coughing like sheep. He roped them ashore, one by one, and drove them before him to rejoin the others.

Wheeler and the remounted Boudreaux and Karnes had driven, coaxed and hauled the rest of the herd successfully onto dry land. The cows seemed immediately to have forgotten their watery ordeal and were now drowsily feeding on the lush riverside grass and bushes. The three men were wearily peeling out of their wet clothes. Karnes's and Boudreaux's hats had begun to disintegrate. The tacky glue had dissolved; the crowns were no longer blocked, but blobs; the brims were frazzling around the edges. Foyt shoved his animals toward their fellows—now making a total of thirty-three head— himself dismounted and began to undress.

"I tell you, pards," said Karnes, getting out of his tent-sized long-johns. "I've got half a mind to go back to working for a living."

"Oh, shoot," murmured Wheeler. "This wasn't nothing much, Mistuh Gideon, suh."

"Eli's right," said Foyt. "Try it sometime with maybe two thousand head, up at that North Pole end of the Panhandle, through some river that's twice as wide as this one, half froze over and colder'n a dead Eskimo's dick."

They laid their clothes, their saddles and blankets and their firearms out in the sun to dry, and decided to take advantage of the wait to get themselves spruced up a little. Foyt brought out a brown bar of Fels-Naphtha soap and they all went back into the Sabine for a swim—for a bathe, rather; the Cajun was the only one who'd been around water often enough to have learned even a dog paddle. When they came out, uncrusted and unsmelly for the first time in recent memory, their gear was still gently steaming. So Karnes gathered dry grass, lit a small fire, heated up a pan of water and, taking turns with Foyt's and Wheeler's straight razors, they all took their first shave of the trip.

Then they lay nude in a row on the warm grass and toasted

themselves in the sun. Wheeler had scarcely any body hair, but the other three were downright shaggy. The dark-hairy Cajun, the red-hairy Karnes and the silver-hairy Foyt looked like a medium-sized black bear, a gigantic cinnamon bear and a very lean polar bear all basking side by side. Boudreaux and Karnes, having been accustomed to working in hot places and with as little covering as possible, were tanned over most of their bodies. Foyt and Wheeler, like all cowboys, were birch white except for their mahogany hands, faces and necks.

After a long, sleepy silence, the Cajun sighed and said, "*Ma foi,* I begin to feel like a real cowpuncher, me." Foyt gave him a sidelong glance of mixed amusement and contempt. Boudreaux went on to say that, speaking of cowboys, he'd been wondering something for quite a while now. "Right from de first, I notice, L. R., how you wear your pistol inside dat bib of dem overhalls. I t'ought all cowboys carry dere gun in a holster belt—like Gideon's doing—and wore dem kind of big flappy pants."

"Chaps, you mean, Moon," said Foyt. "*Chaparejos,* them leather flaps that go over your reg'lar britches. Well, yes, they wear 'em further out west, for protection against the cactus and chaparral. And they wear 'em in Wild West shows just to look like what folks expect a cowboy to look like. But there ain't no cactus or chaparral over here in East Texas. And the weather's warm and them chaps would git damned hot and heavy and uncomf'table hereabouts. No, you won't see no East Texas cowboy wearing 'em, unless he's plumb ignorant or some kind of dude. Denim's more practical."

He reached over and fingered his own denim garb; it was just about dry.

"Some fellers wear Levi's jeans, but most will agree that these plain old Sears, Roebuck bib overhalls are really best for the job. More pockets to carry things in. More covering when you're wrassling some old mossy-horn all plastered with mud and shit, or helping a springer cow with the messy business of dropping a calf."

As for carrying his Billy-the-Kid revolver inside his bib, well, said Foyt, that too was a matter of pure practicality. Nobody but the actors in Wild West shows ever did that face-off-and-*reach*-pardner performance. If you had reason to shoot a man, it was far more sensible to dog him unawares and shoot him in the back—and such a procedure would be admired by all and sundry as evidence of your sagacity. But if it ever did come to a face-to-face encounter, it was blamed foolishness to have your gun hanging out where your opponent could see you grab for it.

"O' course, when a man's working cows, he likes to have his iron handy, and most of 'em hang it around their waist. But they only use it to make noise with, to stir up the critters. Or to shoot their hoss when it breaks a leg or falls on 'em and is about to thrash 'em to death. Or to shoot holes in a saloon ceiling when they're full of redeye. The av'rage cowboy ain't no gunman; he couldn't hit the ground with a fistful of gravel.

"Now I'm not talking about the real professionals, like that Bubba feller. They sling that gun in a holster from a belt full of cartridges and tie the holster bottom to their leg to give 'em a firm, fast draw. But hell, they do that to *advertise* what they are, same as lawmen do, and it'd be a damn fool that tangled with 'em. So them professionals, they hardly never have to draw, noway."

However. Say that you, an ordinary, nonprofessional somebody, had to throw down on somebody—as Foyt had had to do, now and again—you had a notable advantage if you carried your gun inside the bib of your overalls and used it like so. First you looked away from the other fellow, maybe over his head, and looked thoughtful, as if you'd just discovered you had a flea in your chest hair, then you stuck your hand inside the bib to scratch yourself, and then you brought your hand out full of pistol.

One time, said Foyt, in one particularly tight and tetchy situation, he hadn't even had time to bring his hand out; he had simply shot through the overall bib. The other fellow had looked considerably surprised as he dropped his own gun and fell over. And, as the bystanders carried him off bleeding, he confided to Foyt that he had just learned something that would come in useful in future—if it turned out he had a future—and he was much obliged to Foyt for demonstrating that technique of itch-scratch-and-shoot.

The Cajun was so impressed by all this advice that, instead of getting back into his corduroy pants, he wheedled the loan of Wheeler's other pair of Sears, Roebuck overalls. He put them on over his union suit and his flannel shirt, tucked his pipsqueak derringer down the bib, and stayed dressed that way for the rest of the journey. The other three also got up, brushed grass seed off their buttocks and got dressed. They all saddled up, stiffly remounted and once more pushed their herd into its slow westward march.

3

The days were pleasant and the country was pleasant: rolling grasslands liberally patched with forests, mostly shortleaf pine but a lot of red maple, bois d'arc, shellbark hickory and other hardwoods. The deciduous trees were turning brown and shedding, the grass was going tan and going to seed, but there were still more than enough evergreens—holly, magnolia, live oak—and late-autumn flowers to offset the brown and tan with dazzling blazes of color: the rose-purple spikes of gay-feather; the flat-topped azure heads of mistflower; the big, flared red blossoms of trumpet creeper; masses of shaggy rose asters; blue, pink and purple morning-glories; whole meadows colored lavender with cosmos, others solid to the horizon with glowing yellow sunflowers.

Even the plants that were packing it in for the winter were still bright with colorful seeds, berries and pods. There were clusters of the lovely purple fruit of the beauty-berry, and the big, hard, brilliant red seeds of the frijolillo shrub. Foyt called these—most people did—"big-drunk beans," because the Indians allegedly used to grind them down and brew them into some kind of potent, brain-decaying liquor.

Some of these fruits that the wayside shrubs flaunted, to attract birds to come and carry them away and plant them elsewhere, served instead to augment the diet of the four riders and their animals. The men picked and the cows and horses browsed on wild plums, blue-black farkleberries and stretchberries, mustang grapes and applelike may haws. Eli Wheeler, unnoticed by the others, was also collecting and stowing in a saddlebag the supposedly medicinal pleurisy root, the sticky burs of gumweed, the leaves of Indian mint, Santa Maria, rattlesnake master, quinine weed and Adam's-flannel, and the roots of gay-feather, blazing star, Texas milkweed and black sampson.

During the day, curiosity brought flying squirrels gliding out of the trees, over the men and their herd, and made cottontails sit up on their haunches to peer through the grass at them. There were always two or three copper hawks hanging high in the air above and just behind the herd, their wings unflapping, pacing their speed to that of the procession, hoping its shuffle-along would startle a field mouse or a pocket gopher out of hiding and into the open where they could pounce on it. Once, the men spotted two gray foxes being, for a change, not predatory but playful. On a hillside covered with cosmos like a haze of lavender smoke, the two foxes were merrily chasing each other in a circle. Foyt's natural inclination was to take a snap shot at such varmints, but they were having so much innocent fun that he couldn't bring himself to do it.

With the dusk, countless invisible bobwhites began to call perkily "bob!" and "white!" and "bobwhite!" back and forth at each other. These cheerful chirps were interspersed with the melancholy moans of poorwills—Foyt unsentimentally called these by their local name of goatsucker, and insisted they were not saying "poor Will!" at all, but "pour me one!" Evening bats fluttered overhead, and the men thought they were the most noiseless of all the creatures that came to inspect them, until, one twilight, a great horned owl ghosted by, and they knew what noiselessness really is.

Karnes and Boudreaux were so calloused on the bottom by now that even they could take pleasure in the ride. One or the other would occasionally rear back and start singing, partly out of sheer high spirits, partly to drown out the interminable and nerve-rasping whistling of Wheeler and Foyt. The Cajun sang Cajun songs like *"Dansez, mes enfants,"* old ballads like "Jinny Git Around" and modern ragtime stuff like "Mopsy Massy of Tallahassee"—and the mockingbirds in the woods around them seized the opportunity to show off, imitating Boudreaux's clear tenor with an almost spooky perfection. But then Karnes would let fly with "When Big Profundo Sang Low C," and the mockingbirds would simply shut up, hopeless of mimicking that rumbling summer-thunder bass. Instead, every time Karnes reached down among his bowels for that low C, half the cows in the herd would raise their heads and join in, with a moo that was almost as booming as his.

Foyt occasionally whiled away a piece of the long ride by spinning a yarn about some aspect of the country they were passing through. One day he remarked to Boudreaux, "Remember, Moon, how we was talking a while back about gunfighting? I've seen two men git so mad at each other that they've fought it out with worse things than guns."

He gestured more or less southward. "Down thataway a piece, where two trails cross, there's a little one-hoss, one-lung town called Gary. I seen in the latest *Texas Almanac* that Gary's got an elevation of two hunderd and ninety-three feet above sea level, and I'll bet anybody that that's exactly how many people it's got in it, too. Don't even have a saloon—or didn't, the one time I seen it. Had a moonshiner that come through ev'ry noontime and sold his essence of scorpion by the Mason jar out of the back of his wagon. The only real business establishment in town was a seed-feed-and-hardware store."

Boudreaux listened raptly to this long prologue. He had evidently decided, now that he was dressed like a rooting, tooting, shooting cowboy, that he ought to study up on gunfighting and every other kind as well.

"Wellsir," Foyt went on. "The day I was pooting through turned out to be a red-letter day for Gary. There was these two farmers out in the country, see, that had been feuding for as long as anybody could remember—so long that nobody could remember what their original grudge was. Anyhow, they both bought their necessaries, natur'ly, at that hardware store I mentioned. But they'd sort of arranged it, years back, that they'd drive into town on diff'rent days. One come on Fridays, as I recall, and t'other on Saturdays—so they'd never have to meet and bring the feud to a head. They kept their kitchen calendars marked real careful, so as not to make no mistake. But—the way I heard it later—one of 'em had used up the mail-order catalogue he kept hung up on a nail in his privy out back, and there wasn't another piece of paper on the whole farm 'cept his calendar. That calendar, by the way, was presented to its customers ev'ry New Year's by that selfsame hardware store. Well, after this feller'd used it, either he didn't want to hang it back in the kitchen, or it was too smeared to read, I dunno. Whichever, he got his dates mixed up, and breezed into town the same day his mortal enemy did."

By this time, Wheeler and Karnes had also ridden alongside to listen in.

"And wouldn't you know, they bumped into each other right in front of that selfsame hardware store. Well, they started talking real quiet and deadly, but highfalutin at the same time, like a couple of stage actors. *So,* Dudley Meacham, you finally dared to show your two-faced face in daytime! And *so,* Roscoe Suggs, you finally screwed up the nerve to come and look me in the eye! (Maybe I've got the names wrong, but they was something on that order.) And *so,* Dudley Meacham, I reckon I'll peel you rightchere and now, so these good folks of Gary can see the yeller stripe down your back! And *so,* Roscoe Suggs, once I've skint you down to your black and white stripes, these good folks'll know you for the skunk you are!"

With an apt sense of the dramatic, Foyt paused to start rolling a cigarette, doing it deftly without either stopping his horse or dropping his reins.

"Well, they carried on like that for a good while. After all, it had been a long-drawn-out feud; it deserved a long-drawn-out, jumbulacious showdown. Besides, all the other two hunderd and ninety-one local yokels was crowding around 'em by now—ninety-two, counting me—and it wouldn't of been mannerly to cheat that mob out of a good show by killing each other too abrupt like. Anyway, they neither one had come to town with any kind of weapon. They could of both gone home and got a gun and come back—I've

known men in a real walleyed fury to do just that—and the crowd
would of waited for 'em if it had took a week. Or they could of
gone at each other bare-knuckle or bite-and-gouge. But for a long
time they just stood and reviled each other, gitting louder and
louder. You never heard such lowdown names called. Till finally
one of 'em said you son of a bitch, and o' course them's *the* fighting
words."

He licked the cigarette paper, rolled and sealed it, stuck it in his
mouth, scratched a match behind him on the cantle, lit up and inhaled a long drag.

"I've said they was standing in front of the hardware store. And
like all hardware stores, it had a show of its goods stacked out front
—plows and buckets and shovels and chamber pots and all. Wellsir, them two fellers reached out and each of 'em plucked a brand-
new pitchfork outa that display. One hand on the haft and one on
the handle, they raised them clean, shining, terrible tines up to waist
level and went lunging at each other. Boy-hydee! All the men in the
crowd grunted like they'd got them tines in their own gut—me
amongst 'em—and I think all the women in the crowd swallered
their snuff."

"*Dis donc,*" said the Cajun, wide-eyed. "You mean dey killed
both demselves dat same minute?"

"Oh, no. Not quite. I dunno if you've ever looked at four pitchfork tines, point on, with an enemy behind 'em. I never have, but
I'd damned well sooner look down the muzzle of a forty-five. Them
two fellers lunged but they dodged at the same time. I know I'd
of done the same. So they caught each other with just the one outside tine apiece. One of 'em—say Dudley—was wearing just a single gallus to his britches. Roscoe's jab didn't do no more'n snap that
gallus, and Dudley's britches fell down around his feet. Meantime, *his*
jab caught Roscoe at the waist, where he was wearing inside his
underwear one of them patent electro-medico-magnetic metal belts
—to cure, uh, you know, male complaints—and it was wired up to
a cautery battery that he wore hid under his shirt. Well, that steel
pitchfork tine just short-circuited the whole works, and Roscoe went

off like the Fourth of July in an election year. Sparks, fizzes, colored smoke. Alongside Roscoe Suggs that day, Roman candles and Bengal fire wasn't *in* it."

He grinned, shook his head reminiscently, and rode on a way without adding anything more.

Finally the Cajun said, exasperated, "Dat's *all* de story?"

"Well, just about. While some of the folks was helping Dudley hitch up his britches, and others was disconnecting Roscoe from his burnt-out machinery, that moonshine peddler drove up with his wagonload of guar'nteed, sure-fire pacifier. Them two pitchfork-fighters sat down on the edge of the town horse trough, both of 'em purty shaky, and had a drink, and had another drink, and had another, and by damn, that years-long blood feud ended right there. The townsfolk was purty bitter about that. It had been Gary's only distinction."

Karnes looked disgustedly at Foyt, said, "I never listened to such a pointless story in all my life," and rode off to his position on the flank of the herd.

"Well, that's Gary for you," said Foyt, still grinning. "Here I try to fill y'all in on some of the local joggraphy, and them's the thanks I git."

11

1

ONE MORNING, as he edged Lightning into position at the tail end of the herd, Foyt said suspiciously, "What's happened to them cows now? They've done stopped smelling like cows."

"It's that old yellerback yonder, suh," said Wheeler. "He was limping real bad, so I rubbed him down with some liniment, and now he moves along right spry."

"Liniment? Where'd you git liniment way out here?"

"You had some in your saddlebag, suh. Not much, but enough."

"*Mine?!* Eli, you used up my good Yager's Liniment on that bone-yard-bound old steer?! Now what'll *I* do, next time I git an attack of the misery?"

Even Karnes was annoyed. "Here Moon and I've been scouring our asses raw, and all this time you've had a bottle of liniment, and now you've donated it to the Thought-damned *cows?* We sure do thank you, good buddies."

"I been doctoring all of 'em, suh," said Wheeler, his jug ears turning pink. "With Injun cures and old home remedies. I been picking yarbs and roots and things along the way. I brewed yarb teas out of 'em, and made salves with the bacon grease left over from breakfast, and—"

144

"And, by Jesus, next you'll have 'em drinking our coffee!"

"No, suh," he said solemnly. "Coffee won't do 'em no good." He continued stubbornly, "I was thinking, suh, if I had the time to attend to 'em proper, I bet I could turn these into some passable critters."

Foyt glowered out over the herd. The cows still looked like fugitives from a glue factory, but there did seem to be a diminution in the incidence of festering barbed-wire gashes, and the animals weren't staggering quite so drunkenly as before. "You know," he said to Karnes and Boudreaux, "I wouldn't be surprised but that Eli really could do it. I told you, he's got a touch."

However, at next mealtime, Foyt decided to make soda biscuits, and reached for the baking soda, only to discover that Wheeler had pilfered that, too, to make eyewash for the cows with running pinkeye. So he felt it necessary to explain to him—gently—that this herd was only incidental to their project, and would be abandoned when they were through using it, hence wasn't worth Wheeler's concern and attention and affection. Wheeler said, "Yes, suh," but went on doctoring them on the sly, all the same.

There was nothing that could be called a city in that part of Texas, and not a great many towns, hamlets or settlements of any size. Those that did exist were used to seeing cattle being driven through—but always in the other direction: northeast toward Shreveport. So the four men prudently circled around every settlement they came upon, to avoid the why-in-hell-fellers? questions they would inevitably be asked. They could not, however, avoid meeting an occasional traveler on the trail, and for these Foyt had concocted an elaborate explanation of why they were driving their herd ass-backward toward the southwest.

For example, one afternoon they encountered a rider dressed all in black: flat-brimmed, flat-crowned black hat, worn-shiny black serge suit, black string necktie. He reined his horse to a halt, stared at the passing cows in amazement and amusement, then at their herders, and said in a hushed voice:

"Here I went and took Revelations Six for my text just last Sunday, but Great Godfrey, I never in my life thought I'd ever meet them in person—the Four Horsemen of the Apocalypse!"

"I take you to be a preacher," said Karnes, somewhat sourly.

The man introduced himself as the Reverend Josiah Lockard, a circuit-riding pastor to three diminutive Baptist churches that sat in a triangle some forty miles to a side, and he was now en route to Tatum, whose congregation's turn was next Sunday. He glanced again at the herd, and quoted, "And I looked, and behold . . . I heard a voice in the midst of the beasts say . . . his name was Death, and Hell followed with him . . ."

"Now don't go badmouthing our beasts, Reverend," said Foyt indulgently. "Them's God's critters, same as you and me."

"Truly put, Brother. But excuse me for asking. Wouldn't the critters get to meet their Maker a mite sooner if you pointed them the other way? You-all are headed straight *away* from any slaughter-houses."

Here Foyt hauled out his fabricated elucidation. They were herding these cows, he said, all the way west of Fort Worth. Yessir, clear to Thorp Spring, where the Texas Christian University maintained a big experimental ranch, and where these particular animals were to be examined by the resident veterinarians and experts and ologists.

"I see," said the preacher. But he looked at the herd once more and added, "What in creation could you possibly want to know about that bunch that you don't know already?"

"It's a special 'speriment," Foyt mumbled, empty of further lies that would bolster the story. Karnes came to his rescue.

"It's like this, Reverend Lockard. There are"—he snatched a number out of the air—"there are one hundred and seventy bovine ailments that cows can catch. These specially selected cows you see here are suffering from ten or twenty of those diseases apiece. Yessir, among these thirty-three head you'll find represented every one of those one hundred and seventy afflictions." The preacher stared at the herd with new interest. "This is a most important experiment,"

Karnes went on, pointedly, "because at least seventeen of their diseases can be contracted by man, and they are invariably painful,
gruesome and fatal."

The preacher quickly took up his reins, raised his flat hat, bade
the men a good day and wished them a happy culmination to their
journey. Foyt said that that was exactly what they were looking forward to. The Reverend Lockard clucked his horse to a trot and
rode on northward, making a mental note to preach on Revelations
Six again next Sunday at Tatum, this time with illustrative anecdotes
from personal experience.

Foyt had used up all of his precious Bull Durham, and was now
rolling and smoking "Injun tobacco," the dried leaves of frostweed,
and blaspheming every time he did. Their other supplies were getting low, as well, so they decided to stop and stock up at Henderson, the next town of any appreciable size on their route. They
parked the herd a mile short of the place, and Karnes and the Cajun
stood watch over it while Wheeler and Foyt rode on in.

They hitched to an inconspicuous rack at the near end of Henderson's main street and, before Foyt took off for the grocery store two
blocks farther on, Wheeler asked if he might beg one of their remaining dollars for some shopping of his own. Foyt was genuinely
surprised—Wheeler almost never asked for anything, or appeared
to hanker for anything—but he handed over the big bill.

"Whatever it is you're after, Eli, try to haggle for it. Dribble out
that casenote piece by little piece, like it's our last. It prob'ly is."

When Foyt returned to the hitching rack to tie his not-very-bulg-
ing croker sack behind his saddle, Wheeler's horse was still there but
Wheeler wasn't. Foyt went back up the street, peering in the doors
or windows of the stores, leaning down to look under the saloon's
swinging panels—and resisting an almighty urge to go in and relax
over a nickel schooner or two. When he reached the sundries-
sweets-and-drugstore, it was empty of customers, but the proprietor
hailed him:

"He'p you, suh?"

"No, thankee. Just looking for somebody."

"Ah. Young feller with ears and a Adam's apple? Name of Eely Weasel, somep'n like that?"

"That's him."

"He just left. Sold him two bottles o' Peerless Screwworm Formula. Two fer a dollar. Usually fitty-fi' cents a bottle."

"Damn that Eli," muttered Foyt.

He found Wheeler at the rack—he had come a roundabout way, sightseeing the back streets, which is why they hadn't met each other —and Foyt tongue-larruped the young man all during their ride back to where the cows and their companions were.

"Screwworm medicine! Goddammit, while you're dosing 'em for screwworm, they'll be falling over dead of tick fever or blackleg or plain antiquity. Sometimes I think you're gitting simpler, Eli, instead of improving any. That rifle ball must be working around in there and scrambling what little's left of your brains. Now we got sixty-goddam-seven cents left to our name, and we're only halfway home. And, speaking of names, here you go telling yours to just anybody you meet. Try to remember we're *outlaws*. From now on, say you're John Smith, for Christ's sake. Or John Christ, for Smith's sake. Anything but your real name . . ." And so on and so on. Wheeler bore it stoically, but never once said he was sorry he'd splurged on the medicine.

It was only just now midday, Karnes already had a fire laid, and Foyt set about preparing their noon bait, so Wheeler decided to get in a little doctoring on the worse-off cows before they had to move on. Once he got started, though, the other three men began to gag, and then—cursing him with fervor—picked up and moved, cooking fire and all, a good hundred yards away from him and his increasingly odoriferous operation.

Doctoring a screwworm-ridden cow—or even being in proximity to the process—is not for anyone of squeamish sensibilities. The screwworm is not a true worm, like a pinworm or tapeworm, the kind which live in an animal's guts and can be flushed out with a purgative. The screwworm—the larval stage between a blowfly egg and a full-grown blowfly—is better known as a maggot, and the maggot's habits are pretty well known.

A blowfly lays its eggs—inserts them, rather—in any handy organic tissue, living or dead, where, when they hatch, the larvae will have plenty of food to see them through to maturity as a new generation of blowflies. The sole occupation of these larvae, or maggots, or screwworms, is eating, ravenous eating. When they do this in dead carcasses, they perform a useful clean-up function. When they do it in a living host, they make one ungodly mess and eventually kill the creature.

Besides their general and all too obvious debility and torpor, the cows Wheeler was attending manifested their affliction with the open sores being gnawed into them by the screwworms. These sores had deepened and broadened until the infested cows—there were fourteen among the herd—were indented with one, two or several cavities the size and depths of teacups, on their flanks, their bellies, particularly around their navels, that tender place where blowflies are most prone to deposit their eggs. These ulcers were raw red meat inside, rimmed with gray necrotic tissue and brimming with pus. In this nastiness lived the numberless white, blind maggots.

It was necessary for Wheeler to scrape out with his belt knife every trace of that mess from each separate sore on each separate cow. Each scraping liberated a stomach-turning billow of the fetid stench of putrefaction. Once the wound was clean, Wheeler painted the whole cavity and the area around it with his new-bought Peerless Formula.

Wanting to get as many cows treated as possible before it was time to shift the herd, he went right on working without stopping to share the meal with the others. And they, partly to humor him, partly because their stomachs simply wouldn't let them go near him and his patients, let him work on until he was finished with all fourteen. It meant a fretful delay, but Wheeler was so aglow with the pride of accomplishment when he dabbed the last of the Peerless Formula on the last of the sores of the last of the cows that the other three men couldn't bring themselves to grouse at him.

It was well along in the afternoon when they pushed the herd on again, in a bend around Henderson and on westward. And from now on, said Foyt, they sure as *hell* were going to have to avoid getting within eye-reach of anybody.

"Before, we just looked like we'd won all the booby prizes in some crazy kind of a cattle raffle. Now, by Jesus, we look like a traveling menagerie of animal freaks that nobody but the Wild Man from Borneo would recognize."

He had a point. Peerless Screwworm Formula was the color of Mercurochrome. Nearly half the cows in their herd now wore a big splotch, or numerous big splotches, of gay and gleaming red on their hides of dusty tan or gray or buff or brown. Karnes opined that they looked to him like leftovers from some drunkard's case of delirium tremens, and that Sister Maybellyne Dismukes—remember her, Moon?—ought to be taking them around with her on her temperance lecture tours. No, said Boudreaux, it might be even better if Carry Nation, instead of running around wrecking saloons with her axe, could just drive this bunch into each ginmill and turn all the drinkers at the bar teetotal on the instant.

2

Another day, when they and the herd were threading through a pine wood where there wasn't much to look at or remark on, Karnes broached a question that had been in all their minds for some time.

"Not meaning to put the Injun sign on this little venture of ours, L. R., but what if— I mean, what do we do if this venture doesn't come off the way we've planned it?"

"We'll do time," Foyt said flatly. Then he rephrased that. "Lemme put it this way. If things go *really* wrong, and we git hunted down, we'll all either be shot dead as a wedge or we'll all be down at Huntsville braiding rawhide quirts or horsehair bridles in one of the penitentiary workshops. Or after a few years, with good behavior, we'll be let outside to hoe and weed on one of the prison pea farms. But if things just go wrong enough that we can't pull off

the robbery a'tall—if we fudge up our timing, say, or don't stop that
train—well, then, it's just a total fizzle. We won't make a cent, but
at least there won't be no posse chasing us, nor no 'Wanted-Dead-or-
Alive' posters tacked up all over Texas."

"Wanted . . ." Boudreaux echoed hollowly. "Man, dat sounds
scary. My old woman, she always say, ev'ry time my birt'day come
around: well, Euphémon, you done cheated de hangman one more
year."

The other three stared at him, and Karnes said, "Why, Moon.
You're married? I had no idea."

"I *was* married," the Cajun said darkly. "I'm well now."

He didn't seem disposed to elaborate, so Foyt went on:

"Afterwards, we'll be splitting up, I reckon, whether it's a sock-
dolager success or a pure fizzle. If it comes off the way I've figgered
—and I don't see no reason to expect otherwise—we'll head
straight from the railroad down Tehuacana Creek into the Trinity
River bottoms. We'll divvy up the money there, and after that we're
all on our own. I dunno about you and Moon, but me and Eli'll hide
out in there till the hooting and hollering has quieted down some.
Them Trinity bottoms is all full of rattan vines and switch cane
twenty foot high. So tangled and thick that if a hoss bucked you off
in there, you wouldn't hit the ground. So dense and dark that all the
Rangers in Texas couldn't find Jumbo the elephant in there."

Karnes and Boudreaux looked at each other, nodded, and said
they might as well snug down in there for a while, too, until the heat
was off.

"Howsomever," Foyt went on. "If there's some mischance and
our whole plan falls to pieces, and we don't do no robbing a'tall, we
sure don't have to hide out. But we might as well split up, because
we'll damn well never git another opportunity like this again, not in
our lifetimes."

"*Non,*" said the Cajun somberly. "Dis *better* work, by damn."

"But supposing it doesn't," Karnes persisted. "Just *supposing* it
doesn't. Moon and I've both got trades we can go back to. But what
about you and Eli? You said you'd never hire out as hands again."

"Not here," Foyt affirmed. "Not here in the West, where the cow-boy's an obsolete article, and the whole land's filled up and fenced, and civilization has took over, and the damn people are so thick you couldn't stir 'em with a stick. But there's other places, Gideon, that's still frontier. Wide open. Empty and clean. Places where a man can work for wages and still be his own man."

One such place, he said, was Argentina. In the past twenty or twenty-five years, Argentina had become an even more booming beef country than Texas, and its ranchers were combing the rest of the world for experienced and knowledgeable stockmen.

"O' course, they all talk Spanish in Argentina. Down there a cowboy is a groucho. But I've got a smattering of the lingo from when I've worked along the Mexico border. It wouldn't take me long to savvy that palaver. I'd make out."

"How would you get there, L. R.?"

That was the beauty of it, said Foyt; he had already been invited. There were Argentine employment agents lurking in all the bigger towns around the Gulf, from Corpus Christi to New Orleans, look-ing to recruit gringo cowboys for the pampas ranches, and Foyt had run into one of them in Galveston, not long back. The man offered to pay his boat fare to Argentina, and all expenses along the way to the Patagonia ranch he represented, *and*, when Foyt got there, the munificent salary of one hundred dollars a month and found—for doing work no different and no harder than what he'd done all his life up here in the States for less than two-thirds that wage.

"The only hitch was, I'd of had to sign a contract to stay down there on the job for three years. At that time, I didn't feel like sign-ing away three years, because I was already thinking on trying something like this little undertaking we're on now. But that offer's still open; I know where to find the agent; and if this project *should* poop out, me and Eli will sure take a chance on Argentina."

"It sounds like a real long-headed idea," Karnes said admiringly. "Thought damn, I wonder if those greasers need any good riggers down—"

Foyt's gesture hushed him abruptly, and all four yanked their horses to a halt, while Foyt slowly slid a hand down to draw his carbine out of its boot. About two hundred yards up ahead, a young whitetail buck had stepped out from behind a tree to gaze at the passing herd. No doubt the deer had seen cows before, but he had never seen cows like these, and his curiosity was his undoing.

Boudreaux and Karnes had often heard sidearms and shotguns fired, but they had never been sitting on either side of a .30–30 when it went off in an enclosed space like this dense wood. The carbine's jolting, savage, ear-numbing *blam!* made them rock, and even the cows all jumped as if they'd been stung.

"That's Saturday," murmured Foyt, levering out the empty shell and slipping the carbine back into its scabbard.

"How's that?" said Karnes, digging a finger into his ringing ear. "Today's Thursday, L. R."

"Just keeping count of my cartridges, Gideon," Foyt explained, as they rode up to the fallen buck. "This-here's a Winchester Ninety-Four. It holds seven rounds—six in the magazine and one in the chamber—so the Winchester people have a slogan: load her once and shoot all week. I just shot off Saturday's bullet. That's how I keep track."

So they had a meal of fresh meat again, the first since they'd sliced steaks off that defunct brindle steer. They were to have one more meal of new-killed meat—a couple of days later Foyt used his Billy-the-Kid to drop a sleeping possum from a tree crotch. But in neither instance could it have been called fancy dining.

Karnes and Boudreaux had both read, and drooled over, stories by "outdoors" writers which waxed rapturous over the incomparable joy of bagging one's dinner on the hoof—or on the paw or claw or whatever—and the ineffable delight of cooking it oneself over a campfire, and the ambrosial flavor, richness and texture of it, as compared to the mediocre meat of some domesticated animal bought from some commonplace meat market. But Foyt and Wheeler could have told them different. Either those outdoorsy writers had never been outdoors or they had shot, cooked and eaten some little girl's pet lamb.

Except for the tasty and tender liver—which didn't go far for four—the deer meat, unhung, unaged and unmarinated, was just about as blunting to the teeth and blighting to the taste buds as those Methuselah-steer steaks had been. And eating possum—unless it has been carefully prepared by a topnotch cook, and well disguised with seasonings and condiments—is something like eating suet wrapped in lard. After their three meals of freshly dead, freshly cooked fresh meat, Karnes and the Cajun both roundly damned those ah-wilderness! writers, and Boudreaux even stopped muttering *horreur* over Foyt's subsequent servings of salty, brittle bacon, clotty canned beans and saddle-blanket hoecakes.

12

HEY NEVER knew the name of the little town, because when they got there they were too frightened to ask and the inhabitants were too frightened to volunteer trivial information and, later on, the name didn't matter, because there was no town left to need one.

It was Monday, the sixth of November, and they were halfway across Anderson County. For the last few days they had been following what trace remained of the old Comanche Road, detouring off it only once, to sidle around Jacksonville in Cherokee County. They had crossed the Neches River, the Cherokee-Anderson county line, without any untoward incident or any casualties, the Neches being no formidable stream, and all of them by now having had some experience. They were at present traveling alongside the double tracks and pole-slung telegraph line of the Missouri Pacific Rail Road's right-of-way, across a piece of Texas where the hilly land was beginning to flatten out to rolling prairie and the pine forests were beginning to thin out to scattered groves of basswood, hackberry and honey locust.

Every so often—*rumble, clank, clatter, rumble*—a train would swoop by them, going one way or the other. The cows paid these apparitions no heed at all, but the four men would wave and everybody on the train would wave back, from the engineer and fireman up front to the brakeman in the cupola of the caboose (if it was a freight) and (if it was a passenger train) all the people sitting in the coaches and at table in the dining car.

"Take a good look at that engine. That's a Baldwin 4–6–0," said Foyt, when the first of that make came along. "That's what we'll be stopping purty soon."

The others said nothing, but they stared at the locomotive hard enough that, from then on, they recognized each one that came by. They saw many an engine that was bigger and more powerful; the Missouri Pacific ran such titans as the 35 Pacific 4–6–2. But the Baldwin 4–6–0 was big enough, noisy, smoky and steamy enough, impressive enough.

It had four leading truck wheels right behind the cowcatcher; four coupled driving wheels, each as high as Gideon Karnes, under the long black cylinder of the boiler, and another pair of drivers spaced a little to the rear, just under the cab, so there were no trailing truck wheels. Up front, atop the boiler, perched a headlamp that looked as big as a moon. Behind it towered the tall stack, billowing dirty smoke, and two domes like high-crowned derby hats. White steam hissed from the huge, outjutting drive cylinders and from brass valves here and there all over the machine. Yes, it was impressive enough to make the men realize the temerity and enormity of their intention to step out in front of one of these monsters and hope it would stop.

Anyhow, they were on the last lap of their long and sometimes eventful journey, and they had made good time—thanks in large part to Eli Wheeler's attentions to the cattle, which had perked them up a good deal, and speeded them up to some fifteen miles per day. The men were sure now that they would be blocking that stretch of track between Mexia and Teague, three days hence, when the T. & B.V.'s train Number Three came chugging along.

But right at this moment of this morning, none of the four men was manifesting much joy that things were going so well. They were all depressed by the weather, which had turned sour for the first time on the trip. The sky was a solid, low-hanging, surly-looking bank of gray cloud from one horizon to the other, occasionally letting loose a thin, pissy little drizzle. Sometimes this fell on the four riders and their herd, sometimes it was a shred of veil drifting across some other part of the prairie within their view. But, during the showers as well as between them, the morning was hot and sultry, the air so heavy that it seemed simultaneously to impede their breathing and to weigh on their spirits.

"November," grumbled Foyt, sounding worried, "and it's *hot?*" He was wearing a smelly old yellow oilskin slicker for coverage against the showers, but it made him sweat so underneath that he couldn't have got much wetter if he had doffed it.

The nameless little town had been in sight for some time. Now they were close enough to see that it consisted of a single street— which is to say a widened and tramped-hard portion of the Comanche trace they were on—with low buildings wearing high false fronts along just the right side of the street. The first building at this near end had a tremendous sign slung out over the street, "Kickapoo Saloon." The last building at the far end was a small but substantial-looking frame church, even wearing a sort of vestigial steeple. The buildings in between were nondescript stores and such. This being Monday and a workday, the town was practically empty—weekends it might be crowded, when the surrounding country folk came in to shop—and what few people there were on the street today looked as nondescript as the town, and lethargic from this singular spell of weather.

The four men were still a quarter of a mile from the town when Wheeler suddenly said, "Look, suh!" and pointed upward. Foyt tilted his head back and said, "Good Christ!" Karnes and Boudreaux also looked up, but couldn't think what to exclaim. They had never seen anything like it.

The cloud cover had been a solid gray blanket. Now it had darkened to green-black and seemed to have turned to rubber, into which some god far up above was dropping giant bowling balls, one after another. The ugly-colored cloud was bulging here and there into rounded hanging pouches. As the men watched, more pouches came bulging down between the first ones, until the whole sky was clustered with these bizarre gourd-like hanging clouds. Now each pouch began to grow a little nipple at its very bottom. Every goddess of every religion known and unknown was leaning down from Heaven and dangling her breasts. Beautifully formed breasts they were, but eerie and horrible in their close-packed hundreds, all over the sky and all that ominous green-black bruise color.

"Twister coming!" bawled Foyt. "Hit for shelter!"

He jammed spurs into Lightning and took off like a shot, his slicker flaffing behind him, not even looking back to see if the others followed. But, after one stupefied moment, they did; they were right behind him when he hauled Lightning to a skidding stop in front of the Kickapoo Saloon. A quarter of a mile back on the prairie, their cattle had halted and watched their abrupt departure with numb surprise.

In just the couple of minutes it had taken the four men to gallop into town, they had seen the tornado born. Some miles ahead of them, on the other, southwestern side of the town, the nipple of one of those awesome bulging clouds had grown tumescent, had stretched down from the clouds, had changed from a bruise-colored teat to a green-black snake gliding sinuously down toward the earth. Where it touched, they could see—far away though it still was—the earth respond with a little puff of dust. That is, from here it looked like dust. It might well be a welter of boulders, uprooted trees, smashed wagons and houses, mangled animals and people, all seized, crushed, sucked up, flung about, slammed down, when that terrible snake's head struck.

"I seen a lean-to around back," panted Foyt, leaping from his saddle. "Git the hosses in there."

"But the cows, suh!" gasped Wheeler. "What about them poor cows out on the —?"

"What about 'em?" rasped Foyt. "You gonna hold 'em down? Stake 'em to the ground? We'll be lucky if we *got* any cows, time this is over—lucky if *we're* still around. I've seen them big-tit clouds afore. They might drop a *dozen* goddam twisters all over this goddam prairie."

They tethered the agitated horses in the lean-to on the saloon's back wall, then ran again to the front, flinging an agonized look to the southwest as they went. The tornado was definitely coming townward. The undulating storm cloud was not the typical funnel shape but, like a snake, the same thickness all the way from ground to sky. Like a snake, it slowly wriggled and writhed, at one moment even twisting into a kink halfway up its length. They could hear it now, too. It sounded like every locomotive from every railroad in the world, starting up in some distant roundhouse, chuffing, then chuff-chuff-chuffing, then throttling up to a steady low rumble that was getting louder and closer.

They pushed through the saloon's swinging panels and lurched into the room. Everybody in town had likewise seen the tornado coming, and the whole population, some thirty-five or forty people, seemed to have crowded into the saloon. For such a microscopic village it didn't have a bad saloon—all hung with pictures and posters of Indians, presumably Kickapoos, thumbtacked to the walls—and the room seemed quite cozy and safe after the gathering turmoil of the world outside. The morning had darkened so, the saloonkeeper was going about putting a match to the wall lamps. His regular, daylong customers stood along the bar, some of them talking excitedly and knocking it back as fast as they could, a couple already too addled to comprehend what was going on.

One man at the bar was explaining quite calmly and pedantically, "Mammatoform clouds, they're called. Meaning shaped like female breasts. An almost certain sign of a tornado coming—or a whole parade of them." This fellow the others addressed respectfully as Professor. He looked like one, erect and dignified, except that his eyes were like oysters too long out of the icebox and his nose was like an overgrown strawberry.

The rest of the refugees that had crowded into the saloon milled about in confusion, except for one group that stood apart. They were mostly women, and they looked to be prim, proper citizens. They also looked vexed and affronted at being trapped in this den of iniquity.

One man among them was saying in a shaky voice, "The church is the solidest buildin' in town. And we oughta be in thar anyway, on our knees. God's the on'y one that kin pertect us, praise His name."

"But the preacher's the on'y one what's got a key," said another. "Somebody go find him." No one leaped to volunteer.

The man called Professor turned from the bar and said sternly, "If you value your lives, don't go shutting yourselves in that church. Solid or not, God or not, if that tornado keeps coming this way, the church will be the first building to go."

"God or not, eh, Swain?" one of the solid citizens spat at him. "You besotted old reprobate, you know a lot about God, don't you?"

"Maybe not," said Professor Swain, unruffled. "But I know something about tornadoes."

He was going to get to know this one, all right, and intimately; so were they all; there was no longer any doubt of it. The morning had gone dark as night, except for crackling flashes of lightning that came with increasing frequency. A melancholy wind soughed along the street, and bedraggled tumbleweeds bounced along with it. A shower of rain spattered down, stopped, spattered again.

Karnes stepped a little way outside the door, holding tight to his raggedy straw hat, and breathed a prayerful Thought a'mighty. The tornado was a slow-traveling one, still a mile or two away, but still approaching. And now that writhing, sky-high, green-black snake was hung all along its length with lightning of colors Karnes had never seen in lightning before. It was yellow, green, blue, purple, and it was incessant. Its jags and forks and prongs sizzled around the advancing column so unceasingly that the tornado seemed to be draped about with a luminous, multicolored lace.

It was a sight that a man would have paid to see, had he not known that the dazzlingly resplendent phenomenon was bringing a wind tightly coiled and spinning like a drill at maybe three hundred miles an hour—a tube of wind with an irresistible suction insde it, together so mighty and so remorseless that no man and practically nothing man owned or built could withstand the onslaught.

While Karnes watched, paralyzed, the end of the snake that was dragging along the earth topped a rise of ground. On that rise there was a barn. And then there wasn't. The tornado's tube touched it and the barn disintegrated, not into planks and beams but apparently into molecules, and became part of the dust cloud—which was not dust—that accompanied the tornado's ground-end nozzle. The twister was sucking into its column so much Texas topsoil, vegetation and debris that its green-black color was gradually fading to yellow-gray behind its lace of lightning.

Karnes unfroze and ducked back into the saloon. His companions were at the bar, and Foyt was fumbling in his overall pockets for his sixty-seven cents.

"Losh, put yer money away, man dear," said the barkeep in a quaver, his face shamrock green and his bald head glistening with sweat. "If this be'n't the end of the worruld, sure and it's the end of this town—and me poor Kickapoo Saloon." He began hastily taking the bottles from behind him and setting them along the bar— whiskey, gin, Southern Comfort, rock-and-rye, applejack, everything in stock—and urged the crowd at large to 'Dhrink up, byes! Dhrink up on Seamus O'Cluricain! Dhrink it fast and dhrink it all!"

They did, pouring and gulping, or not even pouring but tilting the bottles. All but the Professor, who continued to nip at his drink quite placidly and proceed with his lecture:

"Yes, it's odd, but it is so. Ever since the Midwest has been settled, it's been happening, all up the length of Tornado Alley, from Texas to Michigan. If the twister knocked down just one building in a town, it was the church. If it left just one building standing, it was the saloon. Nobody could figure it out; most people still can't. The pious and the devout have always been especially upset. If God was going to send such a visitation, why would He destroy a house of worship and leave the grogshop standing?"

The Professor had to raise his voice almost to a shout. The noise outside was now a continuous roll of thunder, commingled with sounds like factory whistles shrieking, giant blowtorches roaring and firehouse sirens wailing.

"The reason is," declaimed the Professor, "not the whirling wind. That does damage, but not the worst. There's a vacuum inside that funnel of wind, a suction, like when you sip soda pop through a straw. When that funnel drops over a building, the air pressure around the building falls nearly to zero. God notwithstanding, churches are particularly vulnerable because—"

"You just go right on, Perfessor," snarled one of the men in the group standing apart. "Spout your book-l'arnin'! See whar it gits you. *Hell* is whar! Me, I'll put my faith in the Good Book and the lovin'kindness of my Maker." He turned to the rest of the bunch about him. "Okay, I'm goin' out to find Reverend Shaftoe. He's prob'ly at the church by now. If he's got it open I'll come back and fetch y'all."

He fired one parting shot at Professor Swain. "Most likely you and me won't meet ag'in, you godless son of a bitch. If thisyer twister does git us all, *I'm* prepared. In the fullness of grace and a blameless life and a good churchgoin' upbringin', I'll be embraced by the Lamb. You got a diff'rent destination. You're goin' down when I'm goin' up."

It was magnificent, the way he batted open the swinging panels and dashed out into the tumult and uproar. His fellows called after him, "Good man, Poteet!" and "Bless you, Shadrach!" and "God go with you." To everyone's astonishment, it was the Professor who said that, and added, "You poor, pious, gallant bonehead."

Shadrach Poteet had made a true prediction: he did go up. When the tornado finally petered out, four hours later and forty-one miles to the northeast, it dropped a blob of jelly into a pigpen in Smith County. The blob had been a man. Every bone had been pulverized, every organ hashed, every blood vessel burst, every stitch of clothing stripped off. Only by a distinctive tattoo on the surface of the jelly—the legend "S.P. loves E.V." inside a valentine heart—was the blob identified as the mortal remains of Shadrach Poteet.

Foyt had a bottle of good Tennessee sour-mash bourbon whiskey in his left hand and a bottle of raw Mexican tequila in his right, and was swigging from them alternately. He had got to the point where he couldn't tell one from the other.

"I'll be goddamned and whisked off by that twister," he said to Boudreaux, at his side, "if our little venture ain't the most jinxed and bedeviled and hoodooed job I've ever undertook. This latest piece of luck"—he waved a bottle at the street, where unidentifiable pieces of unidentifiable things were now whizzing past the door—"is just absolutely all we needed!"

Boudreaux nodded, though he had merely seen Foyt's lips move, and had heard not a word. Only the Professor was still shouting loud enough to be audible, still trying to get his explanation across:

". . . pressure inside that spinning funnel drops nearly to zero. But the house has got its own air pressure inside—more than seventeen pounds of it pushing outward against every square *inch* of the walls, windows, roof. Ordinarily the air all around that house is pushing back with the same seventeen pounds to the inch, so everything is stable. It's the same with people. A man is full of air at seventeen pounds pressure, but he's surrounded by air at the same pressure, so he doesn't notice anything. But stick him in a vacuum and he'll pop like a balloon from that air inside him."

It is doubtful that Professor Swain was doing much to educate the patrons of the Kickapoo Saloon, or even that he was trying to. What he was managing to do, though, was to rivet their attention and keep the women from succumbing to panic and hysteria— maybe the men, too. Outside, the infernal noise was climbing toward climax.

"A building pops just the same way. It's usually not the tornado's wind that knocks it down. Instead, that vacuum settles around it and the air inside the house can't get out fast enough, so the whole house simply explodes. It *won't* if it's well ventilated, if some of the windows or doors are open. Then the air can foof out into the vacuum without having to blow off the roof and knock down the walls. Churches aren't ventilated; that's why the twisters tear up so many of them. Except on Sunday, a church is closed and locked up tight. It's a compressed-air bomb, just waiting to go off if a tornado hits. A saloon, on the other hand—"

The tornado hit.

You can look it up: in the whole world there were 48,357 steam locomotives in service in November of 1905. For a moment in that November, all 48,357 of them seemed to be roaring down the one street of that little town, their throttles and whistles all wide open, their big drive wheels all churning, but their brakes all locked and their truck wheels all screeching. The next moment, they were not roaring down the street, they were falling on it.

To the people in the Kickapoo Saloon, the noise was more felt than heard, vibrating not their hearing apparatus, but the bones inside their flesh. They never heard the explosion of the first building the twister touched—the Ark of Restitution Church of God in Christ at the other end of the street. Its clapboards and shingles went to splinters so infinitesimal they could not be distinguished from the splinters of the church's one imitation-stained-glass window. Only the pathetic, stumpy little steeple was ever found intact; it later fell not far from that pigpen, forty-one miles away, where Shadrach Poteet came to rest.

Nor did the people in the saloon hear any of the rest of the cannonade of explosions, as the tornado tore and stomped and sucked its way up the entire row of buildings that lined the street. But they knew when its great gulping maw enveloped the saloon.

For an instant, the shattering thunder seemed sufficient to end the world. The several women's faces were contorted, their hair statically standing on end, their mouths wide open, but not even the God they were screaming to could have heard them in that uproar. The tornado's eerie lace of lightning blazed inside the very room, running across the ceiling and down the walls like liquid fire. Then everyone's eardrums went *plip!,* as if he had come suddenly to the top of a high mountain, and the breath went out of him as if he had been kicked in the solar plexus. All the lamps snuffed out. The saloon's two panel doors jerked stiffly out toward the dark street, and through them went flying, ripped from their thumbtacks, every Kickapoo Indian picture and poster, plus several men's hats, women's poke bonnets and shawls, out into the darkness and away to oblivion. Three or four bottles on the bar fell off and smashed.

It was over. The 48,357 locomotives had gone past and were now headed harmlessly out into the open prairie beyond the town. They still roared and raged and rumbled and howled, but the noise was almost a hush now, compared to that one appalling instant of pandemonium when the tornado had virtually been in the room. The people stared around them, dazed, amazed at still being alive.

"Boy-hydee," murmured one man.

"Mercy," gasped a woman.

"*Taim a' gol amu,*" whispered the bartender.

"*Parbleu. . . .*"

Consciously or not, no one was daring to express his relief at his deliverance with a heartfelt and hearty profanity that might be overheard On High.

"As I was saying," resumed the Professor, "a saloon stands a good chance of thumbing its nose at a tornado. It's open for business all week long, not just on Sunday, and it's open all day and practically all night. And the only doors it *has* are those little louvered flaps." He gestured toward the still swinging panels. "So even if a twister squats right over a saloon, the way this one did—bringing that suction, that near-zero vacuum—all the air in the place can go whooshing out—you all felt it—without doing more than trivial damage. Sorry about your pictures, Seamus," he added, addressing the saloonkeeper.

"Faith and it don't matter," said Seamus, who was looking dolefully out the door. "Me sign's gone, too. Certes, it'll light on some saloon in Chicago—the divil, in *Quee*bec—where they never heard of the Kickapoos." He sighed. "Maybe I'll just rename this place

instid, and redecorate. Chromos of Nora Bayes, maybe. Lillie Lang-
try. The Floradora Gurruls." He sighed even more deeply. "Or
maybe I'll just stack my stock in a lorry and move elsewhere."

A sudden deluge of rain came down, so hard and heavy that its
drumming almost drowned the diminishing roar of the receding tornado. Seamus flinched away from the rain and got back behind the
bar.

"I'd advise all of ye that's still sober to have a good stiff dhrink
—ye ladies, too, and I'm afther meaning it—before ye look out in
the street yonder. No, put yer money away and hold yer whisht. I'll
not be charging still. Jasus dear and merciful, can a man act miserly
whin he's just lived through a miracle?"

They all took Seamus O'Cluricain's prescription, the ladies included, and took it several times over, before they felt steady and
nervy enough to assess the damage outside. Then they left the saloon in a body, to discover that they had just walked out of the only
building, the only man-made object still existing in as much as the
eye could see of the state of Texas. They stood, unmindful of the rain
that drenched them, and stared wide-eyed.

The rest of the town had not been ravaged, or leveled, or scattered far and wide. It was simply *gone*. The tornado had tidily
sucked up and carried off every stick, stone, fragment and sliver of
the wreckage it had caused. All that remained were the concrete
foundations and the gaping cellars of those few buildings that had
had foundations or cellars. Several people, as if saying a silent farewell to their departed town, turned to look the other way, northeast,
where the tornado, dwindling toward the horizon, was barely visible and audible through the rain.

Wheeler, Foyt, Karnes and Boudreaux, after a few seconds of
stunned immobility, darted around back of the saloon and found to
their surprise, relief and delight that the horses were still there, still
alive and each still on four legs. It seemed the tornado, with almost
human capriciousness, had decided that as long as it couldn't snatch
up the saloon it might as well spare the establishment's attachments.
Even the flimsy lean-to roof was still in place. So was the saloon's

two-doored privy some distance away. The horses, after having been brushed by that fugitive piece of Hell, seemed as delighted to see their masters as the men were to see them.

They led the animals around front, to find the crowd of their fellow survivors breaking up—people wandering off singly or in groups, but all looking about them bewildered and unbelieving. The women, weeping fit to break one's heart, and a few men, snuffling tears from their mustaches, hurried to the far end of town, to see if Shadrach Poteet or the Reverend Shaftoe or both might still be alive, however mangled, among the ruins. There were no ruins. There was only a church-sized dark rectangle on the dun-colored ground. There were no bodies; there was nobody. Poteet was found later, of course, but the Reverend Shaftoe never was seen or heard of again.

Kindhearted Karnes wanted to stay a while and help the townsfolk search for remnants, remains, rags—whatever there might be to find—or at least to help them mourn their loss. But hardheaded Foyt reminded him that they were strangers here, and had no right to join in the luxury of the people's private grief, and besides had worries of their own. So they climbed aboard their horses, to ride away from the formerly Kickapoo Saloon, and back along the now muddy Comanche Road, retracing the route they had galloped into town. Of the people they left behind, only Professor Swain took note of their departure. He hadn't drifted far from the doorway of the saloon, and still was drinking from a dark and brimming glass. He raised it to them and they paused to hear him say sardonically:

"The Lord hath his way in the whirlwind and in the storm. The Lord revengeth, and is furious, and he reserveth wrath for his enemies."

A quotation from somewhere in the Bible, and surely he was referring to the tornado, but the line lodged in Karnes's mind and nagged at him. It had sounded uncannily as if the Professor was at the same time pronouncing a portent, and it didn't sound good. Karnes decided he would look up that passage, next time he was near a Bible, and mull over its context.

Arriving back where they had left the herd and, expectably, finding no herd, the four men had to scatter apart and separately quarter the outlying prairie for hours. It was almost night, and the rain had stopped, when they reassembled. But when they did, it was to congratulate themselves on what had turned out to be their first lucky day since they four had first met—a day of incredible and continuing luck. The cows had not stupidly turned tail and stood stolid before this storm. Even cows recognized a piece of Hell when it was bucking around loose. They had skedaddled before it, and most of them had successfully dodged it. When each man brought in the cattle he had rounded up, and they were bunched together, Foyt gleefully counted a round thirty head. The other three had, like the Reverend Shaftoe, disappeared without a trace.

After camping, eating and sleeping—most uncomfortably on the wet ground—the next morning they pushed on again southwestward. And solicitously, or superstitiously, they circled at a chary distance around the onetime town whose name they would never know, where only the single saloon building still stuck up from the empty prairie, solitary, stark, like a tombstone.

13

1

TUESDAY, the seventh of November.

In the afternoon, they crossed the Trinity, where the river bottoms were, as Foyt had said, thickets of rattan vine and switch cane tangled in amongst cottonwoods and willows. In the crossing they lost two more cows—two really feeble ones that Wheeler simply had not been able to nurse back to an approximation of vim and verve.

"The hell with 'em," said Foyt, when the rest were safely on the other bank. "We still got twenty-eight, and that's a plenty to squat on that railroad track and stop that train, unless the hoghead driving it has plumb passed out without letting go of the dead-man's switch. Boys, we're in Freestone County now, just a few-steps-and-a-piece from the scene of the crime. And up yonder way"—he waved up the river to the north—"about twenty-four miles, is where Tehuacana Creek joins this-here Trinity, where the bottoms is even more jungly than around here. That's where we'll be hiding out after it's all over, after we've got the money and got rid of these mizzible cows."

They moved on westward from the river, and Wheeler rode scout, disappearing out ahead of them and the herd, to find and prepare a camping spot for the night. Meanwhile, Foyt outlined for Karnes and Boudreaux the timetable he had calculated:

"You both seen the telegraph dispatch. The Santa Fe's train Thirteen and the T. & B.V.'s train Number Three meet way up yonder at Cleburne at six-thirty Thursday morning. Day after tomorrer. It'll take at least half an hour before that special express car gits uncoupled from the Santa Fe and switched onto the Boll Weevil."

"Onto the what?"

"That's just one more nickname for that sad-ass Trinity & Brazos Valley line. They call it the Boll Weevil because it runs so much of the way through cotton country. And they make all kinds of names out of them initials T. & B.V.—like 'Try and Be Virtuous.' Hell, railroads and railroad men have more aliases than crooks do. You just ain't nobody on a railroad till the other fellers have stuck you with a nickname. My cousin Norwood Foyt is *Spats* Foyt, because his wife Blossom makes him dress like a dude. And I know a station agent called Hop Haskell, and a brakeman Sput Henkelkrug—and Cow Bastrop and Turkey Birtwistle and Nehi McNary and a Chili and a Scutter and a Gooley. Lord, I bet none of 'em don't even *know* each other's real front names. . . . Where was I? Oh, yeah —half an hour to switch that money car onto Number Three."

"I've seen switching done a sight faster than that," observed Karnes.

"Oh, sure. But don't forgit, they got to sign over all the waybills and vouchers and papers of responsibility from the Santa Fe to the T. & B.V. And them REA guards'll want to snatch some breakfast after riding all night. It'll be at least seven o'clock afore old Number Three comes rolling south down the T. & B.V. line. Okay, it'll take three hours to Hubbard City—counting the reg'lar stops along the way. Hillsboro and such. Git to Hubbard at ten o'clock at the earliest. Another half hour, prob'ly more, while they uncouple the money car and git shed of it."

"You mean more signing of papers and all that?"

"Hell, yes. That'll be a real ceremony. Handing it over to the Hubbard station agent and the bank president and the sher'ff and

the mayor. Remember, there's something like a million dollars involved there. I wouldn't be surprised but there's flags and bunting
and a band. And speeches, if any of them cotton-picking Polacks up
yonder savvy American."

"Okay," said Karnes. "That makes it maybe ten-thirty when
Number Three pulls out of Hubbard."

"At the earliest," said Foyt. "And now the crew is all free of
worry and responsibility, and they're hauling out their pints of Old
Muleshoe from their overhalls, and not thinking a thought about
that forty-odd thousand dollars they're still toting in their reg'lar express car."

"I hope," said Boudreaux, "dey don't git so drunk dey decide to
brave it out wid us."

Foyt just sniffed at that, and went on, "Now, it's about forty-
seven miles along that line from Hubbard City to Teague. But we're
gonna stop it at mile forty—the straight and empty stretch I've told
you about, between Mexia and Teague—and that's a two-hour run
from Hubbard. The train should reach that spot about twelve-thirty.
Come Thursday it's bound to be later, what with all them ceremonial
delays, maybe even one o'clock or after. But I've been calculating
on the *fastest* it can possibly make it. Even if it had that twister wind
pushing it from behind, it can't git to our ambush spot before
twelve-thirty. But just to make double-damn sure, we'll be waiting
there at twelve. High noon."

2

Wednesday, the eighth of November.

At midday, the four weary riders and their now slowly moving
herd straggled to the top of a rise and looked down its other slope.
Today was Holdup Eve, they were even nearer to the scene of the
crime, and they were certain they'd be there in good time. But they
had one immediate problem. Men, horses and cows alike were
choking with thirst. In consequence, the men were groggy, scratchy-
tempered and disinclined to exult in anticipation of tomorrow.

None of them had had a drink since leaving the Trinity River. There was plenty of water in Freestone County, but they hadn't been able to avail themselves of it. Being more anxious to stay invisible and anonymous hereabouts than they had been anywhere else along the way, and mindful of their extremely eye-catching, red-splotched herd, they had been obliged to dodge around such settlements as Butler, Red Lake, Turlington, the county seat of Fairfield—and this constant detouring had kept them away from such watering spots as Keechi Creek and the little ponds that the settlements were centered on.

Now they looked down from this rise onto a two-track dirt wagon trail. On the other side of that was a trimly rectilinear fence of white-painted palings and, inside that, a neat and inviting farmstead. The house and the barn were painted a gleaming blue and white. From the chimneys of the house fluttered that most hospitable flag: hearth smoke. There was a tall windmill briskly turning, and, fruit of its labors, a stock tank brimming full of water that glittered as temptingly as sin. The men licked their chapped lips at the look of it and their animals all snuffled wistfully at the smell of it.

"Gotta be Polacks," muttered Foyt. "No Anglo or Tex-Mex would fancy his place up with all that paint."

"I don't give a Thought damn if they're war-whooping Comanches," Karnes said huskily. "I say let's go down and ask for a drink. I favor secrecy as much as you do, L. R. But what good does all this sneaking around do us if we perish of thirst before we even pull off our stunt?"

"Well . . ." said Foyt, deliberating. "If them people *are* Polacks, it might be safe. Even if a posse does come asking 'em questions later, they'd be too tongue-tied in the American lingo to describe us very close."

"*Merde,* man," rasped Boudreaux. "A deef-and-dummy or a blind man could describe dese cows."

Foyt snorted, and dust poofed out of his nose. "Let him. If some posse wants to foller them cows all over Freestone, so much the better. By the time a posse gits after us, there'll be a lot of distance

betwixt us and them cows. Come on. We'll chance it. Even if I hang
for it, I gotta have a drink of water."

Foyt rode down the slope and across the wagon trail to the fence,
while the other three nudged the herd after him. There was a
blonde-haired little girl swinging on the fence gate. She was wearing
a poke bonnet that would have fitted Foyt's horse, and a calico
dress and apron that had obviously been cut down from the garments of some rather large woman, as they were still voluminous.
Fifty yards beyond the gate, at the front of the house, was a woman,
bareheaded and as blonde as the child. She was kneeling down and
setting out cuttings of some kind of plants in a strip of newly turned
soil along the front of the big, homey, welcomey, blue-painted veranda.

"Howdy, Pistol," said Foyt to the little girl. "I wonder if—"

"My name ain't Pistol," said the little girl, getting off the gate and
swinging it shut between them, Foyt on the outside.

"Well, whatever your name is. I wonder if—"

"My name's Feather. Hudspeth. Altdorfer."

"Do tell!" With an effort, Foyt glowed a Santa Claus joviality at
her. "You're gonna have to grow some to fit all that long handle,
Pis— Feather. I wonder if—"

"Not Pissfeather! *Feather!*"

Foyt sighed and said very precisely, "Feather, I wonder if you'd
run up yonder to the front yard and ask your Momma—that *is* your
Momma?—if we could beg a drink of water for our critters from
her stock tank?"

"I don't have to run and axe. Yes, you kin. A nickel a head."

"What?"

"Five cents a head."

"Why, Miss Feather, that just ain't neighborly, putting a price on
water."

"It ain't the water, it's the windmill."

"Hey?"

"Daddy Fritz says if it warn't for the windmill there wouldn't be
no water, and he says Sears'n'Roebuck didn't give him that windmill

and pump for free, and he says them what drinks it oughta share in payin' for it, and when a big herd comes by here we charge 'em a nickel a head, and Daddy Fritz says the windmill's purty near paid for."

"I just bet. But little gal, we ain't no big herd. Look at our cows coming yonder. Does that look like the King Ranch on the move?"

"A nickel a head."

"But there's only twenty-eight of 'em, Miss Feather," said Foyt, really pleading. "And our hosses and us. If we drunk till we busted, we wouldn't lower your tank an inch. We're not the kind of big out-fit your Daddy means for you to skin."

"Then it won't cost you so much, will it, mister?" She stooped and began doing sums with a finger in the dust. "We don't charge for people and ponies, only the cows. So it's—uh—only a dollar'n forty cents."

"Why, you little"—he swallowed—"little gal, I just plain ain't *got* no dollar'n forty cents. And if I did," he added, his hoarse voice rising, "I wouldn't give it to you *if that tank was full of* RYE WHISKEY!"

His horse was suddenly shouldered aside by that of Karnes, who had ridden up. Karnes gave Foyt a scathing look and muttered, "Yessir, folks, there's Jesse L. R. James to the life. Tomorrow, la-dies and gents, he'll be twisting the tail of a great big railroad train, yessir, but today he can't wheedle a drink of water out of a teensy tot of a baby girl." He turned from Foyt's scarlet face and beamed down at the staunch little gatekeeper.

"Howdy, Pistol!" he boomed.

"Next person what calls me Pistol," said the girl, "I'm 'o go up to the house and fetch me Daddy *Fritz's* pistol down here and shoot him." She sounded like she meant it.

"Her name's Feather," said Foyt. He also confided to Karnes in an undertone, "And the little hellfry ain't no Polack. I do believe she's a midget pawnbroker in little-girl disguise."

Karnes gave a loud cough to drown that out, and beamed again at Feather. "Missy, just look at those poor thirsty old animals." He waved at the cows, which were jostling and lowing pitifully and try-

ing to wedge their heads through the fence palings. "Suppose they
were puppies. Cute little lost and lonesome puppies that just wanted
a sip of water. Then wouldn't you feel—?"

"Them ain't puppies. Them's cows. And the sorriest old cows I
ever seen come by here. And how-come you got 'em all dobbed with
that [string of gutturals]?"

Foyt blinked at her, shocked. He knew enough of the coarser
words of the Plains Indian languages to know that this small girl
child had just asked why the cows were daubed with shit—specifi-
cally, shit of that color and consistency common to an attack of the
bloody flux. He was about to remark on this singular and alien vul-
garity in one of such tender years, when she shouted shrilly:

"And *now* they're go' push our *fence* down. Shoo! *Scat!*" She
flapped her oversized apron and astonished Foyt again—with the
effect of it: the cattle stampeded.

They jumped back, turned as one and went galloping away up the
wagon trail—faster than they had ever been seen to move—all their
tails sticking straight up like those of cats. Karnes, Boudreaux and
Wheeler went pounding after them, but Foyt just sat his saddle and
stared at this strange and terrible little girl.

For two weeks and close to two hundred miles, those cows had
been shoved, prodded, whacked with things, hollered and whooped
at, cussed at, all without appreciable effect. They had had rocks
chunked at them, guns fired over their heads, thunderous railroad
trains clamoring right past their ears. Through all these circumstances, they had plodded without varying their pace of mechanical
wind-up toys; without evincing panic, emotion or even interest. And
now this half-pint female whistle-britches shook her apron at them
and they bolted.

"Feather, you li'l imp!" said a new voice, echoing Foyt's very
thought, if not the exact epithet he would have chosen. "What've
you gone and done?" It was Momma, come down from her garden-
ing activities at the house.

"This-here man," said the little imp, "didn't have no nickels to
water his cows, so I druv 'em off."

"*You* come here without ary nickel," said the mother sharply.

"Did anybody drive you off?" She raised her head to Foyt, whose scowl turned to a stunned and admiring smile at the look of her. "I'm right sorry, mister. She ain't quite bin tamed yit." Foyt gallantly said oh, no apologies, spunky little gal, full of grit, ha ha ha. The woman shaded her eyes with her hand, peered up the trail and said, "I see your boys've got 'em turned back ag'in. You fetch 'em right on in to the tank, and welcome."

"Daddy Fritz said a nickel a head," muttered Feather, still untamed.

"You hesh or I'll whomp you! Now swing that gate open. *Wide.* Mister, I'm Wilmajean Altdorfer, and I'd be proud to have y'all —when you've done waterin' your animals—you and your crew come and set to dinner with us. Willie Pearl's just now a-fixin' and she kin easy set four more places."

"Why, that's mighty kind of you, ma'am. We ain't et a home-cooked meal since I can't think when. My name's—uh—Jim Haskell."

While the four men, the cows and the horses all shouldered each other at the stock tank, Foyt dealt out aliases to the other three. He made their Christian names easy ones to remember, and for surnames gave them the first that popped into his head—those of the railroad men he'd been talking about the day before.

"Eli, you're John Bastrop. Remember that, now. John Bastrop."

"John Bastrop. Yes, suh."

"If somebody says 'John,' you pay attention. Gideon, you be Joe Birtwistle."

"Hoo*wee*," said Karnes-Birtwistle, hanging his pistol belt on Foyt's saddle horn. "Thanks a heap, L. R."

"I ain't L. R., goddammit. I'm Jim. We gotta remember each other's names as well as our own. And quit moping, *Joe.* It won't hurt you to be Birtwistle for an hour or so. Old Birtwistle's put up with it all his life. Moon, for now you're Jake Henkelkrug."

"*Sacre bleu!* Do I talk like a Jake Henkelkrug, me? Do I *look* like a Jake Henkelkrug?"

"So you've been promoted from Cajun. Enjoy it. Now, I ain't gonna stand here thinking up dudish names when there's good chuck waiting on the table for us. Them names'll do. Just, for Christ's sake, remember 'em."

They freshened themselves up as well as they could, which meant they hung their hats on fenceposts, ducked their heads in the stock tank and combed their hair with their fingers. So they all, hair slicked straight back and sticking out in stiff strands behind them, looked as if they were bucking a brisk wind when they trudged up the back steps to the porch. Wilmajean swung the screen door open, smiling graciously. Foyt-Haskell introduced the other three.

"John, Joe, Jake," said Wilmajean, nodding acknowledgment. "I b'lieve you-all met Feather already. And this-here's our pearl of great price, Willie Pearl."

They all said howdy and Willie Pearl bobbed her turbaned head. The four men stood until Feather and Wilmajean were seated, then took their places at the table—somewhat awkwardly, it having been so long since they had sat in chairs.

"Aunt Willie Pearl," said Karnes-Birtwistle, as she set the plates in front of them, "these fixings smell so good I believe I could almost make a nourishing meal just off the aroma, without even tasting them."

Wilmajean said, with a chuckle, "Oh, you'll taste 'em. And once you do, you'll have a hard time a-stoppin'. Them things in front of you there, Mister Henkelkrug, them's one of Willie Pearl's specialties—armadillo sassage."

She was right; the four men pitched in with such gusto that Willie Pearl raised her eyebrows, went out to the pantry for additional supplies and began cooking another entire meal. (Of course there was no reason for the men to notice, but Wilmajean and Feather no longer ate like animals or Indians. They ate delicately, mannerly and with utensils—fork in left hand, knife in right, in the Continental manner, as Fritz Altdorfer had taught them.)

"Mister Altdorfer won't be j'inin' us," said the lady of the house. "He takes sammidges in a sack when he goes out to the fields in the mornin'. He's afflicted with authoritis, y'see, and it'd be a long trudge back and forth to come to noon dinner."

"Sorry to hear that, ma'am," said Foyt-Haskell. "Myself, I'm sometimes troubled with the rheumatiz. That's to be expected, at my age. But a young man, that's a pity."

"Oh, Mister Altdorfer ain't no *young* man," Wilmajean corrected him. "He's some older'n me. Matter of fack, I'd reckon him to be older'n you, Mister Haskell."

"Indeed, ma'am? Well, I count him a lucky feller, then, to have such a young and handsome and strapping missus, and such a— such a bright youngun."

Wilmajean blushed at the compliment, but corrected him again. "Feather ain't Mister Altdorfer's dotter. Him and me, we only got married-up a week back."

All four men struggled to swallow their bulging mouthfuls, and chorused hearty congratulations and how-*about*-that and *bonne chance* and best wishes. Foyt-Haskell was privately assuming that Altdorfer must have got this woman as a mail-order bride from one of those heart-and-hand advertisements—and had by no means got a pig in a poke. But Wilmajean's next words set him straight.

"I was took by the Comanches when I warn't much older'n Feather. We just got loose from 'em not long back, and Mister Altdorfer took us in. He's a good, kind man, and not partic'lar about what—"

Willie Pearl deliberately interrupted what seemed likely to be an overly frank and naïve autobiography, by bringing another armload of provender to the table and making a fuss and clatter, spreading it up and down the board. Each of the men had already eaten enough for two others; now each of them dug in to feed a third and fourth.

"So he axed me to marry him and I did," Wilmajean concluded abruptly and modestly. She didn't elaborate further. She didn't have to. Foyt-Haskell had already heard Feather blurt that indecorous Comanche phrase, and also had spotted the trace of bay in her complexion. He could figure out the rest. He was old enough to remember many such cases of white girls being kidnaped by the Indians in the bad old days, and to know what squalid, slovenly squaws most of them had become and had never recovered from being.

But this one seemed to have survived her captivity with scant visible damage. Any white man—if he wasn't too scrupulous about her past—would deem her a prize catch as a wife, and Foyt-Haskell said so:

"I can't do more'n repeat, ma'am, that Mister Altdorfer's a lucky man. I wish we could hang around and meet him, and clap him on the back and tell him that, but . . ."

"Well, why don't you?" Wilmajean said cordially. "Your cows look purty drug-out, and you-all look like you could use a set-down for a spell. Surely you ain't in no hurry?"

"If this was an ord'nary drive, no, ma'am," said Foyt-Haskell, and then gave her his invented story about having to get these animals to the ologists at Texas Christian. "We do figger to stop someplace and rest 'em till midnight maybe. But then we got to push on."

"Then let 'em rest rightchere," urged Wilmajean. "They all look happy enough, layin' down around the tank yonder. And they kin graze in the medder beyond, when they feel like it. And you kin water 'em ag'in for the road, afore you leave. Why, I wouldn't *hear* of you lookin' for no other place to settle for the evenin'!"

"Well . . ." said Foyt, looking around at the others. He had been telling the truth about holing up until midnight and then pushing on, because it would be a steady twelve hours' drive from here to their noon rendezvous. The others all nodded eagerly. "Well, thank you kindly, Miz Altdorfer, I reckon we'll take you up on that. If we-all can just stretch out under your pee-can trees for a spot of shut-eye . . ."

"Naw, suh!" put in Willie Pearl, so loudly and unexpectedly that even Feather jumped. She shook a wooden spoon at them. "Y'all smell wuss'n dem cows you brung. If y'all are stayin' heah till midnight, dere's time for me to bile dem clo'es of your'n."

Wilmajean said, in some embarrassment, "Mister Haskell, Mister Bastrop, you-all, don't take no offense. Willie Pearl just can't stand to see *nobody* miss a chance to warsh. She done the same to me and Feather when we first come."

"Y'all ain't go' stretch out by dem pee-cans neither," the pearl of

great price went on. "Y'all goin' up to de spah bedroom and hand
me dem overhalls and things out de door. How y'all manage to
sleep in de one bed is you-all's bizness. But you'll have clean clo'es
when you git up."

The four rough, tough, evil-intentioned, stop-at-nothing outlaws
meekly said well, all right, to the spoon-wielding brown woman.
Three of them—Wheeler-Bastrop, Karnes-Birtwistle and Boudreaux-Henkelkrug—followed her upstairs. Foyt-Haskell excused
himself momentarily to pay a call on the privy out back. When he
returned to the house, he walked around the outside of it just to
admire it, and found Wilmajean sitting on the front porch steps,
vigorously shaking a Mason jar full of milk.

"Makin' some clabber for biscuits for supper," she explained,
with a light laugh. "Our churn sprung a stave, is why I'm doin' this
poor-folks' fashion. We can't git a new churn till we make our next
market-day ride into Teague."

"Y'all sure do have a first-class spread here, Miz Altdorfer," said
Foyt-Haskell. "I once said I could draw a pitcher of the kind of
spread I'd like to have myself—I could see it so clear in my head.
But I'll be durned if I ain't seeing it right now, rightchere, like I had
drew the pitcher and it come to life."

"Oh, it lacks some things," said Wilmajean deprecatingly, as did
all country people when they were praised about something. "It
ain't really no spread. We don't have no stock, 'ceptin' the two plow
mules and a milch cow. Couple of pigs and some chickens. Mister
Altdorfer had to give up raisin' beef. With his mis'ry and with no
he'p to be got, it's all he kin do to farm what li'l bit he does farm.
And he'd done let the yard here go. I bin puttin' in flowers as fast as
I could git and plant 'em."

"I seen you doing it. That's a good thing, it is. Anybody passing
by, they see a yard full of flowers, they know that house has got a
good missus in it."

"Well, Mister Altdorfer ain't one for complainin'. But Willie
Pearl, she told me how much he was missin' havin' flowers around.
And he don't say so, but I know from his look that he 'preciates
me puttin' 'em in."

Foyt-Haskell was pretty sure that any of Altdorfer's looks at his wife signified appreciation of a lot else besides, but he refrained from saying so and maybe seeming brash.

"Amongst other things," Wilmajean went on, "I'd admire to have a rockin' chair. Bring it outchere on the front porch in good weather. For one reason"—she laughed again—"it'd make it easier shakin' this jar of clabber."

"Oh, here, lemme do that for a spell." He took it from her and started some fancy action, the way he'd once seen a bartender in New Orleans shake up a drink called a Sazerac Cocktail.

"There's a rockin' chair a-settin' in the show winder of Drumgoole's Furniture Emporium in Teague right now," said Wilmajean, waving her hands limply to relax them. "You oughta see it, Mister Haskell. All rosewood and paddin' and the nicest *kind* of plum-colored plush. It tooken my eye the very first time I ever was in Teague. An old lady name of Granny Ashabranner ordered it bespoke to her design, all the way from St. Louis. She had good taste. And then she up and died of the greensickness afore it got here, so Drumgoole's is stuck with it." Wilmajean smiled, looking wistful, wishful and a little mischievous, as she added, "I keep hintin' at Mister Altdorfer. I just bet you anythin' you please, I git that rockin' chair for Chris'mas."

"Well, I sure hope—"

"Mistuh Haskell!" boomed Willie Pearl from indoors. "Whar *you?*"

"You better hustle in yonder and unshuck," said Wilmajean, still smiling. "Or I guar'ntee you, she'll come out and do it to you right-chere."

In the upstairs bedroom, he found the other three looking like plucked chickens, standing around in only their boots and filthy union suits. He took off his own overalls, opened the door a crack and handed them out.

"Ain't none of *y'all* wearin' underwear?" shouted Willie Pearl from the hall.

"Aunt Willie Pearl, suh," said Wheeler-Bastrop, "we can't take ev'rything off. We'd be *nekkid.*"

"You hand me out ev'y blessed thing you wearin'," said the implacable woman. "Or I don't warsh dese clo'es, I *burn* 'em, and den where'll you be?"

Hastily, they complied. Somewhat less severely, Willie Pearl suggested, "Now, if y'all lay crossways on dat bed, y'oughta be able to sleep some. I got a kettle full of Packer's Tar Soap *and* ammonia *and* lye already a-b'ilin', and de sun is shinin' bright. Dese clo'es be clean and dry, time y'all wake up. Den you look somep'n better'n hoboes."

They were awakened, just as night was falling, by Willie Pearl's knocking on the door. She called through the panel to say that their garments were warshed, renched, dreened, dried, ironed and piled in the hall—along with a tub of soapy hot water, in which she strongly recommended that they bathe before putting the clean clothes on again. All the females, she added, would stay downstairs in the meantime to assure their privacy. Again the four desperadoes meekly complied. Wheeler-Bastrop took the first bath, dressed, went outside to the horses and brought back his and Foyt-Haskell's razors. By the time the others had bathed, the water was notably scummy and cooled-off, but they all managed to shave with it, and they were quite a different-looking bunch indeed when they trooped downstairs again—to meet the just-come-home master of the house.

"My husband," said Wilmajean, as regally as a queen introducing the king. "These-here gentlemen are Mister John Bastrop, Mister Joe Birtwistle, Mister Jake Henkelkrug and Mister Jim Haskell."

To them, the elderly Fritz Altdorfer looked nothing like a king; he looked like any other squarehead Polack they'd ever met. But, of course, they had not known him before. They could not realize how much straighter he stood, how much less was the look of stifled pain and how fewer the lines in his face. It was his gnarled, once useless right hand that he extended to them, easily and without a grimace. The reason for all this improvement was plain at least to anyone who had known him for long, like Willie Pearl. For the past two weeks or so, Fritz Altdorfer had had the best medicine there is; he had been loved, and in love, and happy.

The four men stepped forward one at a time, to shake his hand and repeat their names so he could sort them out.

"Jim Haskell, sir. Mighty pleased to make your acquaintance."

"Joe Birtwistle, Mister Altdorfer. A downright pleasure."

"Jake Henkelkrug, me. *Enchanté.*" Altdorfer cocked an eyebrow.

"John Wheeler, suh." Foyt-Haskell winced at that and, unseen, shook a fist at him.

Fritz Altdorfer said a warm *Willkommen* to them all. Apparently he was not dismayed by this invasion of ill-assorted strangers; if his Wilmajean had invited them in, that was commendation enough for him. Nor did he seem to have noticed Wheeler-Bastrop's slip of the tongue. He did, however, remark mildly on the coincidence of their all having Christian names that began with J, and turned to ask Foyt-Haskell if he were any kin to Hop Haskell, the T. & B.V.'s station agent at Teague.

"Could well be," Foyt-Haskell drawled with exaggerated uninterest. "Don't know the feller, but there's Haskells all over East Texas."

"The next time I am in Teague," said Altdorfer, "I will mention having met you. Hop might know of some relationship between you." And Foyt-Haskell silently cursed himself for having picked local names.

They all sat down to supper—Willie Pearl's heavenly chicken-fried steaks were the *pièce de résistance*—and bowed their heads while Altdorfer said a rather lengthy grace in German. Everybody sat stolidly through it, except Boudreaux-Henkelkrug, who felt obliged to pretend to understand, and hoped he was nodding and looking pious at the proper places.

Maybe he wasn't. In the middle of the meal, Altdorfer turned directly to him and asked him if, as a fellow German, he felt much irritation or resentment at always being called a Polack by the Anglo Texans. But he asked this in French.

Boudreaux-Henkelkrug shrugged and replied indifferently, "*Je m'en balance. C'est leur pays—bande de voleurs.*"

Altdorfer, switching back to English, complimented his fellow

German on having a command of French as well. Boudreaux-
Henkelkrug had sufficient presence of mind and grasp of geography
to explain that his parents had come originally from Alsace-Lor-
raine, and so had brought him up polylingual.

Foyt-Haskell, sweating slightly in the realization that they were
dealing with no typical Texas yokel, jumped in for fear that Altdorfer would start quizzing the Cajun in German next. He told his
confected story of their specimen-cow drive to Texas Christian. But
that appeared to be a mistake, too. Their host gave him a sharp look
and commented:

"From Shreveport, you say? You are taking a roundabout way
to deliver your cows, are you not? Thorp Spring is directly, precisely west of Shreveport. Here you are sixty miles south of the
straightest way."

Karnes-Birtwistle put his two cents in. He repeated that these
cows were specially selected for their peculiar afflictions. "So we've
got this list of ranches to call at," he explained, "to pick up particular animals. All over this end of Texas. That's why we've doglegged
way down here. Now we'll be heading northwest. I agree with you,
Mister Altdorfer, it's an unusual kind of a drive."

Altdorfer seemed to accept that and to dismiss his suspicions; at
any rate, he changed the subject. "And what are your plans, gentlemen, after you deliver your herd to that college ranch?"

"Well, a cowboy don't plan ahead much," said Foyt-Haskell.
"We'll prob'ly just ride the chuck line till we find some spread that's
looking for hands."

"*I* am looking for hands," said their host. "There are none to be
hired in these parts. Even the most worthless drifters that come
through here can find work on the railroad at more money than I
can offer."

"I wouldn't never work on no railroad," said Foyt-Haskell. "Not
for any amount of money." He looked around the table, and his
three partners all shook their heads in agreement.

"I can pay what a stockman would consider top wages," said Altdorfer, "but I cannot match what the T. & B.V. will pay him just for
snipe work. If you gentlemen are really determined on remaining

cowboys, why not come back this way after you are through at Thorp Spring?"

"Well . . " said Foyt-Haskell, wondering how to say no politely.

"Or better yet," said Altdorfer. "It should not take four grown men to haze those few cows the rest of the way. Why do not two of you stay? I can put you to work and on wages first thing in the morning. This is the eighth. I will pay a full month's sixty dollars apiece, and you will only be working three weeks for it. Then the other two of you—if you care to—can come back here after Thorp Spring. I can use all four of you." His eyes glowed and he turned to smile at Wilmajean. "*Himmel,* we could put this spread back in the cattle business, instead of this *tollkühn* truck-farming." He swung back to Foyt-Haskell. "But in the meantime, to tell the truth, just with what work there is now, I am desperate for two hands."

"Yes, why *don't* y'all do that?" implored Wilmajean. "We've got a plenty to keep you on, if you keer to stay."

"It's like this, ma'am," Foyt-Haskell said, gently but firmly. "We've come this far together, we'd like to finish this job together. And then, once we're at Thorp Spring, well, we'll be a far piece from here . . ."

Altdorfer said nothing to that, but looked around the table at them, from one face to another, his own set solemn, thoughtful and somehow sorrowful. He pushed his chair back—they had all finished their pecan pie—and said, "We have a little custom in our house, gentlemen. After supper we always read aloud a chapter or two from the Bible. You are welcome to listen, or go outside for a smoke or a chew, or what you please."

They all four said they'd be pleased to listen, so the whole company, Willie Pearl included, trooped into the front parlor. Fritz Altdorfer took down from the mantel a big, heavy, gilt-edged Doré Bible bound in scuffed old leather, and sat down on a horsehair loveseat. Wilmajean snuggled close against his side and Feather knelt at his feet. Willie Pearl and the four guests settled on straight-back chairs against the walls.

"My usual practice is just to let the Good Book fall open by itself, and read whatever God has chosen for me to read," said Alt-dorfer. "But tonight—perhaps one of you gentlemen—do you have a favorite book, or chapter, or verse?"

Karnes-Birtwistle cleared his throat and said in a shy rumble, "Not long back I heard a fellow quote something from the Bible. I don't know what part, but it's stuck in my mind ever since."

"Tell me what you can remember of it," said the host. "If I cannot identify it, I can look it up in the Concordance."

Karnes-Birtwistle remembered it, all right. He repeated Professor Swain's post-tornado parting salute, word for word.

"Ach, ja," murmured Altdorfer. "That is in the Book of Nahum, but I believe . . ." He thumbed the worn pages with easy familiarity. "Yes, your fellow paraphrased slightly. The Book of Nahum is only two pages long. Shall I read it all?" He glanced around and everyone nodded, silent, awaiting the vision of Nahum the Elko-shite.

"God is jealous, and the Lord revengeth;" read Altdorfer, "the Lord revengeth, and is furious; the Lord will take vengeance on his adversaries, and he reserveth wrath for his enemies." He flicked a look up at Karnes-Birtwistle, as if wondering why the big man had chosen to hear this thundering diatribe. "The Lord is slow to anger, and great in power, and will not at all acquit the wicked: the Lord hath his way in the whirlwind and in the storm, and the clouds are the dust of his feet."

There is no knowing what Wilmajean, Feather or Willie Pearl—or, for that matter, Fritz Altdorfer—got out of that night's Bible session, in the way of spiritual comfort or uplift or instigation to live right and be good. But the prophet Nahum's vehement, accusatory, fin-ger-pointing poetics seemed to make the four guests cringe against the walls.

"The horseman lifteth up both the bright sword and the glittering spear: and there is a multitude of slain, and a great number of car-cases; and there is none end of their corpses; they stumble upon their corpses . . ."

When he came to the very last verse—he must have known it

by heart—Altdorfer was not reading from the Good Book, or even looking at it. His face was again turning from one to the other of the four men, sad and somber and almost pitying.

"There is no healing of thy bruise; thy wound is grievous: all that hear the bruit of thee shall clap the hands over thee: for upon whom hath not thy wickedness passed continually?"

3

"Yessir, that was a real wall-banger," Foyt snarled at Karnes. "Why didn't you just ask him to read the funeral service from the Book of Common Prayer? It would of been a sight cheerfuller."

"Oui," grunted Boudreaux, "I wouldn't feel like risking a picayune at *bourrée,* me, not after a send-off like dat. I don't want to spend eternity in Hell de rest of my life. And here in twelve more hours we be risking our immoral souls."

"Immortal," Foyt said absently.

They had roused the cows, some from sleep, some from grazing, and were now mounted and getting the reluctant herd started down from the stock tank toward the front fence gate.

"I'm sorry, pards," said Karnes. "I didn't know it was going to be all doom-crying." After a moment he suggested helpfully, "If you say it over, with Thought instead of Lord and God, it doesn't sound so ominous."

Feather was holding the gate open, and even said a mannerly "Goodbye, misters," as they rode through and headed the herd up the wagon track. Karnes scroonched around on his saddle-pad and raised one of his long arms to wave back at the house. The Altdorfers had stayed up well beyond their usual bedtime to see the men off at midnight. He and she stood side by side on the front porch, silhouetted against the windows' lamplight. They were holding hands; they waved farewell with the hands that weren't intertwined.

"Meks you feel good, meeting people like dem," said the Cajun.

"Yes, *suh,"* said Wheeler. "Nicer folks I never run across."

"Closer'n the Siamese Twins, them two," said Foyt. "Stand 'em in the sun and they wouldn't throw but one shadder. It *was* nice knowing 'em—'cept it makes a man feel so lowdown bad and sad. To see what he's been missing out on, hisself, and prob'ly always will."

"Yep," said Karnes, with a sigh. "You know, boys, I almost wish we *were* taking these cows to Texas Christian and coming right back here."

Foyt had been riding slumped over and old-looking. Now he sat upright and said, "Hell, are we gonna *mope* all night? Let's think about *tomorrer* night. By then, we'll be well fixed to live happy ever after ourselves. Moon, why don't you and Gideon strike up a tune?"

4

"I do wish we could of talked 'em into stayin'," said Wilmajean. "They sho are nice men. And devoted hard workers, too, you kin tell. You'd think that silly job they're on is the most important thing in the world to ev'ry one of 'em."

"Yes," said her husband, somewhat grimly.

"I bet we never see 'em ag'in. We'll prob'ly never even hear of 'em ag'in."

"I don't know about that," murmured Fritz Altdorfer. But the last he ever did see of them was the one man turning on his horse to wave. The Altdorfers returned the salute. Then Feather was shutting the gate, the four men and their cows were gone, and there drifted back through the night the tenor and bass voices of Jake Henkelkrug and Joe Birtwistle harmonizing—briskly, beautifully and a little forlornly—

> "The fox went out on a chilly night,
> Prayed for the moon to give him light,
> For he'd many a mile to go that night . . ."

14

1

HEY WERE THERE at high noon, all right, but it had been push-shove-hustle all the way. The cows were staggering and their tongues lolling out. The horses were stumbling, their necks drooping. The men were equally fagged-out, their eyelids gritty despite the nap they'd enjoyed at the Altdorfers' the afternoon before. They turned the animals loose to scatter up and down the right-of-way, where they could drink from a water-filled ditch and, if they still had the energy, graze on the grass and shrubs roundabout. "We got plenty of time afore we have to bunch 'em up," said Foyt.

They had stopped just short of a bend in the track. The other way —northwest, toward Mexia, where Number Three would be coming from—the track was as straight as Foyt had promised, and there were no houses or any other sign of human habitation. Here at the bend was a copse of flame-leaf sumac trees, under which the men immediately sprawled to rest. But all around was open prairie, and they had an unobstructed view of at least two miles of the track: a single pair of rails, the ties laid on a low bed of crushed rock, stretching northwest to where it bent again and disappeared around another patch of forest. Strung on poles alongside the roadbed, a single strand of telegraph wire likewise disappeared in both directions. With the sun directly overhead, the rails glittered so brightly they were hard to look at, and there couldn't possibly be anything coming along them for quite some time, but each of the men squinted up the gleaming track every minute or so.

After a while, Foyt sat up and cautioned the others, "Don't stay spraddled out too long or you'll stiffen up." He tugged his Ingersoll from a pocket, looked at it and said, "Quarter past noon. We got at least fifteen more minutes afore we can even hope to hear her blow for any crossing up the line. But we might as well git some things arranged."

He untied the latigo thongs that held his carbine boot to Lightning's saddle flap and retied the Winchester onto Wheeler's horse. He plucked his Billy-the-Kid from his overalls' front and spun its cylinder to check that it was fully loaded. Karnes did the same with his Peacemaker.

"You still got your peashooter?" Foyt asked Boudreaux, who patted his bib and nodded. "Just remember now, all of you, nobody pulls iron—nobody reaches for his gun, nobody even *looks* at it— till you see me pull mine."

"Yes, suh," said Wheeler, and the other two looked as solemn, severe and *semper fidelis* as a U.S. Marines recruiting poster.

Twelve-thirty came and went. Karnes, Boudreaux and Wheeler no longer kept glancing up the track; now they had their gaze fixed on it, squinting against the brightness and almost going cross-eyed when they looked all the way to the two rails' merging point in the far distance. Foyt, although he consulted his watch every couple of minutes, maintained an imperturbable calm. He even got his bedroll off his saddle, undid it and set about tidying it up. He removed burs and dead leaves, laid his tarpaulin to air, began sorting through the few other belongings he carried in it.

"Something just occurred to me, L. R.," said Karnes, without shifting his gaze from the railroad. "Is it likely that any of this train's crew will recognize you?"

"No," said Foyt with assurance. "Time was, they would of. But I was just a sprat in them days. Ev'rybody I knew on the T. & B.V.

back when I lived hereabouts has died by now, or retired, or got promoted to the station or the yards or the home office in Houston. I won't have to tie no bandanna around my face. Neither will none of you-all."

"Just as long as you're sure."

"I'm sure. Oh, I used to know 'em all—ev'ry man on the line. Buddied with 'em, drunk with 'em, wenched with 'em. A rowdy lot, them railroad fellers—almost as boisterous as some of the cowpokes I've caroused with since."

To liven the long, slow and increasingly nervous-making wait for the train, Foyt spun some yarns about the railroad men he had known. Among them:

"I'll never forgit old Lampasas Rawls, one of the hogheads. That man had the biggest pecker I've ever seen that wasn't on a hoss. And I've traveled some. He was proud of it, natur'ly—had a right to be. Claimed it was the hugest this side of the Mississippi, and I wouldn't be a bit surprised. His house was just a mile or two yonder towards Teague, right alongside the tracks, and ev'ry time Lampasas drove past it, he'd toot the whistle and his wife'd lean out the winder and wave. Nine toots he'd give, ev'ry time. Nine toots. One for each inch, he always said. Oh, he bragged considerable, you bet. All about how much more satisfied and gratified his wife was than anybody else's, and how sweet and pleasant to him, and never naggy like ev'rybody else's. At least, he *used* to brag, till old Lemoine Waskom shut him up for good one night."

"How was that?"

"Well, old Lampasas was at his locker that night, after a run, changing from his overhalls into his going-home clothes. And, as usual, he was waving that whang around for the boys' admiration, and quoting his usual statistics about length and girth and endurance and so on. Then old Lemoine—he was a conductor—he piped up and said *he* wouldn't want to be hung like that. Wellsir, Lampasas Rawls stopped in mid-brag with his mouth open, and somebody else said, 'Good God, man, why wouldn't you?'" Foyt stopped to chuckle at the memory. "Lemoine shook his head and said, 'I'd just hate to think my woman had a hole in her that big.' Well, *laugh* . . . ?"

Foyt brought out his watch again: one o'clock straight up.

"*Laugh?* I thought ev'rybody in that room would bust. And from then on, they'd all giggle and snort and elbow each other ev'ry time they'd pass Miz Rawls on the street. And old Lampasas evermore changed his clothes real modest, behind his locker door. Some said it was because his old lady give him hell on account of all the snickering at her. Others said Lampasas had to hide his dick now, because it had shrunk to a nub just from sheer humiliation. All I know is, from that time on, whenever he drove an engine past his house, he never give but two quick little too-toots. Let's git them cows up on the track now."

That took some doing. The cows were happy where they were, grazing or lying down in the prairie grass. They had to be kicked and cussed and larruped up the low embankment to stand in a bunch on the crushed rock along the rails and the ties between. But they were so long-suffering that, once there, the cows stayed where they were put. Several of them resignedly lay down on the uncomfortable surface.

"By damn, that heap of meat oughta stop anything that rolls," said Foyt with satisfaction. He peeked at his watch again: 1:32. "But where the hell *is* old Number Three?" He was beginning to look anxious; the other three looked even more so.

Karnes jerked a thumb at Foyt's watch and inquired acidly, "Is that old turnip working as well as everything else has on this venture so far?"

Foyt ignored him and, as they all sprawled again under the trees, went back to sorting his bedroll contents. He scattered some odds and ends on his blanket—a corncob pipe, some loose cartridges of various calibers, a spool of black thread, a few needles and safety pins—and now picked from among them something bright and shining. Karnes asked him what it was.

"You didn't know I was a cowboy hee-ró?" said Foyt offhandedly but with evident pride. He handed the thing to Karnes. It was a scrap of royal-purple ribbon, with "First Prize" printed on it in gilt. From the ribbon dangled a large gold-plated tin medal of sunburst design, most of the gold long ago worn off by fond handling. Karnes turned it over and read aloud the engraved legend:

" 'Grand Riding and Racing Contest Celebrating the Close of the Judith Basin and Shonkin Roundup. Fort Benton, Montana. Eighteen eighty-four.' Well, I'm Thought-damned, L. R. Congratulations."

"Yessir, biggest rody-o I ever took part in. And come out with top prize. Fifty dollars. I wore that medal all the way from Fort Benton back to the GeeKay spread where I was working"—to demonstrate, he pinned the thing onto the left upper breast of his overall bib—"and lemme tell you, it got me *more free drinks* in ev'ry saloon I stopped at, the whole time I was in Mont—" He stopped abruptly; he had just noticed a number of the cows look down curiously at the rails at their feet; the rails had begun faintly to hum. Then Wheeler shouted:

"Old Number Three! Yonder she comes, suh!"

2

All but Foyt scrambled immediately to their feet, though the train wasn't even visible yet—just its plume of gray-black smoke puffing up above the treetops at the bend two miles up the track. Foyt looked one last time at his watch—1:41—and remarked that there *really* must have been some ceremonies and theatrics along the way. Then the engine rounded that far bend and came into view. Foyt lazily got up and began to re-roll his pack. The others ran for their horses.

"Don't bust a blood vessel," said Foyt, tying his bedroll behind Lightning's saddle. "That train'll be another five-six minutes gitting here to where we—" He broke off and frowned. The engine had negotiated the curve and was coming toward them down the straight stretch, while the rest of the train trailed around the bend after it— and something about that train, distant and toy-sized though it was, seemed subtly wrong. Foyt counted in his mind: engine, tender, express car, mail car, four coaches—in all, eight pieces of rolling stock. Maybe, he thought, seeing it so far off had fooled him—he couldn't count the cars at that distance—but somehow that train looked too *long*. Mildly puzzled, he climbed aboard his Lightning and directed the others to their positions.

"Gideon, us three'll stay on this side of the track. You cross over to cover that side of the train. But stay well out ahead of the engine, and so will we, so we can all keep each other in view. I'll do all the talking. And—one more time—don't nobody make any move till I do."

He still sensed something was wrong. Surely the hoghead had seen their cattle blocking the track by now. Any normal engineer—which is to say a man constitutionally cantankerous, self-important, overbearing, ill-tempered and probably half drunk—would have been swinging his whole weight on his whistle cord by this time, and raising a banshee wail that would have had every wild creature on the prairie streaking for the far horizon.

Foyt backed Lightning several yards away from the roadbed so he could watch the train approaching from a less acute angle—and sure enough, the train was longer than it ought to be. Between the coal-and-water tender and the passenger coaches, there should have been two cars with side-mounted sliding doors—the express car and the mail car—but there were three. Furthermore, the locomotive was chuffing and grunting on this easy straightaway as if it were straining up a steep mountain grade. Could it, Foyt wondered, have picked up somewhere an extra car full of ingots or heavy machinery or something? Now the engineer opened the drive cock, steam spewed from the drive cylinders on both sides of the engine's front end and, unpowered, the train was coasting, losing way, idling up to them.

Foyt could see the hoghead in his long-billed cap leaning out the cab window shaking his fist and working his mouth. And now Foyt could also see, emblazoned on the side of that puzzling extra car, the number 1120.

"Lord a'mighty!" he breathed to himself. "Eleven-twenty—the special REA car. *The money car!* They didn't drop it off at Hubbard. Great God, are we gonna have to rob that whole million dollars?!"

He clucked Lightning up alongside the roadbed again, as the engineer eased his air brakes on and brought the locomotive hissing to a stop at the cattle blockade, its cowcatcher nearly touching the nearest cow. The whole herd had turned to look at the train, but without any great interest, and none of them had moved out of its way. Wheeler, Boudreaux and Karnes gazed up at the engine, too, in some awe. A Baldwin 4–6–0 looked a sight bigger and blacker and more fearsomely fire-breathing when it was right on top of you than when it was just passing by. After one final hiss of steam and compressed air, the engine fell silent enough for the hoghead to be heard bawling at Foyt:

"Officer, why'n *hell* ain't you clearin' them bums and thar cows off'n this right-o'-way? Great *Jesus,* Officer—!"

Foyt suddenly realized that he was still wearing his rodeo prize pin, and the engineer had mistaken it for a lawman's badge.

"Oh—uh—I was just doing that, but—"

"Man alive, this is an *eemergincy!* We bin robbed!" bellowed the hoghead, his face maroon under its smears of soot and grease. "I gotta git to Teague and report!"

"Robbed?"

The engineer grabbed the handhold and swung down from the cab to the ground. So did the fireman on the other side of the engine, where he began chattering excitedly to Karnes over there. All down the length of the passenger coaches, smoke-smudged faces were leaning out the windows, peering up forward as if to see what-now? The conductor and a brakeman came trotting along the embankment from somewhere at the back of the train.

"Robbed! Held up! Bushwhacked!" shouted the engineer. "Now these goddam cows have made me lose all way. It'll take me two miles to git up any speed ag'in! I gotta git to Teague to report!"

"Robbed?" repeated Foyt.

Though the hoghead now stood beside Foyt's horse, he was still shouting. "You git a-movin' and spread the word! I reckon it's just as well I run into another lawman. All the telegraph wires are down. You kin he'p spread the alarm!" He hadn't yet noticed that Foyt's badge proclaimed him no more than a First Prize.

"Robbed?" Foyt said again stupidly. "At Hubbard City? Somebody robbed the money?"

"We never got the money *to* Hubbard City!" shouted the hoghead, spraying spit when he talked. He also exhaled whiskey fumes. "They caught us eight miles short of thar. Near Malone. Four of the bastards, and real experts, lemme tell you."

"Four of the bastards," repeated Foyt, sounding as witless as Wheeler. "Who was they?"

"Who *was* they?" frothed the engineer, practically dancing. "Well, thar was Pres'dent Roo-sevelt and Gov'nor Lanham and the Grand Poobah of Jibib . . . ! Goddammit, Officer, you think they wore *signboards?* They all had kercheefs over thar faces! It was just like the Old West all over ag'in."

"Robbed you," Foyt said once more, still stunned. "They took ev'rything?"

"No!" snarled the engineer. "They did leave me my overhalls!" He thumbed the bib of his greasy gray pinstripes. "Will you lemme tell you, for Chrissake? They shot two of the special guards and disarmed the other two. We dropped them poor fellers off in Hubbard. One of 'em may be dead by now. And I tell you them bandits was experts. Lookayonder!"

He pointed. Atop the engine's boiler, near the cab, one of several copper tubes was twisted loose, and from its torn end came a wisp of steam. On the other side of the track, the fireman was pointing at it, too, and Karnes was soberly shaking his head.

" 'Magine train robbers carryin' a monkey wrench?" said the hoghead. "They wrenched loose that line to the whistle, so's I couldn't blow no alarm, and they cut the cord to the bell. With that whistle line busted, the steam just went a-whooshin' out of it and I lost all pressure. Had to do some fancy valvin' and patchin', I tell you, just to git under way ag'in, and we been limpin' along ever since."

The conductor pitched in, panting from his run along the embankment. "Took us 'most an hour to git the eight miles to Hubbard City, and them poor guards a-bleedin' all over the floorboards the whole way. Ev'rybody at Hubbard was already havin' the fantods. Old Belcher, the dispatcher thar, he didn't know *whar* we was. He'd got an OS on us the minute we left Cleburne with that special express car, but not a click of his key after that. Them robbers had ev'rythin' timed just pree-cise. Soon as we was clear of Cleburne they had somebody cuttin' the telegraph wires all up and down the line."

"So even when we reached Hubbard," resumed the hoghead, "thar warn't no way to report this shockin' tragedy to nobody— 'cept by word of mouth. The Hill County Sher'ff was in Hubbard to meet the train, and he sent riders off at a stretch-out gallop to fetch the Texas Rangers from Waco. Natur'ly we didn't take time to uncouple that special car. What the hell, it's empty now. We come right on. And we've done stopped at Mexia since, and thar's a posse a-formin' up thar, too. But them bandits is long gone. They knowed what they was doin'."

"Me, *I* wouldn't want to join no posse chasin' after 'em," put in the brakeman. "One of them guards they shot, they shot him right in the face. If he lives at all, he's gonna walk around the rest of his life without no head above the collar. Them was *mean* sonsabitches."

"That's right," said the conductor. "They didn't have to do no shootin'. When they throwed down on us, not even them special guards went for their hardware. Ev'ry man on this train was a-reachin' for the clouds. Not a one of us wanted to trade hisself for that carful of money. Hell, it's insured; we ain't. But them bastards shot them two fellers just to show us they meant bizness."

"And they got ev'rything?" Foyt asked dully.

"Ev'rything they wanted," said the brakeman. "Which was money. The Hubbard bank's money and the railroad payroll. They didn't yank wallets and watches off the passengers, if that's what you mean. And they didn't even open the U.S. Mail car. They knowed that's a fed'ral offense. Them was experts, all right."

"De payroll, too, eh?" said Boudreaux, his shoulders sagging.

Foyt spun around at him and barked in a voice of authority, "You and them other two waddies git these goddam cows off the track! You heard—this is an emergency!"

The Cajun looked startled and stung, but he, Karnes and Wheeler hastened to comply. The fireman, deprived of his audience, crossed the track to join the circle around Foyt's horse. The whole crew, now that they had had to stop anyway, seemed disposed to take a morbid pleasure in dwelling on their experience.

"Fust time such a thing has ever happened on the T. & B.V.," said the conductor, but added almost pridefully, "Puts the old Boll Weevil up thar in a class with the Santa Fe and the Union Pacific and such, what's allus bin held up by the Jameses and the Hole-in-the-Wall Gang and all."

"Prob'ly be the *last* time it happens, too," said the brakeman. "After this-here calamity, nobody'll even let us freight thar hawgs no more, let alone thar money. They'll send that by old ladies—in thar carpetbags—with knittin' needles to hold off any bandits."

That scornful remark was obviously addressed to the Railway Express guard reguarly assigned to this run, who had just climbed down from his car and joined the group, a sawed-off shotgun in the crook of his elbow.

"Don't go blamin' this mess on me," he said, breathing whiskey like the rest of them. "If four of the agency's hand-picked special troubleshooters, all a-bristlin' with weapons, couldn't stop them robbers, what was I s'posed to do?" He looked up at Foyt and his badge. "Deppity, you know what that bunch took? I seen the papers on the consignment. More'n twelve hunderd thousand dollars for the Hubbard City bank and more'n forty-seven thousand for the railroad payroll. That's nigh onto *one and one-quarter million dollars!* It's *got* to be the biggest train robbery thar ever was!"

Foyt looked impressed and appalled and dismayed. He didn't have to exert himself to do it.

"And *ain't* we gonna ketch Billy Blue Hill from ev'ry snipe and gandydancer on this line?" muttered the fireman. "Not to mention ev'rybody we know in Teague, when we show up to report we've misplaced all thar wages."

"Screw them," said the brakeman. "Tomorrer's *our* payday, same as thars. I'll ketch enough hell from my old lady."

"Well, report it we gotta do," sighed the engineer. "Teague won't of got no OS on us neither, not since that 'departed seven-oh-five' from Cleburne this mornin'. Them cows is off the track. Let's try to git some steam up and move along."

"Yep," said the conductor, also sighing. "Old Spats Foyt must be havin' a shit-fit. He was gonna hold all northbound traffic at Teague to give us a clear track all the way from Cleburne down. I bet he's got trains a-settin' caboose-to-cowcatcher halfway back to Houston by now."

"And Old Man Wiggins is waitin' in Teague, too," said the hoghead dolefully. He explained to Foyt, "That's the Pres'dent, Gen'ral Manager and Super'ntendent of the Trinity & Brazos Valley line." Foyt murmured that everybody knew that. "Old Man Wiggins was a-comin' up from the Houston office to Teague today, just to congratulate us on this special run. Fust time the T. & B.V.'s ever bin trusted with such a big job. Now we gotta tell him how it fell through. Oh, well . . ." He consulted his big railroad watch. "Mebbe he won't take it too hard. It's well past two o'clock now, and the Old Man's always fuddleheaded drunk by noon." Foyt murmured that everybody knew that, too. The engineer said, as he grabbed the handhold and swung up into the cab, "Be obliged, Marshal, if you'd spread the word hereabouts and start a-roundin' up a posse of your own."

"I'll git right on that," said Foyt dispiritedly.

The crew climbed back onto the train. The fireman began vigorously shoveling coal into the engine's firebox, while the hoghead twiddled valves and yanked levers. The stack's trickle of gray smoke became a belch of black. Steam billowed from the drive cylinders. The big locomotive went *chuff!* and jerked a few inches, chuff-*choof!* and moved a foot or two, then the chuffing became continuous, the drive rods pumped slowly but steadily back and forth, the drive wheels rolled ponderously, and old Number Three continued to move, though at a snail's pace.

It was several minutes before the last coach rumbled slowly past the four men and their twenty-eight cows, and around the bend, to disappear beyond the sumac trees where they had rested. All four simply sat still and silent on their horses—even when a couple of smoke-stained passengers halfheartedly waved at them from the rear coach's platform—and watched Number Three go out of their lives.

3

"Well," said Foyt at last, unpinning his prize medal. "This has sure cut our cinches."

"Yep," said Karnes. "We bet our all on a bob-tailed nag."

One after another, they dismounted and turned their horses loose to join the cows, which were again grazing or lazing in the grass. The men sat down under the same sumac tree as before, and for a long time no one said anything.

The silence was finally broken by Wheeler, usually the silent one. "There's sure to be a ree-ward, suh."

"Sure will," said Foyt sourly. "We'll draw straws to see which one of us turns the other three in for it."

Silence fell again, a long and dreary one.

"It's way past time for noon chuck," said Karnes.

More silence.

"I ain't hungry, me," said the Cajun, though he was gnawing the fringe of his mustache.

More silence.

Karnes said he really didn't know why he'd mentioned it; he wasn't hungry either. He reached for his cut plug, bit off a mighty hunk and chewed moodily.

More silence.

"Hell," said Foyt. "There ain't nothing left to eat but them raisins and dried apples, nohow. I figgered that grub and doled it out just to last us to here." He took out his Bull Durham and began rolling a cigarette. "By now I expected to be buying out the whole stock of some grocery store to have us a feast when we camped down in the Trinity bottoms. Canned peaches, whiskey, store-bought bread, *cheese*. Lordy, how I had my mouth fixed for some cheese."

More silence, except for some muffled sniffling.

Karnes suddenly stood up, to his full and formidable height.

"All right, pards, we can go over yonder and lay our heads on that railroad track and wait for another train to come along and put us out of our misery. Or we can do something positive. Now, L. R., you've been the leader of this expedition all the way. And you've been a good one. Topnotch. First-rate."

"I ain't never aspired to be perfect," Foyt said sullenly. "I'd settle for splendid."

"Well, it's not your fault the whole thing turned out to be a Thought-damned frost. You're still the leader, as far as I'm concerned. So what do we do now? Split up, like you said? Each of us head for a different point of the compass?"

"After divvying up all our worldly goods?" Foyt asked sarcastically. "Okay, there's seven sick cows apiece. Take your pick. But I ain't got the education to figger out how to split sixty-seven cents four ways."

Boudreaux suggested timidly, "Dere's dat job dem nice Polacks offered us."

"And there's always Argentina," said Foyt. He also got to his feet, though not very spryly. "I got to do some tall thinking, fellers. But first we need some grub and some walking-around money. Let's ride on into Teague and I'll see can I put the bite on old Norwood for a small loan."

"What about dem sick cows?" asked the Cajun. "I be glad to see de last of dem."

Foyt started to say hell yes, leave them to rot. But he saw the look of real anguish on Wheeler's face, and reconsidered.

"No, bring 'em along—for a while at least. If we don't wind up eating 'em, maybe we can sell 'em to some tannery in town for their hides—what hides they got left, in between all them brands. If we can git just three dollars and thirty-three cents for the whole bunch, that'll give us one nice round silver dollar apiece."

He hawked and spat fiercely on the ground. "That only leaves each one of us shortchanged by nine thousand, nine hunderd and ninety-nine dollars."

15

1

THEY FOLLOWED the railroad into town. Of course, crippled though it was, Number Three had got there before them and, now that the track was cleared, they were passed by other trains—one passenger and two long freights—released from their enforced holdover at Teague and highballing like hell toward the north. The trains were followed by a handcar heaped with workmen and coils of telegraph wire. Four of the men were pumping its seesaw handle and pushing it along at a furious clip.

Foyt stopped just outside town, at the peach orchard of an old acquaintance, Abner Broadnax, to ask if they could park their herd in an adjacent meadow for the rest of that day and possibly the next. Broadnax said sure, and welcome; although, after seeing the cows trudge in, he inquired mildly whether Foyt shouldn't be parking that bunch of freaks in the County Museum over at Fairfield instead.

Wheeler, no doubt because he still feared that the others would decide to abandon the herd, volunteered to bed down with the cows and watch over them until time to move on.

The other three rode into Teague at twilight, to find the town all commotion and conniption. Horsemen were galloping in both directions along Main Street, their purposes or destinations impossible to guess. Other men were gathered in knots on the street corners, excitedly talking and gesticulating. The few women in evidence, their faces drawn and frightened, seemed to be hurrying through the dusk to get safe under cover somewhere. There was a crudely hand-lettered cardboard sign in the window of the Emerson-Marlow Produce store: "You're Credit Is Good! Till Next Payday!"

The T. & B.V. depot was absolutely surrounded by tethered horses, buggies, wagons and buckboards. The downstairs waiting room and trackside platform were chockablock with men, these also waving their arms and talking—or shouting above all the other talk going on. The smoke in the waiting room was almost thick enough to support a swimmer, and the platform outside was almost too slippery with tobacco spit to walk on. Oddly, the veranda of the Yoakum Hotel across the street was empty of loungers for a change, except for four cats who sat in a row, watching with placid cat-curiosity all the goings-on over at the depot.

The three men managed to wedge their horses in among the horde of others, then Foyt led Karnes and the Cajun around behind the building and up an outside staircase to the second floor, thence into a room containing two men. One was a clerk wearing pince-nez and pawing through the drawers of a filing cabinet. The other man sat at a vast desk covered with papers, charts, maps and half a dozen telegraph keys, all of which seemed to be chattering simultaneously, and to none of which he seemed to be paying any attention. Tall and bald, he wore a green celluloid eyeshade, but otherwise was dressed so nattily—Norfolk jacket, Ascot tie, spats over his pointy-toed yellow shoes—that he might have been President Old Man Wiggins himself. He glanced up idly as the three entered, went back to his papers, then his head jerked spastically up again and his face turned nearly as green as his eyeshade.

"Lancelot Royal!" he gasped. "Great snakes, what are you doing *here?*"

("Lancelot Royal?" murmured Karnes and Boudreaux, *sotto voce*, behind Foyt's back. "Lancelot . . . ? Royal . . . ?")

Foyt turned and gave them a look that silenced them forever on that subject.

"Relax, Norwood," he said to the man at the desk. "It wasn't us." He gave a significant flick of his head toward the clerk.

"Uh, Hiram," said Norwood. "How about running around to the Greek's? Fetch some java and sinkers for my cousin here and, uh, his friends." The clerk obediently disappeared.

"It *wasn't* you?" said Norwood, his color gradually returning.

Foyt glumly shook his head. "Now you know, Cuz, I wasn't after enough plunder to buy Fort Worth. And you oughta know I wouldn't shoot nobody to git it. No, somebody jumped the gun on us, by about two hours and about forty miles up the line."

"That shoot-'em-up part did worry me. I've got communications now as far as Hubbard City"—he gestured at the still-racketing telegraph keys—"and we got teams out hunting the other cuts in the wire. I just got word from old Belcher at Hubbard that one of them guards is dead and the other soon will be. About the money that was stole, well, a lot of it is in bank certificates and drafts and other kinds of paper them robbers can't spend—but they still got maybe half a million in cash. Oh, this is a *turr*'ble thing, Lancelot!"

"Yes, it is," Foyt said, and then introduced his two partners to his cousin. The cousin took out a pack of Piedmont ready-rolls and offered them around. Each of the men gratefully took one and lighted up.

"I'm sorry," said the cousin, "that you fellers missed your chance. But hell, what you-all had in mind was small potaters—practic'ly innercent highjinks—compared to what's happened. I can't say I'm sorry you-all ain't mixed up in it."

"I thought I'd see Old Man Wiggins running around tearing his hair," said L. R. Foyt. "I heard he was here."

Norwood Foyt snorted. "Him and his varicose brains. When we got the news, the Old Man acted with his usual lightning confusion. You know how he is when he's drunk."

"Nobody knows how he is when he *ain't.*"

"Well, right now he's over at the Yoakum Hotel. They got one of them telephones there now. Oh, this-here town has gone *modern*, Lancelot, since you last seen it. And the Old Man's telephone-calling ev'rybody from Gov'nor Lanham on down to maybe the State Board of Embalming for all I know. He's called the Texas Rangers at Waco *and* at Austin. He's even called in some private deteckatives from Fort Worth. The Bynum-Allnutt Agency. They're on their way down here right now on Number Five. Sher'ff Roper just bustled in from Fairfield. But we had to send a man for him; there ain't no telephone in Fairfield. Backward town, that."

"I take it," said Karnes, "they're all figuring there'll be a reward posted?"

"Oh, there will be, there will be," said Norwood. "And no lack of bounty hunters, no doubt, looking to claim it. I bet Old Man Wiggins'll be putting through a call to the White House next, and I wouldn't bet ag'inst Teddy sending out his Rough Riders. Anyhow, whatever happens, the Old Man is enjoying hisself. Ev'ry drummer rooming at the Yoakum is crowded around watching him yell into that telephone box. So, to show off, he's calling ev'rybody he can think of—like the Lord bellering out of the burning bush." He turned his head. " 'Scuse me, fellers, here comes something from Houston."

He cocked an ear toward one of the telegraph keys, evidently having the knack to filter out its clickety-clacking from the seemingly identical clickety-clacking of all the others. He grinned broadly, and began to write in block letters on a pad of paper. Thinking that it might be news of the capture of the train robbers, the other three men peered over his shoulder. This is what they read:

YOUNG MAN SPENDS NIGHT WITH BEAUTIFUL INTELLIGENT
TALENTED EDUCATED CHARMING WHORE. NEXT MORNING HE
ASKS HER HOW DID A BEAUTIFUL INTELLIGENT TALENTED
EDUCATED CHARMING GIRL LIKE YOU WIND UP IN THE
WHORING BUSINESS. SHE SAYS JUST LUCKY I RECKON.

                                                    F. U.

Karnes asked impertinently, "What in Thought's name is that?"

"Oh," said Norwood, turning slightly pink. "That's just old Flewellen Upshur down at Houston sending along a joke."

"I didn't think it sounded official. People send *jokes* over the railroad's telegraph lines?"

"Hell, man, didn't you ever wonder how jokes get spread around so fast? You can hear a brand-new one in San Antone one night, take a train to Dallas, git there the next day, and the first person you meet'll tell you that same joke. It got there faster'n you did. It's the railroad telegraphers. Ev'ry new joke they hear, they tap it out on the key for ev'rybody on the line. I bet even a New York joke gits to Frisco just as fast."

"But you talking about new jokes," said Boudreaux. "Dat one had whiskers when Adam was a pup."

"Oh, shoot, I know that. But old Flewellen has led kind of a sheltered life. Houston's about as backward a town as Fairfield."

The door opened and Hiram the clerk came in with four mugs, a tin bucket of steaming black coffee and a grease-spotted paper bag of about three dozen doughnuts, still warm. The visitors started wolfing them, their first food since breakfast, while Norwood got rid of the clerk again by ripping the penciled joke off his pad and handing it to him.

"Here, Hiram, show this around amongst the fellers downstairs. It might help cheer 'em up a little."

While they all munched doughnuts and sipped coffee, L. R. Foyt asked Norwood Foyt what else—besides the train robbery and the telephone—was new in Teague since he'd left town.

"Well, lemme see. I reckon you know the firehouse burnt down."

L. R. Foyt said he didn't even know Teague owned a firehouse. Norwood said oh yes, the town had a real efficient fire-fighting system. Or *had* had. The city fathers had erected a frame firehouse at the corner of First and Main, with a siren fixed outside, where any civic-minded person who spotted a fire could crank it and summon the volunteer fire department, which consisted of just about every man in Teague who wasn't too old or spavined to come running when the siren howled. Then they'd bought a brand-spanking-new, brass-bound LaFrance pumping engine—worked by a seesaw handle on the principle of a railroad handcar—and two husky, big-bellied, imported Clydesdale dray horses to pull it.

However, fires being fairly infrequent, but garbage being a day-to-day municipal problem, the city fathers had cannily put those expensive and hearty-eating Clydesdales to double duty. Most of their time was spent hitched to the trash cart driven by the town character (also town drunk, town poet and town garbage collector), Sonky Dudley. But if and when the firehouse siren sounded, Sonky would drop his trash can or his bottle or his Muse, and simply yank the whiffletree pin from his cart's tongue. Wherever in town they were at, the two horses—believe this or not—would automatically gallop straight for the firehouse, harnessed side by side, their reins and traces flapping and the whiffletree bouncing behind. Once they arrived, the firemen had only to attach that whiffletree to the fire engine's tongue, and off they went.

"That surely sounds efficient," said Karnes. "But how did the firehouse come to burn down?"

"Well, the firemen got a call—feller rode in to report a smold'ring brush fire out near Abner Broadnax's orchard; hell, Abner could of peed that out—and when they went tearing off, one of the boys just pitched away his seegar, and it landed in a pile of rags they was always polishing up the brass on that pumper with. So, by the time they got out to Broadnax's, their own firehouse was on fire. Lots of people noticed it, o' course, and jumped for the si-reen to call the boys back. But they just couldn't crank it. The cylinder inside wouldn't turn. What it was, see, it'd been so long since the last fire, a fambly of warblers had moved in and built a purty hefty nest inside the si-reen. Afore the folks could git that nest picked out of there, twig by twig, the firehouse was falling down around 'em in blazing chunks."

L. R. Foyt said, with a trace of sarcasm, that he was glad to hear that his old hometown was still as brimming with drama and thrills and excitement as he had remembered it.

"Well," said Norwood Foyt, a little defensively. "At least them costly hosses and LaFrance pumper wasn't inside when the building burnt down. They're kept in Gooch's Liv'ry Stable for the time being. And now, there not being no si-reen, when anybody spots a fire they run for Sis Veva Magness. She won the women's hog-calling contest last year."

2

Full night had fallen when Foyt, Karnes and Boudreaux left the depot. At cousin Lancelot Royal's request, cousin Norwood had reached into his pocket, with no hesitation, and hauled out a twenty-dollar gold piece. Three dollars of it, he said, would buy all three of them supper, bed and breakfast at the Widow Turnipseed's on Mimosa Lane.

The rest of it, said L. R. Foyt, would see them back to the Altdorfers' spread, if that was where they decided to head, and he'd guarantee that Norwood got the twenty dollars back in jig time. But, whichever way they headed, they'd drop in on Norwood before they did, just to see what news there might be of the robbers.

On all the lampposts and walls along Main Street—and doubtless on trees all over Freestone County—were now slapped up smudgy, still wet posters, turned out gratis by Jennings Press, the town's one print shop. They had been so hurriedly composed (by Mayor Boyd), so hectically typeset (by hand), and so frantically run off (on the shop's single creaky Chandler & Price clamshell job press) that they were one day to become collectors' items of the art of misprinting:

!!! WANTED !!!

DEAD OR ALIVE
FOR TRAIN ROBBERY
AND HOMOCIDE

also assault with deadly weapons, interference with law officers in the performance of their buty, also interruption of pubic commerce and transport, also threats to persons, also abusive and profane language!

¡!! FOUR MEN !!!

male, white, age indeterminated, all dressed like cow-boys, wearing bandanas over lower haff of faces, armed with revolvers, shotguns and rifles. These men are desperate and bangerous! Shooot on sight!

!!! $1,000.00 REWARD !¡

will be paid by the Trinity & Brazos Valley Rail Road for apperhension of these four desperados, fetched in

DEAD OR ALIVE

"Shoo-oot on sight," Karnes read aloud. "Thought a'mighty, there are sure going to be a lot of white male men cowboys of all ages shot dead."

"Only if dey go around in bunches of four," said Boudreaux. "*Ma foi,* I'm glad ol' Eli stayed behind, so we're only t'ree."

"But just take note," said Foyt. "Them four sons of bitches have robbed a million and a quarter dollars, and killed two men in cold blood, and you know they won't stop at killing anybody else that looks at 'em cross-eyed. And here Old Man Skinflint Wiggins is offering a measly one thousand spondulix to the brave heart that outshoots and brings in all four of 'em. Hell, he'd have to offer more'n that to git Sis Veva Magness to hog-call 'em in."

"*Dis donc,*" said the Cajun. "I just t'ink of somep'n. I bet de Turnip Widowseed can't break dat big twenty-dollar coin, but dere's a frien'ly looking saloon right across de street. What say we cash dat gold piece in dere?"

3

They had drunk up rather more of the twenty dollars than they had intended, so Foyt's two companions were still dead to the world and snoring mightily when he slipped out of the Widow Turnipseed's house quite early in the morning, without even waiting for breakfast, and headed uptown. The rest of the people of Teague also seemed to be sleeping off their emotional binge of the day before, and the streets were almost empty.

On Main Street he did see one unusual sight—unusual for Teague, anyway—a bright green Packard automobile, square-built as a shoebox, with high-backed plush seats like sofas front and back, topped by a bright yellow canopy on poles, with a fringe around the canopy like that on a fancy surrey. The thing seemed to stare at him with its big round acetylene headlamps as it approached, and so did the four men it was carrying. They were all identically dressed in derbies, celluloid collars, bow ties and long white linen dusters, except for the driver behind the high steering wheel, who also wore goggles. Every one of the four had a bulldog pipe gripped in his teeth.

Maybe Foyt looked suspicious, out alone so early in the morning. The car chug-chugged past him, stopped some distance beyond, then, with a loud, gritty grinding of gears, chugged backward until it was level with him again. The man on the front sofa beside the driver leaned out, pointed the stem of his pipe and said with crisp authority:

"Good morning, sir. I am Oral T. Allnutt, Field Chief of the Bynum-Allnutt Detective Agency. May I ask who you be?"

"I be L. R. Foyt."

"Ah," said the Field Chief, consulting a piece of paper. "Any relation to Mister Norwood 'Spats' Foyt, Chief Dispatcher of the T. & B.V.?"

"His cousin."

"You live here?"

"Just visiting. Going over to the depot to see Norwood right this minute."

"Ah. Gathering of the clan in time of trouble, eh? Well, you can assure your cousin that we're hard on the job. And making progress. These are my Operatives."

Foyt refrained from remarking that the Operatives might do more operating if they got off their fat behinds and off those plush sofas. He merely bade Field Chief Allnutt good day and went on toward Third Avenue.

He met another inquisitor before he got there. This was an eager-looking young man with a pencil behind his ear, a notebook in his hand and a card marked PRESS stuck in his derby's hatband. Foyt thought for a moment that the fellow had just got his hat back from the blocker and had forgotten to remove the tag, but then the young man spoke:

"Good morning, sir. I am Walter A. Dealey of the Dallas *Morning News*. May I ask who you be?"

Foyt gave him a clenched and humorless grin, said, "I be Theodore Roo-sevelt. How do you like me with my new teeth?" and walked on.

Cousin Norwood "Spats" Foyt said he had been up the whole damned night, and he looked it—his face was about as rumpled as his Norfolk jacket.

"Them hawkshaws got in at midnight on Number Five," he said. "Brought along a dude auto*mo*bile on a flatcar and a whole pack of bloodhounds in the baggage car. Number Five was also full of newspaper reporters from Dallas and Fort Worth. Then Number Two pulled in with another batch of reporters up from Houston. The whole kit and caboodle piled in on me, because I was the most senior employee still awake."

L. R. Foyt said he had just met the detectives, the car and one of the newsmen, but not yet the bloodhounds.

"This-here office was just a-b'iling full," grumbled Norwood. "Oral Allnutt and his bonehead Operatives pawing through all my papers and dispatches. Them newspaper people flashing photographs of 'The Sleuths on the Trail.' I swear, there was more flash powder burnt in here last night than all the gunpowder that's ever been burnt in train robberies since time began. The newspaper men even took pitchers of them damned bloodhounds, when they wasn't pissing in ev'ry corner. The hounds, I mean, not the reporters. And then Blossom come a-raging in to give me hell for not coming home. Oh, it was a reg'lar hoedown. I'd of sicked the whole bunch onto the Old Man, except he had passed out beside the telephone over yonder in the Yoakum Hotel."

The telegraph keys were chittering, and every once in a while Norwood would cock an ear and scribble down some cryptic note like "OS CL No. 3 A 06:30 D 06:37." His cousin asked why the Bynum-Allnutt detectives were poking around here when the robbery had happened up near Malone.

"Why, they're looking for *clews*, Lancelot! They already stopped and got some at the scene of the crime. Found feetprints and made plaster casts of 'em. Bootprints. They scrutinized 'em through their magnifying glasses and dedooced that at least one of the bandits wears a size twelve boot."

"Well, that narrers it down. It wasn't a woman."

"So now they're here to inspect the car that was robbed. Old number eleven-twenty. They spent most of the night dusting the whole inside of it with talcum powder, till now it smells like a baby's crib. Said that was to bring out 'latent fingerprints,' whatever that means and whatever good it'll do anybody. As for them blood-hounds and what they're good for, God knows. Old Gooch says they've et ev'rything in his liv'ry stable short of them two big-bellied Clydesdale draft hosses."

"Speaking of big bellies," said L. R. Foyt, "I ain't seen none of them big-bellied Texas Rangers a-clomping around here."

"Maybe them Rangers ain't so swift when it comes to intellect, but they sure got more sense'n these uppity Operatives. The Rangers ain't out looking for *clews,* they're out looking for the *robbers.*"

"Do they know where to look?"

"They've got a purty good idea. The Rangers figger them robbers'll go to ground till all this hue and cry eases off."

L. R. Foyt nodded. After all, it was what he had planned himself.

"They bushwhacked the train up yonder near Malone. Okay, look at that map on the wall. You can practic'ly figger out for yourself which way they'd head from there to the best hideout place. Straight west into the Brazos River bottoms. That's where the Rangers are beating the bushes right now. I wish 'em luck. You know what them canebrake bottoms are like."

L. R. Foyt nodded again. They were like the Trinity bottoms: a next-to-impenetrable jungle of switch cane and rattan vine. The robbers, whoever they were, might almost have read his own mind and purloined his own scheme.

Thoughtfully, he rubbed the silver bristles on his chin and said, "Norwood, I been puzzling my head over this, most of the night. You know how I got wind of that special shipment. But them other sons of bitches did, too. *How?* You didn't, uh, by any chance, let slip a word to—uh—Blossom?"

"To my *wife?* Christamighty, Lancelot, I wouldn't never say ary word to Blossom about anything I wanted kept quiet."

"Well, I just wondered."

"I don't know why it's any wonderment to you. That consignment

of money was about as secret as a circus parade. I had to send you
a note about it, yes, because you was out cahooting around the prairie. But *anybody* could of eavesdropped on that dispatch."

"Could of, huh?"

"Cousin," Norwood said patiently. "You left town and turned
cowboy afore you could git as crazy about railroading as most kids
do. Maybe you don't realize. Ev'ry kid that lives along a railroad anywhere in the world, if he knows the goddam alphabet, he knows the
Morse Code. When he stands outside a depot winder and hears a
telegraph key dot-dashing, he can read you off the message just as
fast as the telegrapher can."

"Can, huh?"

"I know at least one tad that grew up here when this was still
Brewer's Prairie and—" Norwood broke off, looked deeply medi-
tative and a little troubled. He finally resumed, "And you know him,
too, Lancelot. Now I'm gonna tell you something I ain't told nobody
else."

L. R. Foyt looked interested.

"About a week back, a passenger got off Number Two rightchere,
when I just happened to be down on the platform. He was some
older, and wearing a heavy beard, and dressed purty rough, but
there was something about him that made me look twice. Well, his
only baggage was a valise, and you'd expect him to be carrying it.
But it was a mite heavy, so he'd checked it through in the baggage
car. He had to go to the baggage winder to collect it." Norwood
opened a drawer of his desk and rummaged in it. "After he'd picked
up his bag and gone, I went and got the tag that had been on
that valise. I don't know where the feller went from here—never
seen him since—but I still got that tag."

He handed it to his cousin. The tag was an ordinary rectangle of
buff pasteboard, with a hole for the string, and the usual disclaimer-
of-responsibility and such printed on it. Handwritten in the proper
spaces were the point of departure (Houston) and the destination
(Teague) and the bag owner's name: Thaddeus E. Pickerel. L. R.
Foyt's pale eyes glowed as he looked up from the tag.

"They say," he murmured almost breathlessly, "that when an outlaw changes his name, he almost never changes his initials, because maybe they're stamped inside his hat or on his underwear or something. Anyway, it makes it easier for him to remember his new name. Not that this feller used much imagination in picking a new one. This-here is old T. Eustace Pike, the respectable-banker-turned-desperado, sure as you're born."

"The railroad'd fire me if they knew this, Lancelot, but I sent the baggage agent off on an errand, to give me time to sneak a look inside that feller's valise afore it was handed over to him. Locked, o' course, but a baggage agent has keys to fit most any kind of luggage made. The reason it was so heavy—besides being full of the ord'nary truck like soap and socks—it had two big Colt sixguns, a monkey wrench and two pairs of wire cutters."

"Jehosaphat, Norwood! Eustace Pike just *has* to be the bell-ox of that bunch of robbers. And his brother Jasper must be one of the others. Didn't you *suspicion* nothing about all this?"

"Hell, yes! I suspicioned he was one of *your* gang. I wasn't about to say anything."

"Oh. But now—you still ain't told nobody? You ain't told them deteckatives?"

"No. In the first place, them hawkshaws are too biggity to be *told* anything. They gotta *dedooce* it. In the second place, they're such nincompoops they couldn't track a chimbleysweep through a snowbank. In the third place . . . well . . . I just thought you might like a crack at landing that reward. I only hesitated to tell you all this because, hell, Lancelot, I'd hate to see you risk gitting yourself killed doing it."

"So would I," mumbled L. R. Foyt. "For a crummy thousand dollars."

"It's a thousand dollars more'n you got right now," said Norwood, with a shrug. "But there y'are. It's in your lap. I won't say a word of this to nobody, and there ain't much chance anybody'll find it out on their own. So, unless them Rangers have the world's biggest hunk of luck and stumble on them robbers down in the Brazos bottoms, you've got a good head start. At least you know who you're looking for—them feisty Pike brothers."

4

Karnes and the Cajun were strolling toward the depot as Foyt was hurrying away from it, and they met fortuitously right in front of the A-Double-A Saloon. Foyt at once dragged them inside, plunked them at a table and called for a bottle.

Karnes said, "I appreciate the drinks, L. R. I've got quite a head after last night. But ought we to be guzzling away any more of that twenty dollars?"

"Afore long," said Foyt, "we could pay twenty dollars for a store-bought shave-'n-a-haircut and not miss it—if you boys are int'rested in a new proposition."

He went on to relate everything that Cousin Norwood had just told him. From time to time during the recital, one or the other of his listeners would say they'd be goddamned or they'd be Thought damned. At the conclusion they looked slightly staggered by the magnitude of what Foyt obviously had in mind.

"You obviously have it in mind," said Karnes, "for us to go after the Pike boys and whoever the other two are."

"If you're game. I know Eli'll come along. He's too simple to be scared. That'd be four ag'inst four. It wouldn't be like we was out-numbered."

"The hell it wouldn't," said Karnes, reaching for the bottle. "Two cowboys, one oil field rigger and one swamp logger—up against four *very* experienced, *very* efficient, *very* professional gun wad-dies. We'd have all the chance of a butterfly caught in a sausage machine. We don't even have four decent guns amongst us."

"Now we do," said Foyt. He took one out of his overall bib and handed it under the table, out of sight, to Boudreaux. "I borrered it from Norwood." It was a heavy, long-barreled Colt Peacemaker like the one Karnes was wearing. "Now you can throw away that peashooter," said Foyt. The Cajun looked at the pistol under the table edge, holding it awkwardly and a little gun-shyly, but finally slid it inside his own bib.

"That means you're in, Moon?" Foyt asked him.

"If Gideon's in, I'm in."

"But it could take months, years to hunt them down," objected Karnes. "Just because you know them and can recognize them— how do you know when or where they'll surface?"

"We don't have to wait for 'em to surface," said Foyt. "I know more'n just who they are. Remember, I told you-all I grew up with them Pike boys. I knew 'em when they was mere whelps just beginning to train for the gallows. I knew their favorite fishing holes, their favorite deer stands and duck blinds. I don't just know who they are, I know *where* they are."

Karnes and Boudreaux stared at him.

"The Texas Rangers have gone trailing 'em straight west to the Brazos, because that's the most logical and shortest and most obvious way they'd of gone to hide out. But they didn't. They went directly opposite—east—the longer way that nobody'd expect 'em to take. They went to where *we* would of gone, down Tehuacana Creek to the Trinity River. I know. Them Pike boys and me, we've fished there, we've shot ducks there. Them four bastards are squatting right at the very place in them bottoms that *we'd* be in *this minute* if our scheme had come off. You could blindfold me here at this table, and I could lead you out that door, out of Teague, off across Freestone County and, if you didn't take the blindfold off me, I'd step smack into their campfire."

"I *will* be Thought damned!" said Karnes. He ruminated and frowned for a minute, then shrugged. "Well, in for a penny, in for a pound. After all our trouble and disappointment, we might as well try to salvage something out of this mess."

"That's the spirit! Drink up, and we'll go collect Eli and the cows."

"What?" said Karnes and the Cajun together. Karnes said, "Eli, sure. But *the cows?*"

"Have some sense, Gideon, Moon. If the Pikes and their sidekicks see us coming—four mounted men looking like a piece of a posse—they'll pick us off our hosses afore we even git a glimpse of them. But if all they see is four cowboys chousing a herd of scroungy cows, they *might* just figger we're chuckleheaded and harmless, and let us git close enough that we can shoot first."

Karnes and Boudreaux had to admit they hadn't thought of that. As the three of them stepped out the door onto Main Street, Karnes said, "Then you're taking that 'Wanted' poster seriously, L. R.? About fetching them in dead? Like I said, *I'm* agreeable to salvaging something for all our trials and tribulations. But just last night, *you* were saying what a chintzy reward it is for facing down four desperate killers. And now—"

"Reward?" Foyt stopped stock-still on the sidewalk and gave Karnes a look of utter amazement. "Who gives a flying fart about the *reward?* Gideon, them four men are going to sleep tonight with their heads pillered on saddlebags—or croker sacks, more likely— stuffed full of half a million dollars in cash money. *That's* what we're going after!"

16

ONCE MORE they pushed all through the night. When dawn came, they had backtracked as far as the Altdorfers' spread. Dawn brought little light, though, as the sky was dense with cloud and a heavy, clothes-soaking, spirit-damping drizzle was falling. Karnes's and Boudreaux's cheap straw hats were coming even more unraveled. By now, they appeared to be wearing heaps of sauerkraut on their heads.

In this murk and mizzle, even the Altdorfers' ordinarily cheerful blue-and-white farm buildings appeared gray and sad. As the four men followed their herd along the two-rut wagon track toward the farmstead, Foyt noticed something that made the place look still more depressed, not to say deserted: there was no smoke coming from even the kitchen chimney.

"We gonna stop and say hello, suh?" asked Wheeler.

"They'd feel hurt if we didn't. But let's not leave these cows in the road. Eli, you open the gate. The little gal don't seem to be collecting tolls this morn—"

And then he saw the little girl. She was standing in the rain at one corner of the house, in one of her mother's flower beds, and she appeared to be digging. Something about that rained-on, dejected-looking little figure, working fumblingly but with intense concentration, gave Foyt a pang of alarm. He told the other men to herd the cows inside the fence, and, as soon as Wheeler had the gate open, cantered up to the house and leaped from his saddle.

She was trying to dig with a straight-edged shovel instead of a spade, and had barely managed to scrape away a patch of flowers and make a shallow dent in the ground. She was still wearing her voluminous cut-down dress and apron, both of them drenched through and hanging deadweight, which added to her look of being bowed, shrunken and miserable. But she had also put on a hat—probably one of Willie Pearl's or the late Hannelore's. It was a severe, matronly, going-to-church hat, a flat black straw adorned with a bunch of artificial grapes. It was so much too big for her that it came down to her eyebrows, and her face was streaked with a mixture of rain, tears and purple dye draining off the grapes.

Foyt flashed a look at the house; its silence practically shouted emptiness. He looked down again at the little girl and said gently, "Howdy, Pistol."

Without raising her head, she snuffled, said, "You know my name," and went on clumsily scraping with the shovel.

"Sure, Feather. I was just funning. Now, what is all this?"

"This is a fun'ral."

Foyt swallowed and knelt down to her level. He said huskily and hopefully, "A cat? A doll?"

She shook her head, sobbed once, and said, "Daddy Fritz and Aunt Willie Pearl."

Foyt managed to gulp out, "What . . . ? What . . . ?"

"What?" echoed Feather. "I'm gonna bury 'em under these-here flowers. They both liked flowers."

"I mean, what *happened?*"

"Some men shot 'em," Feather said simply.

"Oh, good Jesus. Where are they?"

"They all rode off just afore daybreak."

"I don't mean the men. I mean your Daddy and Willie Pearl."

"He's in the kitchen. She's at the foot of the stairs." She looked

up for the first time. "Mebbe y'all kin he'p me fetch 'em outchere?"
Foyt muttered a curse and bounded up the front porch steps. Just
in case Feather was wrong about all the men having gone, he took
out and cocked his Billy-the-Kid before opening the front door. He
nearly stepped on Willie Pearl, who lay in the hall at the bottom of
the staircase leading to the second floor. She was a heaped and
wadded tumble of skirts, apron and petticoats, and her turban had
come unwound, revealing a head as bald and shiny as a sevenball.
An iron skillet was clutched in her hand. She had been shot in the
chest, and apparently had rolled down the stairs in consequence.

Foyt went on through the house to the kitchen. It looked as if a
tornado had passed through, cooking itself a messy meal on the
way. The once shining copper pots and pans that had hung on the
walls were now scattered on the table, the sink and the floor, their
copper outsides blacked and their insides clotted with congealed
food. The big coal stove, still warm, was splotched with cooked-on
drips and dribblings. Fritz Altdorfer sat in a chair at the table, leaning forward, his head pillowed on his crossed arms. There was no
back to his head, where the bullet had come out. Foyt didn't move
him to look at the front of it.

He returned to the entry hall and, pistol still at the ready, quietly
climbed the stairs. The spare bedroom, where he and his companions had once slept, looked untouched. So did the little room that
was obviously Feather's. But the tornado had made its way into the
main bedroom—that of Fritz and Wilmajean—though it hadn't
stopped here for a meal. All the bottles and jars and other feminine
fripperies had been swept off the dressing table onto the floor. The
mirror over the dressing table was a splintered spider web. One of
the legs of the bed had given way and the bed sagged sideways. The
sheets were tangled, torn, smudged here and there with swipes of
dust, mud and boot blacking, and were disgustingly spotted with little dried white crusts. In one of the rents in one of the sheets hung
the torn-loose rowel of a spur, its loss evidently unnoticed by its
wearer in all the excitement.

Outside again, Foyt found the other three grouped around Feather, all looking as stunned, aghast and outraged as he was himself. Feather had the shovel—almost as tall as she was—standing on its blade and her head bowed on her hands gripping its handle.

". . . so Momma said she'd go with 'em, if they'd leave me alone and leave me here. But I know she didn't want to go."

Foyt led the little girl into the shelter of the front porch, hunkered down beside her and asked her to tell them, from the beginning, how it all had happened. Only occasionally letting out a sob that she couldn't stifle, or snuffling back a drip from her nose, Feather told them, quite clearly and succinctly:

Just at last nightfall, four mounted men had come along the wagon trail. The only description Feather could give was that two of them were bushily bearded, one was fat and bald, one was ordinary-looking—but all were big and fearsome. Without a by-your-leave, they opened the gate and rode right up to the back porch. Still without knocking or announcing themselves, they tromped into the kitchen.

There Fritz Altdorfer was eating a solo supper, having come in late from the fields, after the women had dined, and was teasingly asking Feather what she'd like Saint Nicholas to bring her for Christmas—maybe a doll-size rocking chair to match the one her mother yearned for?

When the men came through the door, Fritz looked up from his plate and said, quite calmly, that he supposed they were the train robbers on the run. He was in the middle of saying that he'd been expecting a different foursome, when one of the men pulled a pistol from his holster and shot Fritz in the face. The shot knocked him and the chair over backward and Fritz slid halfway to the wall. But the four men picked him up, all joking about how the man of the house ought to sit at the head of the board when entertaining guests, and replaced him in the chair at the table.

Feather faded out of sight into the pantry while this was going on; the men had not even noticed her. But now her mother and Willie

Pearl came running in from the barn, where they had gone to worry over the family cow, which had a slight case of the bloat. Wilmajean, Indian-trained to stoicism and inscrutability, simply stood and stared at her husband's dead body, but Willie Pearl went into hysterics. One of the men said she'd better shut up her screeching and fix them something to eat. Another of the men, looking at Wilmajean, said eating could wait. He had just decided he was hungry for something else.

So all four of them took Wilmajean by the arms and led her out of the room, she moving along like a sleepwalker. At that, Willie Pearl came out of her fit and chased after them, snatching a skillet off the stove as she went. She lumbered up the stairs behind them and, at the top, one of the men turned and shot her. Willie Pearl literally flew down the staircase without touching one step, until she lit halfway down and then rolled the rest of the way.

Feather had crept out of hiding to see that much of what happened, but she didn't dare go up the stairs. She could only listen, and hear a deal of noise—as if the men were breaking things and throwing things around and laughing uproariously. After a long time, one after another of them came downstairs again, but her mother stayed up in the bedroom.

In the kitchen, the four men grumbled at each other. Feather, in the pantry again, watched through a door crack. One of the men cussed another one because he'd killed the cook. Still another one groused that the lady of the house wouldn't be up to cooking, either, for a while. So they all fixed their own suppers, which was why the kitchen now looked like a pigsty.

When they had eaten, they sat around the kitchen—ignoring Fritz Altdorfer's corpse in their midst—and rolled smokes and chewed tobacco and spat on the floor, and talked about what-next? Move on again before it got light, they decided, and take the filly with the matching yellow mane and tail along with them. Yes, said one, she'd come in handy to have between them and the guns of any posse. And, said another, between them and the hard ground, too, eh boys, haw haw haw.

One of the men went up and fetched her down. Wilmajean had her clothes on all hind-part-to and disheveled, and one of her eyes was blacked and swollen shut, and her hair was a mare's nest. She looked as draggled and worn and wretched and ugly as Feather remembered her being, back in their Indian days, when John Blackwater used to get drunk and beat up on her.

Another of the quartet went out to the barn and brought both of the plow mules to the back porch. He also brought Fritz's battered old saddle and a pack harness. Each of their riding horses was loaded with a bedroll and a couple of lumpy sacks. These they transferred to the mule they had strapped the pack harness on. The other mule they saddled for Wilmajean to ride.

That was when Wilmajean said all right, she'd come along with them if they just wouldn't hurt her little girl. The men said what little girl, and Feather stepped out in view for the first time. They all said well they'd be damned. One of them told Wilmajean she was coming along anyway and to hell with her brat. Another one said why not bring the squirt, too; if they had to hide out for very long, she'd grow big enough to be worth keeping.

But finally one of them pointed out that a .45 cartridge cost twenty-four cents, and, rich as he might be these days, he wouldn't waste twenty-four cents just for the pleasure of plugging a little half-pint bitch of a Polack. So they all mounted up and, leading the pack mule and Wilmajean's mule, rode off eastward to disappear into the rain and the dark. As soon as daylight broke, Feather went to the barn, found this old manure shovel and started to dig two graves.

"Now let me git on with it," she said, almost fiercely. "They bin dead too long, without no place to lay down and stretch out and be easy."

Foyt, choking slightly, said, "I don't think I'd put 'em in the flower bed, Feather, honey. So close to the windmill and the water supply. Let's lay 'em to rest yonder in the medder. Come spring, they'll have plenty of flowers over 'em."

"But they'll have the cow walkin' over 'em, too, and the mules, if Momma brings 'em back. That's where they graze."

"Your Daddy Fritz won't mind that. He'll like it. He was a stock-man afore you ever met him. He'll *want* to keep an eye on his stock. And whatever he'd like, you know Aunt Willie Pearl'd like, too. Now—let us do the digging, Feather. It's too much work for a little gal. You run off and we'll call you when it's time to say good-bye to 'em." He stood up and whispered to Wheeler, "Eli, you've got a way with young animals. Take this one off somewhere and distract her."

"Come with me, Miss Feather, suh," Wheeler said persuasively. "Let's you and me go to the barn and see can we help that sick cow some way."

"You fellers," Foyt said to Karnes and Boudreaux. "Go hunt up a spade and a pick and dig a couple of graves yonder in the med-der, whilst I see what I can do about laying-out them poor people decent and proper."

The Cajun was scandalized. "Bury a white man side-beside a nigger?!"

Foyt said Boudreaux could shove his southern-gentlemanly scruples up his coon-ass. "Them two lived and died not far apart from each other. Saint Peter can sort 'em out, if he wants to, when they git to the Pearly Gates. Anyway, Moon, I defy you to dig 'em up a year from now and tell me which one was which color. Now git moving."

The bodies were cold and stiff when he carried them, one at a time, into the front parlor and laid them on the carpet. It took all Foyt's strength to crack the rigid ligaments and unbend the knotted muscles, to straighten Fritz Altdorfer from his bowed and seated posture, and Willie Pearl from her untidy heap. There was no ques-tion of making coffins for them, but he found some clean sheets in a linen closet and rolled the bodies in these for shrouds.

He was bent over, tucking in the last loose ends of the sheets, when he was suddenly brought upright by a noise from way down at the front gate. When he stood, his pistol was almost magically in his hand and his thumb was on the hammer. The noise had sounded

queerly like a goose honking in anger. It honked again, several
times. Foyt stepped to the parlor window and looked out toward the
wagon track.

That green Packard stood there, at the gate, no longer shiny, but
plastered with mud where it wasn't coated with dust. The fringed
yellow canopy sagged, full of water. The four Operatives still sat in
it, and the man beside the driver was impatiently squeezing the
rubber-bulbed brass horn mounted on his side of the car. Muttering, Foyt tucked his pistol away, left the house by the front door
and trudged down through the drizzle to the still open gate. All four
men in the car were now wearing goggles, so dusty and mud-speck-
led that he couldn't see their eyes.

"Good morning, sir," said the horn-squeezer. "I—"

"May I ask who you be?" Foyt barked. The man looked slightly
taken aback.

"I am Oral T. Allnutt, Field Chief—"

"We don't need no Feed Cheese. And people with manners come
up to the house and knock. Even peddlers."

"We're in a hurry, man! I am *Field Chief* of the—"

"Then don't let *me* keep you. Hurry right along."

Oral T. Allnutt raised his goggles and glowered at Foyt. "I am
Field Chief of the Bynum-Allnutt Detective Agency of Fort Worth.
Me and my Operatives here are on the trail of the four men that
held up a T. & B.V. train, robbed more than a million dollars and
shot two Railway Express guards to death."

"Well, keep on a-trailing," said Foyt. "They ain't here."

"You haven't seen four men ride by?"

"No."

"Are you the proprietor of this establishment?"

"No, I just work here."

"I'd like a word with your employer."

"So would I," said Foyt. "But he's down sick, and that's why I
ain't got time to stand here in the goddam rain talking to you. I got
work to do—his chores now on top of mine."

"I've seen you somewhere before," Allnutt said suspiciously. He narrowed his steely eyes. "Didn't I once pick you up for breach of promises made to the Widow Peavey over at Mineral Wells?"

"No," Foyt said flatly. "*Are* you in a hurry, mister, or ain't you? I am."

"I warn you," said Allnutt, his color rising. "I *recognize* you, and I never forget a face. I have a photographic memory, and I've got the faces of every miscreant in the Rogues' Gallery of every county in Texas filed away in my brain. Now you just stand there while I recollect."

"Hell, I'll help," said Foyt, even more menacingly than the detective. He leaned his head under the canopy, nose to nose with the Field Chief. "You dumb son of a bitch, you met me on the street in Teague just yesterday morning." Allnutt blinked. "I'm L. R. Foyt, first cousin to Chief Dispatcher Norwood Foyt, and I'm gonna see that Norwood reports to Old Man Wiggins just how all-fired efficient you stupid gumshoes are." The four Operatives looked at each other. "Right this minute, you're trespassing on private propitty." Foyt casually took out his pistol. "If you ain't gone in one more minute, I'm gonna shoot the innards outa this fancy auto*mo*bile, and y'all can walk back to Teague in the rain." The driver hastily worked the gearshift. "Now *piss off!*"

The driver yanked his foot from the clutch and the Packard sprang forward, spraying mud. The detectives pissed off in a hurry, up the wagon track and out of Foyt's sight.

He slopped back up to the house, around it and out to the meadow where Karnes and the Cajun were working, and streaming with rain and sweat.

"That's deep enough," Foyt decreed. "Now let's hurry up and git them bodies planted afore these holes fill up with water."

On the way to the house, Karnes nodded toward the wagon road and asked, "Why'd you get rid of the detectives? Four more guns would have been useful, I'd think."

"Not no four guns with them four leather-headed yahoos behind 'em. Allnutt and his men are purty poor pickles, but I'd hate to be the one to git 'em all shot."

"Better dem dan us," Boudreaux said. "Some of de shooting be shot *dere* way. Be dat much less lead *we* have to dodge."

Karnes added, "You know what we're going up against, L. R. You heard what-all Feather told. The men we're after are not just robbers that're too quick on the trigger. They've got to be insane— mad dogs—the way they're killing everything that crosses their path."

Foyt said, kindly and as if he was laying out a lesson to be learned, "Gideon, it's purty hard to work yourself up to kill a human being. But once you've done it, the next one comes easier, and the next easier still. And if you kill a hunderd, they can only hang you for one. They can't hoist you an inch higher and you won't fall an inch deeper into Hell."

"But besides that—Thought damn it—think of what they did to that poor woman!" Karnes shook his big head, looking shocked and nauseated. "What they'll go *on* doing to her!"

"Doing that has killed many a man," said Foyt equably. "But it never killed no woman. That one, especially. She'll just think she's back amongst the Comanches."

Karnes stopped and turned squarely on Foyt, his face gone suddenly pale, so that his pink forehead scar stood out like a brand. "I never realized it until now, L. R. You're a *hard* man."

"No, Gideon," said Foyt, still kindly and teacherly. "I'm a realistic man. Realistic and practical. If you live long enough, you'll learn that's a damn sight harder thing to be than *hard.*"

"Then I hope I don't live to be it."

"I'm as sorry as you are that they kidnaped that woman," said Foyt. "But not for no sentimental reasons. For a practical one. I'm not gonna weep about her, not now. I know she can take anything them thugs dish out; she's been kidnaped before. What I'm thinking of is that she's gonna be standing smack in between their bullets and our'n. When that happens, that's when I'll weep."

After they had laid the two swathed bodies in the graves, Foyt shouted for Wheeler and Feather to join them. Wheeler was pleased to report that there was nothing seriously wrong with that bloated cow. She had just eaten some larkspur or sneezeweed, most likely. He had milked her and slopped most of the milk to the two pigs, saving some for their own breakfast. Foyt said he was gratified for the report, then held up the big Doré Bible he had brought from the house.

"Miss Feather," he said, taking off his hat. "Fellers." They took theirs off, too. "I don't know the proper services to say. But Feather, your Daddy Fritz once told us he'd just let the Good Book fall open and read what it felt like showing to him. Is it all right with ev'rybody if I do the same?"

They all nodded.

Foyt closed his eyes, opened the book at random, stabbed a finger at the left-hand page and opened his eyes.

"Ye shall not round the corners of your heads, neither shalt thou mar the corners of thy beard." He stopped and mumbled that *that* wasn't very applicable; maybe the pages were damp and had stuck together. He closed the book, closed his eyes and tried again. This time he seemed satisfied.

"I returned, and saw under the sun, that the race is not to the swift, nor the battle to the strong, neither yet bread to the wise, nor yet riches to men of understanding, nor yet favour to men of skill; but time and chance happeneth to them all."

He looked up and motioned to Feather. She bent down, clutched a handful of moist earth from the dug-out pile, and sprinkled a bit of it into each grave, onto each shrouded corpse impartially. Karnes murmured, "Ashes to ashes, dust to dust . . ." Feather murmured something in Comanche.

"For man also knoweth not his time:" Foyt went on, "as the fishes that are taken in an evil net, and as the birds that are caught in the snare; so are the sons of men snared in an evil time, when it falleth suddenly upon them. Amen."

Karnes and Boudreaux pitched in again to fill the graves and then

pat the mounds firm with the flat of their spades. But the drizzling
November rain was already softening their rectangular outlines,
smoothing them, blending them into the meadow.

"Now, Feather," said Foyt. "You run on in the house and change
out of them wet clothes. And warsh that grape stain off your face.
While you're at it, pack yourself a carpetbag or something. Whatever you'll need for a little trip—say a day or two. Then come down
to the kitchen and maybe you can lend me a hand fixing some grub
for us all."

She nodded obediently, and sloshed off ahead of them to the
house. As the four men carried the digging tools back to the barn,
Boudreaux asked, "How-come you tell her to pack a bag, L. R.?
Where you gonna send her?"

"She's coming with us," said Foyt. The other three men gawked
at him. "She can hitch on behind your saddle-pad, Gideon. You got
the bulk to shield her."

"Now there speaks the realistic, practical man," Karnes said sarcastically. "You mean you intend to take that child with us into that
nest of vipers?"

"Yes. I'm *being* realistic. We can't leave her here by herself. And
I ain't about to spare one of y'all to set and tend her. Besides, I'm
figgering on a real practical use for her."

"You must be out of your mind!" Karnes sputtered. "As if it's
not idiotic enough, us four greenhorns tackling four killers that are
professionals and blood-crazy to boot. Here we're going tippy-toe
into the Trinity bottoms, but we're taking along a Thought-damned
herd of shuffling cows that'll let those men know we're coming a
mile away. Now you want us to bring a helpless little girl along besides! *Won't* we make a fine-looking bunch of bounty hunters?!"

Foyt said crisply, "You once said I was the leader, Gideon. Okay
—Gideon, Moon, Eli—I'm leading. I got reasons for what I'm doing." His voice dropped to gruffness. "As for bounty hunting, I give
that up a couple hours back, when I seen what's happened here. I
don't give a good goddam if them robbers use the million dollars
for a campfire or for wiping paper. *If* we git it, fine. And we'll share

it out with Wilmajean and Feather Altdorfer, *if* we git 'em home alive. If we don't do neither one, well . . ."

He looked up, at each of them in turn, with something like a challenge.

"I ain't quit being a realistic man. But now I'm a realistic and a *wrathful* man, and I'm going into them Trinity bottoms for a realistic and a practical reason. It'll improve this planet and this century when them four butchering bastards are dead. I can't speak for none of the rest of you—but me, I'm going to see that they git dead."

17

1

JUST over that hump yonder," said Foyt, "we'll turn off this track and make camp."

"Why?" asked Karnes. "We've still got a good three hours of daylight left."

"Because we've arrived," Foyt said simply. "Other side of that hump in the road, there oughta be the jagged trunk of a lightning-blazed live oak tree. At least there was, thirty-odd years ago, when I last come duck shooting hereabouts. That marks where me and the Pike boys used to make our way down to the river. Where I'm gambling they're at right this minute."

Since dawn, the fivesome and their herd had been following a quite easy-to-travel wagon trace northward from the hamlet of Sand Hill, where they had camped the previous night and where they had been told that the trace went all the way up to the market town of Kerens in Navarro County. Foyt said it had been hacked through sometime since his last pass through these parts. It was as near being a real road as that two-rut wagon track that went past the Alt-dorfers' place, and would even have been negotiable by the Bynum-Allnutt Packard. But Foyt's phrase "hacked through" was apt.

Traveling the trace was like traveling along a canyon bottom, so high and dense was the growth on either side.

For most of this day, they had been moving parallel to the Trinity River, never farther than a pistol shot away on their right, but they had not seen so much as a gleam of the water. The growth on both sides of the wagon trail consisted of trees—mainly cottonwoods, black willows and black gums—seemingly straining to stretch their crowns above an endless brake of switch cane, in places as high as a horse's head, in others twice as high—the inhospitably thick cane interspersed with clumps of cruelly saw-toothed sotol grass and with formidably thorny shrubs like shaving-brush thistle and wait-a-minute mimosa—and all of this lush bottomland growth was tied together, intertwined and enmeshed by loops and twists and coils of tough rattan vine. Either side of the wagon track was a land of keep-out and touch-me-not.

Foyt let the cattle amble on ahead, and got down from his Lightning. "Lemme show y'all the lay of the land." Wheeler and Boudreaux also dismounted. Karnes and Feather watched from atop their horse; they had to. Feather had been inclined to doze now and then, and loose her hold on Karnes's mackinaw; so he had tied a rope around both their waists.

Foyt found a stick, hunkered down and drew a large S shape in the dirt of the trail.

"That's the Trinity River," he said, and pointed eastward, to their right. "This track we're on cuts straight up alongside the left side of that S, and we're just about here." He pointed at the bottom tail point of the S. "Tehuacana Creek is up ahead of us. It flows in from our left, crosses this-here trail and hits that S of the Trinity right in the middle where it bends. That's the way we'd of come here—straight from the railroad and down the Tehuacana—if our original scheme had worked out."

He paused for a moment of silent mourning for their original scheme.

"Now, if I've figgered right, them fellers are camped down here inside the belly-bend of this-here S, on the riverbank. That's where we used to go shooting. What with all them bends, there's a lot of quiet backwaters where the ducks and geese'd come down to feed and rest amongst the reeds. Okay, if them men are there, they got water around 'em—the Tehuacana and the Trinity—on three sides. We're gonna close the fourth side by pitching camp rightchere." He indicated a spot in the open space exactly midway between the center bend of the S and its bottom tail point. "That's just over that hump in the road ahead. And that hump is the highest piece of ground anywhere around here. When we go over it, they're gonna see us coming."

"What if dey don't?" asked the Cajun. He added, rather hopefully, "What if dey ain't dere a'tall?"

"We'll soon know," said Foyt. "If they are, they're bound to be keeping an eye out along this trace. When we stop and camp, they're gonna get nervous—or peevish. It won't be long afore one of 'em shows up to make it plain that we're unwelcome. Is ev'rybody armed and ready?"

Karnes patted the butt of his Peacemaker, which he still wore holstered, gunfighter style, low on his right thigh. Boudreaux patted the bib of his overalls, where he kept the twin to Karnes's Colt. The Winchester carbine was still booted on Wheeler's saddle. Feather asked anxiously, "Where's Daddy Fritz's pistol?"

"It's here inside my bedroll, Rooster, don't worry," said Foyt. "But I don't reckon we'll have to use that except in a real emergency."

He hoped not. Feather had insisted on their bringing it, but it was a most impractical weapon: a dragoon pistol, literally long and heavy enough to require carrying, like the carbine, in a saddle scabbard. Of Civil War vintage, it was an old brass-framed percussion-cap revolver, and didn't appear to have been fired since Appomattox. Its caps, nipples and buckshot charges were probably so long ago corroded that the hand cannon was more likely to blow up and kill its wielder than to shoot anybody in front of it.

Foyt had a private word with Wheeler, then they moved on again to catch up with the cows, everybody mounted except Wheeler, who trailed a little way behind, walking and leading his horse. They topped the rise in the road—half expecting a hail of bullets—to find Foyt's marker tree was indeed still there, on the left of the track, though now weathered and worm-eaten down to a rotted and riddled stump. Karnes looked from it to the right, toward the presumed belly-bend of the S of the Trinity River, and said, "I don't see any trail going that way. That canebrake's still solid wall, it looks to me."

"I hope you didn't expect they'd lay a flagstone path for us," said Foyt. "No, it'll take some wiggling and crashing through. But it *is* easier to git through rightchere than most places in these bottoms. If you stood on your saddle, so you could see over them canes, you'd see that there's at least a break in the trees and thornbushes. A narrer alley between 'em, all the way to the river. You have to buck the switch cane and rattan, but that's all."

It took some hearty cussing and larruping to make the cows turn reluctantly off the easy trail, and push and lunge their way into the malevolently resistant undergrowth. The cane stalks sprang back into place immediately the herd had shouldered through, so the mounted four—Foyt, Boudreaux and Karnes-and-passenger—trailing at the rear of the herd, were whipped and slashed and stung by the flailing cane. Wheeler, afoot behind them, was having an even harder time of it. Karnes asked why he was walking.

"Well, for one reason," said Foyt, "when we topped that rise back yonder on the road, Eli wasn't sticking up ag'inst the sky, the way we did on our hosses. He's still less of a target than we are. I'm hoping any lookout, up in a tree or wherever, will of seen just three men coming. But besides—I told you—Eli's an old infantry sojer. On hossback, he's only a fair shot. But standing planted on his feet, he can shoot the beak off a musketeer so it starves to death."

They kept pushing the herd until they were a couple of hundred yards off the wagon track and well into the belly-bend of that S. Then they choused the cows around in a milling circle until they had stamped the canes and vines passably flat for a camping place.

"Now lay out our soogans," Foyt told Karnes and the Cajun, "like we're here for the night. Feather, you gather up some of the drier burnables. I'll light a fire and make out like I'm fixing to cook up some chuck. Then all we do is wait. If them men are down there, one of 'em'll soon come calling."

So that's what they did: wait—the three men and the girl around the smudge fire, Wheeler still somewhere invisible in the jungle—while their cows moseyed grumpily around the perimeter of this flattened-down space, nipping peckishly at the local vegetation. Among all this lush growth, little of it could be considered fodder.

And then suddenly there was a man on a horse, tall in the saddle, looking down on the camp and campers. He had come from the direction of the river, and come as silently through the canebrake as if he and his horse had lived in it all their lives. He was about Foyt's age; he was dressed in cowboy denims, hats and boots; his face was considerably obscured by a heavy, curly, salt-and-pepper beard; he wore a holstered pistol and carried a double-barreled shotgun casually cradled across his left elbow, his right hand on the stock and the trigger. He said howdy and they all said howdy back.

"Peculiar place y'all picked to camp," he said conversationally. "Not very comf'table. Nothin' for the cows to eat."

"The hell with the cows," said Foyt, in an equally uncaring voice. "We're hoping to bag us a bird for our own supper." He pointed upward, to where a flock of great white birds with black-tipped wings were circling high, evidently having spotted the numerous men and animals in the bottoms and being hesitant to come down to the water.

"Them's snow geese," said Foyt. "A challenge to shoot and damned good to eat. Surprised *you* ain't banging away at 'em, Jasper."

The man sighed and said, still conversationally, "I was hopin' the beard would put you off, Lancelot," and he flipped the shotgun over in their direction. He pointed it directly at Karnes, who was the only one with a gun actually in sight. But the four were hunkered close around the fire. The scatter of shot from those two barrels would annihilate or incapacitate all of them.

"When I spotted that li'l piss-ant brat," said Jasper Pike, "I figgered you wasn't just a-trailin' a herd. You shouldn't of follered us, Lancelot. If you was lawmen, now, or a posse"—he shrugged— "but I do hate to plug an old chum of my childhood."

"I wondered if you would," Foyt said offhandedly.

"Oh, I would. And I will. But the others'll want to be in on this." Jasper put two fingers of his free hand into his mouth to give a whistle.

"Okay, Eli," said Foyt, still without raising his voice.

From somewhere in the canes nearby came the appalling, ear-clapping *blam!* of that .30–30. Everything about Jasper flew wide: his mouth and eyes went as open as they could get, his arms and legs jerked out in an X, the shotgun went sailing, and all in the same instant Jasper whisked backward off his horse, as if it had been galloping full speed and a low limb had caught him in the stomach.

Foyt got slowly up from the fire, dusted off his overalls and went over to where Jasper lay on his back, a good ten feet behind his horse. The others followed, but stopped at a respectful distance as Foyt knelt down beside the fallen man.

"Damn it, Lancelot, that was a gut shot," Jasper complained. "The painfulest way there is for a man to die. Soon as the numbness wears off, I'll be squirmin' and a-screamin' for hours. We ain't even totin' no whiskey I could take to dull it down. I do think you might of showed a little consideration."

"Don't fret, Jasper," said Foyt. "You'll go out right quick and easy. That was my old Winchester that shot you, and all the bullets in it are dumdummed the way you and me used to do 'em for deer hunting. Remember? File off the point of the bullet and cut a cross in the blunted end. So that slug went all to pieces whilst it was going through you. There's a hole in your back I could put my fist in. You won't suffer long."

"Oh. Well, that's okay then. I am obliged, Lancelot." He shifted his body to get more comfortable, and his face contorted. "Now," he said, "you-all better cut and run while you got a chance. The

other boys surely heared that thutty-thutty go off, and they know I
warn't carryin' one."

"I'm counting on that," said Foyt, unperturbed. "We're after
them, same as they'll be after us. We'll just wait for 'em to creep a
little closer and then we'll make our next move."

"Well, good luck," said Jasper. "You won't ketch them boys off
guard, like you did me. I'd hate to be in you-all's boots."

He lifted his eyes from Foyt's face a little higher, to the sky,
where the big ,ghost-white birds were still circling indecisively.

"Yessir," he said. "Them's snow geese, all right, come all the way
down from the Yukon. Don't often see so many in a flock no more,
now the country's gittin' all crowded up. I kin almost smell one a-
roastin' for Christmas. It'd be nice to have a good oldtimey Christmas ag'in, with roast goose and ches'nut stuffin' and all."

"I remember the day you brung down a double, Jasper," said
Foyt. "Purtiest shooting I ever seen. One barrel, *bang,* and then
swing and *bang.* Both of 'em dropped damn near at your feet."

Jasper smiled, nodded and winced slightly. "I remember that,
too, Lancelot. Ain't the sort of thing a man forgits. Eustace never
done nothin' like that. Neither did you."

"I never had but a single-shot gun back then."

"You're right; I'd forgot. But I recollect the time you fired *that*
off at Hicks Spring—right inside the pavilion, you idjit—at the First
Annual Encampment of the United Confed'rate Vet'rans. Them
old sojers of the Seventh Texas thought they was back at the Battle
of Franklin, Tennessee. Scared the shit out of 'em, you did. You
was drunk as a coot, Lancelot."

"Me?! Jasper, you was too drunk to of been invited to a skunk
wrassle. I recall how you livened up the reunion some, too. When
the Mexia Silver Cornet Band stood up to play 'Dixie,' you got in
front of 'em sucking on a lemon. They all puckered up so they
couldn't of blown a good fart."

"And you and Eustace slipped the ratchet on the merry-go-
round so it went a-whizzin' like a spinnin' wheel, and all the gals was

a-screechin' and their skirts was flyin' up above their panta-
lettes . . ." He winced again. "Yep, them was some funs and mis-
chiefs we used to have. A man only remembers the *good* times
when . . ." He squinted. "Don't see them snow geese no more.
Reckon we've skeered 'em off."

Foyt looked up; the snow geese were still up there circling. He
looked down; Jasper was dead.

Foyt stood erect again—and again did it slowly—now looking
rather old and tired. "Well, that's one down," he said. "Three to
go."

2

Wheeler stepped out of the canebrake to join them, calmly levering a new cartridge into his carbine's chamber. Karnes and Boudreaux seemed a little fidgety.

"We jes' wait?" the Cajun asked. "You sho don't figger dey so
stupid dey come one by one?"

"No, we'll have to meet 'em halfway," said Foyt. "But they're
coming, all right." He pointed. A short-legged, flop-eared dog had
appeared and was sniffing curiously at Jasper's corpse. Foyt turned
to Feather and said, "You didn't tell us them men had that sawed-off
hound dog along."

"I forgot, mister," she said apologetically. "It stayed outdoors
with their ponies."

"What's it matter?" asked Karnes.

" 'Count of we know that dawg, suh," said Wheeler.

"Eli's right," said Foyt. "That-there's a basset hound, Gideon, and
there ain't many in these parts. But our last boss—that cheating bastard Toad Walsh—always had one at his heels. Now we know who
the third of them robbers is. I reckon old Toad wasn't satisfied with
just the money he bilked us out of—he had to try for a real big
wad."

"Me, I don't cotton to jes' standing here," said Boudreaux nervously. "What now, L. R.?"

"Now Feather does her stuff." He went and clapped a knobbly hand on the girl's slender shoulder. "Feather, I don't know what kind of Comanche medicine-making it is you do over them cows, but you're the only one I know can do it. I want you to stampede 'em ag'in, just the way you done at your gate that day. You reckon you can?"

She nodded with the haughty assurance of a medicine man.

"Okay. I want to run 'em down thataway, straight through the cane where old Jasper came out of, and on down that narrer alley between the trees. Got it?"

"Got it," said Feather.

"Now, when them cows go running, us fellers are gonna foller after 'em." He went and collected Jasper's unused sixgun and shotgun, and checked their loads. "You stay here with our hosses, Feather. You're gonna hear some shooting from down yonder way, but don't let it worry you. With luck, it'll be us that's doing the shooting. Whatever happens, none of them other crooks knows you're here, so nobody'll be coming after you. *However*." He held up a stern finger. "If so be things go bad for us, and we're not back here by dark—that's a couple of hours off—I want you to climb on my old Lightning yonder and head back down the wagon trace towards Sand Hill. Is that clear?"

"Yes, mister," she said. "But I could sneak along after you-all and—"

"You do no such a thing! You do what I tell you! For one reason, you're responsible for keeping our hosses from straying, in case we have to come back running and make a fast gitaway. But—*if we don't come back*—you ride to Sand Hill. You're a brave gal; you can ride by night; you'll be there by sunup. Tell the first person you meet that there's at least one dead train robber up here"—he indicated the late Jasper M. Pike—"and maybe more. They'll send a posse up here in a helluva hurry. If ev'rything goes like I'm hoping, the posse'll find your Momma alive and safe—and us, too, I trust. Anyhow, there'll be a big cash reward for you and your Momma. You hear me, now? You promise you'll do as I say?"

"Yes, mister," she said, but pouting. "I promise."

"All right." Foyt handed Jasper's Colt to Boudreaux and told him to carry it in his hand. He slung Jasper's shotgun in the crook of his own arm. "You and me, Moon, we'll keep our other pistols hid as long as possible. Okay, Feather, go to it."

Like a surveyor taking a sighting, she peered riverward, in the direction Foyt had specified, then looked at the half-drowsing bunch of cows, then painstakingly moved into position—putting the herd between her and the canebrake aisle that led down through the trees.

"*Shoo! Scat! Shoo!*" Fearther suddenly shrilled, flapping her big apron.

The Comanche medicine, if that's what it was, worked again. The cows all gave a terrified blat and leaped from a standing start into a headlong gallop. The basset hound scrambled out of their way. About four abreast, the cows veered around Jasper's body and crashed into the wall of canes as if they were circus animals jumping through a paper hoop. Barking excitedly, the basset hound chased after them, serving to drive them even faster. All the animals disappeared, with a gradually diminishing racket of barking, mooing and crunching, and left in their wake a four-cow-wide walkway for the men to follow. They waved goodbye to Feather and, guns at the ready, stalked warily down the alley toward the Trinity.

Karnes and Boudreaux had often, with a thrill of horror, read in "real Wild West" dime novels how some luckless cowboy or somebody would fall in front of a stampeding herd and get mashed flat by the thundering hooves. But Foyt and Wheeler knew that to be an overworked fiction. Such an occurrence was considerably more rare than a cowboy or somebody getting shriveled to a raisin by a bolt of lightning out of the blue.

True, there are individual killer horses, cows, even swine. But a herd of wild animals on the run, encountering a man prone and helpless on the ground, will do its best to avoid stepping on him. Every animal in that herd—whether it be cow, horse, buffalo, caribou or zebra—and no matter how maddened or terrified it may be by whatever caused it to bolt in the first place—and no matter how tightly wedged among its fellow creatures it may be—will try its utmost to step around that fallen man, or jump over him, or turn a somersault or a cartwheel, anything to keep from trampling him.

However, the Feather-stampeded cows had no such option of maneuver. They went crashing through that tangle of rank growth hemmed in by the banks of trees on either side, running as close-packed as if they were going through a stockyard chute. Walling their eyes backward at the yappy hound dog chasing them, running blind through that jungle of towering, vine-entwined cane stalks, they didn't even see the man until they were on top of him. And then they were past him.

So Karnes and Boudreaux, with a thrill of horror, and Foyt and Wheeler, with grim satisfaction, came upon the grisly remains of Toad Walsh, squashed like a toad under a wagon tire. At least, they guessed who it was, because what had been the body had been lard fat and what had been the head had been buzzard-bald. Otherwise, it was scarcely identifiable even as having been human. Its tongue now protruded from one eye socket and . . . But their stomachs made them move on without examining the mess too closely. One thing they did notice was that one of its spurs was lacking its rowel.

"Two down, suh," murmured Wheeler. "Only two to go."

3

They became suddenly aware that they were standing in the midst of a gentle snowfall. A green snowfall. Big green rectangles of paper were drifting down among them, blowing about overhead in the breeze, getting caught in the canes and vines and impaled on thorns. Boudreaux snatched at one and exclaimed, *"Nom de dieu! A hunnerd-dollar bill!"*

"I'll be damned," breathed Foyt. "Them cows've stampeded the pack mule with the croker sacks of money."

Karnes, Wheeler and Boudreaux were cramming their pockets with every casenote within reach on the ground or in the air. Foyt himself tucked away a couple of fifties that came floating past him, but reminded the others, "We still got to spend a couple more bullets to stake our claim to this-here money. Keep moving."

When they came out at the end of the aisle the herd had made, they were at the opening of a clearing on the riverbank. The cows had come to a halt at the edge of the water and were now idling up and down the bank, cropping at the rather better feed here. Among them were the robbers' other three horses, Wilmajean's riding mule and the pack mule. The latter was carrying just two croker sacks, one slung on either side of its wooden packtree—these, as it turned out, loaded with gold and silver coin. All the other sacks had been trampled flat or torn to shreds in the bush. The whole clearing was strewn with green bills, stamped into the ground, blowing hither and yon, many of them out on the water, floating downstream like autumn leaves.

The desperadoes' campfire was here, built small and smokeless of dry cane stalks. Their bedrolls, saddles and other gear were distributed at a distance around it. And in front of it, facing the four newcomers, stood Wilmajean Hudspeth Altdorfer. Her face dirty and bruised, her tangled hair hanging down her back, her clothes torn and awry, she looked like hell, but she stood as tall and regal and untouchable as a queen still. She said quietly:

"Well, if it ain't Mister Haskell. I'm sorry to have to tell you this, but you and your crew are under the gun. There's at least two of 'em p'inted at you. If'n you don't chunk all your own guns out in front of you on the ground, you-all and me will be shot dead this instant."

If it had been the two remaining outlaws confronting them and telling them this, the four men might have tried some desperate shootout. But Wilmajean's quiet and melancholy advice carried conviction. Foyt and Wheeler tossed their long guns out in front of them, the Cajun flipped away the Colt in his hand, and Karnes unholstered and threw his.

Only then did the two outlaws step out of the canebrake, one from each side of the cow-trampled aisle. Eustace Pike was almost the twin to Jasper, only a little older, his curly beard a little grayer. The other was a younger man, of medium height, medium face, medium hair, medium garb. Even if his photograph had been on every "Wanted" poster in Texas, he would have been so undistinctive as to be unrecognizable—except that the four men had seen him before. At last encounter, Bubba had been lying unconscious in the mud and manure of the Shreveport stockyards. Eustace carried a double-barreled shotgun, Bubba a cumbersome old ten-shot Volcanic Repeater pistol. Both guns were cocked, aimed and practically aquiver with readiness to let loose.

Bubba didn't recognize the men until he moved in front of them to guard the discarded armament, and spotted one of the Peacemakers as his own. He looked up at them, his lip curled, and he snarled, "You're the sons of bitches that snuck up and tried to knock my head off!" He might have started plugging away at them right then, but Eustace said, "You kin git your revenge after a while, Bubba. After they've did some work for us. But you're right; they're sneaky. Hold your gun on 'em whilst I frisk 'em. You-all put your hands straight up, *far* up, as far over your heads as they'll go."

He grinned at Foyt. "Mebbe you didn't think I'd remember your habits, Lancelot—or is it Haskell now?" With a chuckle of satisfaction, he slid Foyt's Billy-the-Kid and Boudreaux's other Colt out from inside their bibs, and tossed them on the ground with the other arms. He found nothing else on Wheeler or Karnes, and stepped away from them again.

"Now you kin put your hands down. Way down, becuz you bastards are gonna pick up ev'ry one of these greenbacks that your goddam cows spilt around. And meantime, Bubba's gonna—show 'em, Bubba."

With his free hand, Bubba seized Wilmajean by the wrist and twisted it in an armlock behind her, so fiercely that she let out a little cry of pain. He jammed his big pistol's muzzle hard into the bulge of her right breast and she cried out again.

"The first wrong move any of you make—the first time you slow down in your pickin'-up work—I'm go' blow this li'l lady's purty tit right off. And it *is* a purty one, lemme tell you! Make another move, or another slowdown, or even look mean at me, and I'll blow off the other'n. If'n you still misbehave, *guess* where I'll ram this pistol bar'l up in her and shoot next!"

"Now," said Eustace. "Pick up ev'ry blessed bill that's loose in these bottoms. When you got an armful, hand 'em over to me and I'll roll 'em in our soogans. Put 'em in my left hand, becuz my right'll be holdin' this-here scatter-gun, and remember there ain't one of you gonna git out of range of it. All right, you shitheads, *git to it!*"

Boudreaux, Karnes, Wheeler and Foyt all started glumly picking up the bills around them; there wasn't much else they could do. The basset hound frisked about among them, happily joining in the game. Bubba still held Wilmajean in that armlock, standing directly over the pile of their confiscated weapons, with his own still cruelly prodding her breast. Eustace Pike stood by one of the bedrolls, where he could effectually cover the whole clearing with his shot-gun. As each of the money-pickers accumulated a sizable wad, he would deliver it to Eustace—to his unarmed left hand, as specified —Eustace would deposit it on the bedroll, and then flip a fold of the blankets to cover the money and keep the breeze from getting at it again.

The four men stooped and moved and picked-up as slowly as they could without provoking either Bubba or Eustace into shoot-ing the woman or one of them. They knew that this was bound to be the last exertion—or activity, or fun, or anything—they'd evermore get to do, this side of plucking harp strings or stoking Hell fires. As soon as all the money was gathered—or all of it that wasn't beyond retrieving—they would certainly be rubbed out before the two des-perados moved on. And the prospect of dying was particularly unpleasant because—from what Foyt knew personally about Pike and Bubba, and what the rest of the men had seen of Pike's and Bubba's previous sadisms—they had good reason to believe that they'd have to do their dying inch by tormented inch.

4

Gideon Karnes had never worn a pistol in his life until he'd buckled on Bubba's gunbelt some while back. He had never felt comfortable with that thing, and he had never used it, except to fire skyward once in a while to stimulate the slow-moving cows. All his days, in all his fracases, Gideon Karnes had relied on the brute strength of his massive body, and indeed had had to restrain that somewhat, to keep from hurting his adversaries beyond repair. His physical strength was now, he figured, the only weapon he and his buddies had left to them. He decided to rely on it one last time, and stake all their lives on it.

In his stooping and picking-up and moving-along, he unobtrusively followed a scatter of bills that led riverward—and led him imperceptibly behind Bubba's back. When he finally had Bubba between him and Pike's shotgun, Karnes suddenly dropped his collection of soiled greenbacks—and sprang, with surprising agility for such a big man.

He wrapped his huge arms around Bubba in a bear hug from behind, forcing Bubba's hands and gun away from Wilmajean, and pinning them to the man's sides. Now Karnes squeezed as hard as he could—the bear hug became a grizzly hug—and there was a subdued crunching sound, muffled by Bubba's yell of agony. Wilmajean lurched away from them, one hand holding the arm Bubba had kept locked.

Eustace whipped his shotgun up to his shoulder, but hesitated; he couldn't shoot Karnes without riddling the shielding Bubba. In that moment, though, Bubba fired the big pistol he held pointed straight downward, and shot into Karnes's instep. Karnes grunted and involuntarily eased his squeeze just enough for Bubba to leap free. Bubba turned as he leapt, and shot the big man in the chest.

Karnes dropped to one knee. He muttered something and struggled erect. Bubba shot him again, in the head this time. Karnes fell again, muttered again, and again flailed to his feet—but now his eyes were closed and he was groping blindly before him, a sightless Samson. Bubba fired again and again.

Like a mighty tree falling, the big man toppled slowly, then rapidly, to crumple full length on the ground and lie still. The hound dog came to sniff at him. Though whimpering from the pain of her own twisted arm, Wilmajean murmured, "Dear Mister Birtwistle," knelt beside the fallen giant, took his bloody head into her lap and let her long blonde hair fall over him like the final curtain of a stage-show tragedy.

Bubba was staggering about, his own arms now wrapped around his chest, and cursing vehemently in a curious sort of squeak, as if his voice was coming from a punctured bellows. "Eustace," he managed to say. "I think all my ribs are broke. Splintered. I can't breathe. It's like knives. *God!*"

"Whose goddam fault is it?" snapped Eustace. "Stupid bastard, lettin' him git behind you. Now stop your whinin' and git useful ag'in."

Bubba made a mighty effort, his mouth twitching, his breath still whistling, and slowly peeled his gun arm from hugging his chest, to point the Volcanic Repeater at Wilmajean.

"I told you," he wheezed to the others, "what I'd do if anybody made a wrong move." He cocked the pistol, stepped to Wilmajean's side, where she was in profile to him, and placed the muzzle precisely at her left nipple.

There were two shots, though scarcely louder than popcorn popping, and Bubba backed away from Wilmajean, looking puzzled. Two tiny holes had appeared in his forehead, one above the other, like a colon: his eyes rolled up and backward, as far as they would go, as if he was trying to see what had stung him. A trickle of blood ran from the two dots down his nose and dripped off the end.

Bubba lowered his arm, dropped his pistol and began to walk restlessly around in a small circle, only the whites of his eyes showing, and his whistle-squeak voice saying urgently, as if he had to convince everybody of something important, "Eating easy even Easter . . . evil east . . . easy even . . ." He sighed, sat down with his back against a tree, added tiredly, "Warning warm . . .

when we walk warble . . . weather . . . warm . . ." and died.

There was a similar colon of two holes in the bib of Boudreaux's overalls, with a wisp of smoke coming from them. The Cajun withdrew his hand from inside the bib, holding the little whorehouse derringer. He stared at it and said with mild surprise, "Both dem bar'ls went off de same time."

Everybody had been watching Bubba's deranged and dying performance with horrified fascination—except Wilmajean, who was still grieving over the body of Karnes-Birtwistle—and except Eustace Pike. The moment Boudreaux showed that pipsqueak pistol, Eustace swung the shotgun on him and let fly. The *ba-loom!* shook the whole clearing, stirred a few greenbacks from the ground, and picked Boudreaux up like one of the ill-fated croker sacks, to fling him bodily into the canebrake. He didn't cry out at the terrible wound that is inflicted by a charge of double-O shot at close range, nor could he have, and he didn't move again, nor could he have.

Immediately, Eustace dropped the shotgun, which had only one load left in it now, and snatched up two Colts from the pile of weapons beside Wilmajean, one in each fist.

"You sons of bitches!" he blazed. "You really reckon you've put paid to my gang, don't you? But there's still me to reckon with. And you-all won't be around long enough to do much reckonin'." His voice got almost cheerful, as he added, "Come right down to it, you've did me a favor. I don't have to share out the plunder with nobody. Christ knows how much of the money's gone west, but there's still a lot more left than I'd of got from a four-way split."

"You're holding the guns, Eustace," said Foyt. "But we're still three to your one. You can't watch us all while we pick up them bills for you."

"I know it," said Pike. "But I don't need you to pick 'em up. It's gittin' dark purty soon, anyway. I'll do that in my own good time— take a week at it if I need to—and make sure I git all there is. I don't need you-all a'tall no more. Lancelot, you must of figgered by now that this is the end of the string for all three of you. I can't take no more chances."

"Yes, I figgered that," said Foyt, weary, submitting, finally defeated. "I reckon I'd do the same, was I in your boots. But can we have just a minute, Eustace, to say goodbye to each other? We're all rightchere in your sights. You ain't taking no chance."

"O' course, Lancelot," said Pike, almost benignly. "You know I always bin a good Babtiss. Y'all take a minute. Say a few prayers if you keer to. But only a minute."

Wilmajean let Karnes's big head down gently to the ground, and stood up, her dress front crimson with his blood. She came to Foyt, put her arms around his neck and leaned her head on his chest. Her Indian stoicism and fortitude had just about worn out, and she was crying quietly. Wheeler stood close beside them, looking resigned, his Adam's apple drooping.

"Your little gal is all right, Miz Wilmajean," Foyt said softly. "We seen to that. She'll be well provided for, too. And we buried your mister and the colored woman, proper and decent, with the Good Book read over 'em."

Wilmajean nodded her thanks, not trusting herself to speak without bawling. Her tears ran down Foyt's overall bib.

After a short silence, Foyt said to her, "Old Gideon—uh, Mister Birtwistle—was mumbling something there at the last, when he was gitting shot all them times. You was close beside him. What was he trying to say?"

Wilmajean sniffled. "The first time he got up, he was sayin', 'God he'p me.' When he got shot ag'in and got up ag'in, he just said 'God . . .' and then he got shot some more and fell down dead."

"Is that a fact?" Foyt said wonderingly. "God, eh. Old Gideon must not of been thinking."

"That's time enough!" Eustace snapped suddenly. "Y'all kin turn around t'other way, if you want to."

Slowly, one by one, they turned their backs to the executioner, and held out their hands to each other. They were all holding hands when Pike cocked both his pistols.

18

IN THE NAME OF THE LAW," boomed a commanding
voice from somewhere in the canebrake, "drop both your guns or
get shot where you stand!"

Eustace started violently and swiveled his pistols in that direction. His three about-to-be victims turned their amazed faces that
way. The dog began barking madly.

"*I am Oral T. Allnutt!*" boomed the voice, as Feather Hudspeth
Altdorfer made her way through the last few cane stalks and stood
at the edge of the clearing.

Eustace stood stunned for an instant by the apparent anomaly
of that deep, imperious voice coming from that little girl child. His
instant's hesitation was an instant too long. With both hands,
Feather swung up the heavy, formidable, buckshot-charged dragoon
pistol and, with a grimace of effort, squeezed the rusty old trigger.
T. Eustace Pike went all to fibrous, squashy, pink pieces, like an
overripe peach slammed with a mallet—his beard, for instance, with
jaw attached, flew all the way to the river—and Feather was jolted
by the recoil back out of sight among the canes.

Foyt and Wilmajean ran to her, and met the four Bynum-Allnutt
Operatives just struggling their way out through the brake. Being

251

bulkier, they hadn't been able to wriggle through as sinuously as had Feather. A couple of them had lost their derbies, and their torn spats flapped around their mud-caked shoes. The Operatives went to inspect the disaster area, and question Wheeler, and deduce things, while Foyt and Wilmajean bent over the little girl.

She was lying on her back, blinking, looking stupefied, and shaking her head to clear the ringing in her ears. Wilmajean clasped the girl to her breast, while Foyt gingerly felt along her arms. Finally he said, "Well, I reckon you're lucky, Rooster, that you didn't break your collarbone and your neckbone and God knows what-all. But you *have* done broke one wrist and the other'n's swelling like it's sprained bad."

"It don't matter," Feather said faintly but staunchly. "I got that man what shot Daddy Fritz."

2

"I don't suppose you'd have heard, Mister Foyt," said Field Chief Allnutt jovially. "But that reward has been substantially increased. Between them, Railway Express and the insurance agency have upped it by five thousand. That makes a grand total of *six thousand dollars,* and I figure you and Mister Wheeler are entitled to half of that."

"Yes, that sounds fair," said Foyt. "Them Altdorfer women certainly deserve the other half."

"Er, heh heh, I'm afraid you miscomprehend me, friend," said Allnutt. "It'll be paid, of course, half to you and half to the Bynum-Allnutt Agency. If you want to split your half with the widow and—"

"Er, heh heh," Foyt echoed him, mirthlessly, "I'm afraid you miscomprehend me, friend. Me and Eli and the Altdorfer women git it all."

"*What?!* Now see here! We've been on the trail of this bunch—"

"*You* see here!" rasped Foyt. "I've lost two—no, four—good friends to this butchering bunch." He had retrieved his Billy-the-Kid, and now began making ominous clicking noises with it, cock-ing the hammer, twirling the cylinder, lowering the hammer off cock. "I don't know how much of that scattered money you and your Operatives are gonna pick up here in the next week or so, or what it'll amount to by the time you turn it back to the Hubbard City bank. But I'm prepared to swear in court that it ought to of been *twice* as much as you hand in."

"Why, you old f—!" Foyt did some more clicking with the mechanism of his pistol. Allnutt looked at it, swallowed, and said, with less bluster, "That's out-and-out blackmail."

"Maybe," Foyt agreed. "And maybe I won't have to resort to that. You-all've been paid by the day—well paid, I gather—to do a job that a little nine-year-old gal finally did for you. When my cousin Norwood taps out *that* joke on the key to ev'ry other telegrapher on ev'ry other railroad in the United States of America, y'all can change the name of your deteckative agency. Its new name'll be Mud."

Allnutt appeared on the verge of apoplexy.

"That's why me and Eli and Miz Altdorfer and little Miss Altdorfer git the whole reward, to split as we see fit, *ain't* it, Mister Allnutt? And that's why you'll go back to gumshoeing breach-of-promise suits for lovelorn widders, *ain't* it, Mister Allnutt?"

The Field Chief turned several colors, ground his teeth, choked, struggled for speech, finally nodded, demolished.

"One more thing," said Foyt. "We already got hosses to tote our dead out for burial, but I'm appropriating two of them outlaws' hosses for the ladies to ride home on. What you do with the rest of this garbage is up to you. Goodbye, Mister Allnutt. I'll call on you the next time I have a suppeeny to serve on some crippled old saloon swawmper, and I'll send little Feather to help you."

3

" 'Pears like that basset dog's done attached hisself to us," said Foyt. "Reckon you can keep him, Feather, if you want him. Toad Walsh called his name Casey."

Feather said she'd keep the dog but she (Comanche cussword) sure wouldn't keep any name that (Comanche cussword) crook had called him. She would rename the dog Fritzwillie, in honor of the two departed.

It was almost dark and they were on the wagon track again, heading back the way they had come, via Sand Hill toward the Altdorfer spread. They were pushing that same little herd of well-traveled and woebegone cattle ahead of them, and Fritzwillie was yapping and nipping at their heels, pretending to be a herd dog.

Foyt rode between Wilmajean and Feather, mainly so he could do the steering of Feather's horse. Allthough they had splinted and bandaged the girl's injured wrists, he didn't want her to use her hands until a doctor had tended to them properly. Trailing behind, Wheeler rode on his own horse and led two others, across whose saddle-pads were slung the tarpaulined bodies of Euphémon Boudreaux and Gideon Karnes, and behind the horses the two Altdorfer mules. However relieved and grateful the live riders assuredly felt at their own deliverance, this was a mournful procession.

It had been Wilmajean who suggested that they take Karnes and Boudreaux back to be buried alongside Fritz and Willie Pearl. (All the names had been straightened out by now; Foyt told Wilmajean they had been traveling under aliases only while they were tracking the Pike gang all the way from Shreveport.) Even Feather and Wilmajean couldn't help thinking how, under other circumstances, this journey would have been enlivened and made enjoyable and made to seem shorter by the singing of a trail song. Foyt especially remembered old Karnes's bass voice rumbling "Big Profundo," and the Cajun's tenor caroling "*Dansez, mes enfants . . .*" and the two of them harmonizing "For he'd many a mile to go . . ."

He swallowed the lump in his throat and said, "Miz Altdorfer . . ."

"Oh, please call me Wilmajean," she said. "I reckon we-all've bin through enough together not to go on bein' formal."

She had tidied herself up considerably. Though her clothes were still filthy and bloody, and her face bruised, she had washed herself in the river and arranged her hair, and was again almost as handsome as when Foyt had first seen her.

"Wilmajean," he said. "We're all gonna be fairly well fixed now, what with divvying that reward. But you once offered us fellers a job at your place. You reckon you'd still want what's left of us?"

"More'n ever now," she said sincerely. "Me and Feather couldn't begin to manage even a corner of that place by ourselves. I was hopin' you'd consider signin' on."

"Well, to tell the truth," said Foyt, "I was thinking even further'n that. Your late husband wanted to go back into stock-raising, and so do me and Eli. If we pooled our share of the reward money in with you-all's, and stocked the place with these-here cows we've got, well, we'd have a *start*. I grant you, this ain't much of a herd. But I reckon the first oldtime cattlemen that come here to Texas— Kinney and O'Connor and all—they prob'ly didn't have much better to start with. Nothing but yeller-backed old longhorns. With Eli's touch, I wouldn't be surprised but what we could make a beginning with these, and later on buy some good breed bulls and . . ."

"I think it's a real fine idea, Lancelot," she said warmly. "We'll talk some more about it when we git home, and make some plans."

It was the first time since his boyhood that Foyt could remember anyone suggesting that he had a home to go home to. After enjoying this new notion in silence for a while, he asked:

"Would you mind, Wilmajean, if we went home by way of Teague?"

She looked puzzled. "Why . . . no. It's only a little out of our way. But what for? Don't you reckon we ought to push on as fast as we kin?"

"I don't see no great need for hurry. Your cow'll be bawling to be milked, and the pigs'll prob'ly of busted out of their pen by now to root for mast. But a few hours one way or t'other won't matter. And it's chilly enough that Moon and Gideon will keep till we git there. Reason I asked, we can get Feather straight to a doctor, instead of waiting for one to come out to the place. And—well—while we're there in Teague, I'd kinda like for you to show me that-there plum-colored plush rocking chair you once told me about."

4

Back at that S-bend confluence of Tehuacana Creek and the Trinity River, all was quiet at last. The survivors and the detectives had gone, and had taken with them their honored and dishonored dead, their cows and horses and mules, their dog and automobile.

High above, the patient snow geese circled a while longer, to make sure there were no more perturbations in store, then tilted their great wings to lose altitude. They came down to a backwater that was safe and serene and secure, and they came down gratefully, after their long passage and their ceaseless spiraling, finally to rest.